ON PRESIDENTIAL ORDERS

G. D. COVERT

Preface

Thank you to the many readers who have read Hawkeye Ridge. ON PRESIDENTIAL ORDERS is a stand-alone book, but the characters flow from book to book. If you have not read Hawkeye Ridge, I hope you feel compelled to discover how the saga began. I appreciate your kind comments and encouragement to expand the characters into a series.

Readers have accused me of being prescient in forecasting what became the devastating wildfires in Oregon over the last two years. It was eerie to see what I wrote as fiction in Hawkeye Ridge happening on the evening news.

I pray the events described in ON PRESIDENTIAL ORDERS do not also come to pass. Unfortunately, they could.

At the end of each book in this upcoming series, I hope you think, "I know that was fiction, but it felt real." I commit to finding fictional stories in the world's headlines to foster that unsettled feeling. Truth is stranger than fiction.

Greg

Disclaimer

My friends and family may occasionally recognize the name of a family member, friend, or loved pet in my life. My use of their name is a feeble attempt to create earthly immortality or memory, and the use of their name is limited to their name only. Any similarity of physical, emotional, or moral characteristics is purely accidental.

With that exception, all characters in this book are purely fictional.

Greg

This book is dedicated to my loving wife, Lisa, for her perpetual love, support, and encouragement.

Prologue 1

January 2003
London, England

Fahim Zaman entered Scotts on Mount Street, located one block from Grosvenor Square and two blocks from London's Hyde Park. Scotts featured seasonal menus, serving the finest traditional fish and shellfish dishes alongside various meat and game entrees. Oysters were a specialty and served at the elegant champagne and oyster bar.

The tuxedoed maître d' said, "It's good to see you again, Mr. Zaman. We seldom see you anymore. Your party arrived before you. Follow me, please, to your private dining room."

"Thank you, Edward."

The service and menu at Scotts were always impeccable.

The First Secretary to the American ambassador rose as the maître d' escorted Fahim into the dining room. "I'm happy to see you, sir. I worried you might not get here."

Taking a deep breath, Fahim replied, "It wasn't a question of my getting here. It was getting here without being followed. To save time, have you seen the menu?"

The First Secretary said, "Not yet. What do you recommend?"

Fahim said, "If you don't mind. I have fantasized about this meal all day. Unfortunately, it may be quite a while before I can return. May I order for us both?"

At the First Secretary's nod, Fahim turned to the maître d', "Edward, I know it's below your position, but could you take our order and see that we're not disturbed?"

Edward replied, "Of course, sir. What could we prepare for you this evening?"

Fahim said, "Could you start us with the mixed tomato salad with basil? It's so light and flavorful. Then I think the rump of Cornish lamb, served medium with the spiced carrot mash and crispy Boulangère potato. I know it's two carrot dishes for side dishes, but it will be a long time before I return. I want to remember the Dukkah roasted carrots with yoghurt and coriander. Your chef may disagree with my pairings, Edward, but please ask him to humor me."

Edward said, "It is my pleasure to serve you tonight. The chef will give you no issues. Would you care for wine with dinner?"

"Not for me tonight. Tonight, is business."

The First Secretary shook his head, "Not for me, either."

As the various courses arrived, they chatted about the food, their families, the London rain, and the tense diplomatic times.

As the meal concluded and dessert declined, the American First Secretary said, "It appears plans are advancing. Are you certain you do not want to bring your family to London now?"

The Iraqi said, "I wish I could. My brother and my boys are already here. I can't get my wife and my daughter out of the country. When will it begin?"

The First Secretary said, "You'll know. Here is a radio transmitter similar to those in planes. When it begins, we suggest you head south out of Bagdad towards Saudi Arabia and fly a white flag on your antennae. We will advise our advance units to watch for you and escort you to the border. Turn the transmitter on as soon as you leave Bagdad so we can identify you from the air. Do you have questions?"

"No."

"Then, may God be with you."

"If Allah wills it."

Prologue 2

Three months later
March 2003
Bagdad, Iraq

The night sky over Bagdad illuminated with explosions as stealth bombers dropped tons of explosives and cruise missiles raced across the countryside. The sound was deafening.

Fahim kept his family's escape bags in his Mercedes. Then, as the explosions began, he gathered a satchel of money and papers and hurried his wife and daughter to the car. Fahim lived on the outskirts of Bagdad and escaped down secondary roads to the south. The main arterials were cratered and filled with crowds fleeing.

Hours later, American Humvees surrounded his Mercedes with machine guns trained on them. Tired, hungry, and frightened, Fahim's wife and daughter cried in the backseat. The lieutenant in command said, "Everyone is searching for you, sir. We are under orders to push on for Bagdad. You should be safe now. Although I have heard reports, the local religious people are searching cars again, further down the road at the Saudi border. I think it's just a shakedown for cash to let people through."

Sighing in relief, Fahim said, "Thank you, Lieutenant. I have cash."

Three miles down the road, Fahim stopped at another roadblock. This time Saudis with full robes surrounded the car. They held automatic weapons and looked with suspicion at his Mercedes.

The mullah in charge ordered everyone out of the car. Holding a photograph beside Fahim's face, he looked at it intensely, "We found you. The reward will go to our mosque."

Turning to his men, he said, "Tie them and take them to our brothers in Africa. Six of you go with them. If our brothers are reluctant to part with the reward, let them know it is necessary." He gave a menacing tap to his weapon, and Fahim's wife whimpered, clutching their daughter.

Chapter 1

Present-day
September
Mahonia Hall
Salem, Oregon

Julia fastened an iron grip on Roman's arm as they walked toward the door of the Tudor governor's mansion, Mahonia Hall.

Nestled in the lush South Salem hills, the neighborhood illustrated the wealth of a bygone era. Mature trees abounded. Majestic Douglas firs, Oregon maples with their huge leaves and native Oregon white oak, provided pedestrian shade. Visible from the street, the grounds contained 100-year-old rhododendrons, camellias, and tulip trees. Beautiful formal gardens, gravel walkways, and boxwood hedges bordered the parking area in the mansion's front.

Roman commented, "These bushes are the size of my pickup. They are huge. In the spring, the grounds must be a riot of color."

"They are."

They made an attractive couple as they walked from his shiny deep red F250 Crew Cab to enter her father's official residence.

Thirty-one years old, six feet tall, and weighing one hundred ninety pounds, Roman looked athletic. He looked fit to handle whatever came his way, well-toned but not bulky. Regardless of his casual dress, his shortcut black hair, brown loafers glistening with polish, well-fitting dress slacks, and crisp golf shirt gave the appearance he was pressed and shined for inspection.

Julia was 28 years old, 5'8" in height, with long suntanned legs shown off by her white shorts. She looked fit with a runner's slender build and a well-endowed upper body straining at the fabric of her designer top. Her honey-blond hair fell loose on her shoulders.

She said, "Please don't let me fall in front of the reporters. I'm shaky from what I just heard. You love me, and I love you? Right? Is that what I heard you say?"

Roman smiled and agreed, "Sounds that way to me."

Squeezing his hand, Julia replied, "I could squeal right here if the reporters and photographers weren't watching. What does that mean?"

Roman replied, "Well, it means I want to spend my life with you, which I think means we should get married? What do you think it means?"

Julia squealed, and spinning into his arms, gave Roman a lingering kiss. The reporter's cameras started flashing.

As they approached Mahonia Hall's entrance, security opened the door and escorted them to a large conference room. Lawyers, police officers, and witnesses to the attempted rape and assassination attempts at Roman's estate filled the room. The conference room felt claustrophobic for Julia.

Governor Stan and Margo Anderson, Julia's mother and father, and Rose Nelson, Roman's mother, came over to hug Julia and determine if she was okay. They knew last night in Salem Hospital; that she underwent humiliating evaluations ordered by the police and her attorneys. Feeling dehumanized, Julia believed the hospital staff was more concerned with gathering evidence than treating the injuries she sustained in the assault and attempted rape.

While reassuring her mother and father that she was okay, she whispered to Margo, "We just got engaged."

Roman looked at Julia and said, "I see where your squeals come from," as Margo squealed and rushed to hug Roman. Rose soon joined the hug with tears of happiness in her eyes for her son.

Stan called for the staff to bring champagne for everyone when Julia's lead attorney, Mike McDuff, interrupted, saying, "I suggest you hold off on the champagne until after the District Attorney has finished asking his questions."

Mike stood 6'3" and weighed 230 pounds with a polished, shaven head. He was the leading criminal defense lawyer in the state, with a high-profile practice in Portland. Friends since their college days, Stan often asked him, "Do you wax your head? Is making it shine part of your intimidation process?"

Mike never answered. As a lawyer, he was at the top of his game. He exuded palpable confidence, dressed in an expensive gray suit that hid his weight, a starched white shirt, and a bold red power tie. He looked like a hungry bulldog, waiting to be unleashed while slobbering for raw meat.

Mike said, "Julia, congratulations. I expect an invitation to your wedding. But we need to make sure you can have a wedding."

Pointing his wood-grained Montblanc pen and looking at the assembled district attorneys and police officers, he said, "Gentleman, let's establish the ground rules. You may ask questions of my client. But, Julia, I may clarify their questions for you before you answer. And before answering any of their questions, please look at me for permission to answer. Do not answer any open-ended questions and do not offer any opinions. Speak only of the facts."

Looking again at the district attorney and his assistants, he said, "Before we get to Julia, I suggest the two U.S. marshals make their statements."

The various attorneys agreed and decided on an open interview process instead of interviewing everyone in separate rooms. When Mike realized that, he grinned. He now knew the district attorney thought the killing was in self-defense, and he was going through the motions of an investigation.

The Marion County District Attorney said, "I think we should start with comments from U.S. Marshal James Stockade."

Chapter 2

Present-day
Mahonia Hall conference room

Jimmy Stockade, known by his SEAL teammates as "Smoke," was 5'11" and 185 pounds, with well-groomed, short blond hair.

Watching Jimmy with a reporter's eye, Roman's sister Alexia thought, *"I expect he grew up poor because of how tailored his clothing is and his impeccable manners. Or, did he grow up wealthy because he wears those fancy clothes like they are second nature? He must have a private tailor the way his sports jacket and slacks fit him. He can't be purchasing them on a marshal's salary."*

Seeing him in action during the attack on the governor, she thought the fancy tailored clothes covered an arsenal of knives and pistols. Itching to run her hands down his back and see if she felt a shoulder holster, she thought, *"That would be an excuse for running my hand down his back... what am I thinking?"*

Sitting behind Jimmy, she didn't need to be discrete in watching him. Her thoughts refused to leave him. *"His polite, soft-spoken manner and beautiful clothing hide the most dangerous man I've ever met."*

That thought forced her to look at her brother Roman. *"Hmm, they're two of a kind. No wonder Jimmy appeals to me. I never considered my brother dangerous until I saw him in action. If Roman's capable of what I saw last night, perhaps Jimmy's the second most dangerous man I know."*

As a news reporter, it was second nature for Alexia to

automatically dig out a notepad and take detailed notes of the morning's questioning.

♦ ♦ ♦

The DA requested, "Marshal Stockade, could you identify yourself for the record, both your current status and your military experience? Then could you tell us why you were on Hawkeye Ridge and what happened?"

Speaking into the recorder, he said, "Yes, sir, my name is James Stockade. I'm a retired chief warrant officer in the U.S. Navy SEALS. My official position is as a U.S. marshal, working on special assignments for the United States president, Alex Myers. President Myers is a close friend and former fraternity brother of Governor Anderson. President Myers knows of three assassination attempts on Governor Anderson and his family's lives, beginning with a car crash on Mt. Hood. Details of those attempts are already on file with the Oregon State Police. President Myers requested I come to Oregon and keep Governor Anderson safe until the police caught the perpetrators."

Pausing for a sip of water, he continued, "I operate undercover and currently function as the governor's driver and special assistant. Yesterday, I drove the governor and Mrs. Anderson to the home of Roman Nelson. After dinner, an alarm system alerted Roman of an incoming drone. Roman shot it out of the sky. Unfortunately, it exploded upon being hit. That alerted us that the individuals responsible for the prior assassination attempts may be in the vicinity." Jimmy held up photos of the pieces of the exploded drone.

Jimmy waited while the prosecutors and police officers viewed the photos before continuing. Finally, he said, "Later in the evening, Roman's security system showed the breaching of his driveway gate and what we assumed were potential assassins staking out the exit road. The exit is a steep logging road and slow to drive, even slower in the dark. It's not a place you want an attack by assassins, as I think the officers at the house last night will attest." He paused and looked at the officers standing in the room, nodding their heads.

The District Attorney nodded at him to continue, "After a discussion with the governor, we decided the safest exit for the Governor and Mrs. Anderson would be down a chairlift from the mountaintop. The chairlift has a bulletproof glass bubble or enclosure and a steel plate on the floor. We explained the safety features to the governor and told him I would be on a zipline in front of the chairlift, and Roman would provide security from the rear. Unfortunately, the attack occurred on our way down as we neared the midway point. The chairlift passengers were Governor and Mrs. Anderson, Rose Nelson, Roman's mother, and Alexia Nelson, his sister. Alexia is a reporter and filmed the ride downhill. I expect you saw a copy of that video."

The District Attorney's face wore a tight-lipped look of frustration as he nodded his head.

Jimmy took a breath and looked around the table before continuing, "As we approached the midway point, shots rang out of the darkness, targeting the chairlift. There were six attackers, all firing various weapons at the chairlift. I know three of the six were firing AR-15s. Randy Miller used a 12-gauge pump shotgun with double ought buckshot. I don't know what the remaining two shooters used. Roman Nelson and I wore digital night vision goggles, allowing us to see the attackers as if it were daylight. When they began the attack, I dropped off the zipline and shot Bruce Miller, Randy Miller, and an unidentified assailant. Roman shot the group leader, Donald Miller, as he prepared to shoot me in the back. The Marion County deputies captured the remaining two attackers as they ran downhill."

Jimmy paused again for another sip of water. Mike, Julia's attorney, said, "Please continue, Chief Stockade."

Jimmy nodded to him and continued, "If you watch the video, you can hear Julia Anderson scream. Roman raced up the hill once we neutralized the attackers. You'll need his testimony on that aspect of the events, and I took the potential victims the rest of the way down the hill on the chairlift to safety. I got an Argo ATV for a quick run up the hill. Alexia rode with me back to the house. When we got there, I saw Roman comforting Julia on his patio. Her blouse hung from her in blood-covered shreds. Her face was covered with cuts and bruises, a bloody nose, and an eye rapidly swelling shut. Julia's violent shaking, I believe, shows up on the videos you have."

The District Attorney thanked Marshal Stockade and commented, "Yes, I saw Alexia's video. I imagine everyone in the state has seen it. If we wanted to get a jury pool for a trial, I don't think you could find twelve people not already prejudiced by those videos. One clip or another from her video has played all night on each of the channels."

Grinning, Jimmy replied by reminding him, "Well, she is the top reporter at the Northwest's number one station. Reporting is her job."

Jimmy added, "And she has many friends in the news industry concerned about what happened in the attack and the news being created now."

At that remark, the district attorney looked outside the window to an ever-growing crowd of news trucks in the governor's parking lot. He called on Roman and asked him to identify himself and his former background.

Chapter 3

Present-day
Mahonia Hall conference room

My name is Roman Nelson. I'm a retired Navy SEAL. My rank was lieutenant commander."

The DA asked, "Why are you being identified as a U.S. marshal? I have not heard of the stationing of a U.S. marshal in Gates. Are you, in fact, a marshal? After you clear that up, please give us your version of what happened last night."

Roman replied, "Upon my discharge from the Navy, the United States president asked me to accept a U.S. marshal's reserve appointment. I became a reserve deputy the president could activate for special assignments in Oregon. When President Myers found I knew Governor and Mrs. Anderson through their daughter Julia, he activated me to assist Marshal Stockade."

Roman continued, "Julia and I, and both our parents, planned a get-acquainted dinner for our families. Unfortunately, events occurred, as Marshal Stockade mentioned. When I heard Julia's scream, I raced back up the hill. Approaching the house, I saw through the window her struggling with two assailants. I entered the home and pulled one off Julia. Somehow, his neck broke in that process."

Roman paused and waited for the DA to acknowledge his obscure comment before continuing. "When I removed the assailant, it broke the second assailant's hold of Julia. She grabbed a knife off the kitchen counter and stabbed him multiple times. Subsequent identification identified the first assailant as Charlie Miller Jr. and the second, the man Julia stabbed, as his uncle, Hank Miller."

Roman continued, "Blood poured from his wounds. There was no way with a kitchen towel to stop the blood flow. It is a thirty-minute drive up the logging road to my home, and the nearest ambulance would be another twenty minutes away. I took Julia outside. She didn't need to stare at dead bodies or a bloody floor."

The district attorney looked at Julia, who shook and sobbed with a black eye, a swollen nose, and scrapes on her face. He then looked at her attorney, Mike McDuff, and her father, the governor, who scowled at him.

Turning to Alexia, the DA asked her, "Would it be possible to get a copy of the videos from last night?"

She said, "I thought you might want a copy," as she handed him a flash drive with the video on it.

The District Attorney looked at Roman and said, "I know you understand the need for our investigators to go over your property and home to complete our investigation. Will you grant us access, or do I need a search warrant?"

Roman responded, "I waive the right to a search warrant for the site of the attack on the chairlift, the chairlift itself, and the kitchen and patio of my home. As a matter of principle, I deny access to the rest of my home. There is no need, as the attack occurred in the kitchen, and the access point was the broken kitchen window. The attackers never got beyond the kitchen. Is that acceptable?"

The district attorney nodded and looked again at a pasty white and shaking Julia. He said, "Julia, I have a couple of questions that I will make as easy as possible for you. I understand you were cleaning the kitchen and doing the dishes when the two assailants' broke a window and entered the home. Is that correct?"

"Yes."

"The hospital took scrapings from under your fingernails, which I expect will match with the scratches found on the assailant's faces, and should establish your resistance. My question is, as they were attacking you, did you fear for your life?"

Julia replied, "I knew if Roman did not hear my screams, Charlie would rape and kill me. I think they planned on brutalizing me before killing me. They talked about wanting to listen to me scream in pain. Charlie kept saying, 'for the sins of the father, you shall pay.' I thought he was crazy. Yes, I was beyond being afraid for my life. I was 100% freaked out."

The district attorney continued, "Governor Anderson, now is the time for you to order the champagne. Our investigators still need to do their background work, process the crime scenes, the autopsies, etc. If everything proves to be consistent with what we discussed today, I will announce a self-defense decision for Julia. I think it's reasonable to expect a finding that both officers acted within their authority to stop individuals involved in a crime."

Looking out the window again, he said, "May I suggest, sir, you and I step outside and talk to the press? The crowd of reporters gets larger each time I look out the window."

Chapter 4

Roman and Jimmy spoke to the deputies. The deputies responded in mass to the original reports of the shootings. They were awake much of the evening securing the premises and photographing scenes until replacements arrived. Nonetheless, they were at the governor's official residence early in the morning. Like Roman and Jimmy, they looked clean, starched, and ironed.

Roman and Jimmy agreed to meet with the deputies later to walk them through the evening's activities. The deputies wanted help cleaning up their reports. They wanted no question of a lack of thoroughness if anyone reviewed the files.

While watching from across the room, Julia thought the young deputies almost looked 'star struck' talking to Roman and Jimmy. She saw the deputies taking 'selfies' with the two of them.

Alexia came over to Julia and asked the first of many wedding questions. "So, when is the wedding?"

Julia's eyes widened, and her voice quivered as she replied, "I don't know. I said yes, just as we walked in the door. Roman and I have not talked beyond that."

"I see. Is this for sure? Before you announce your engagement, be certain. Now, however, would be a great time for an announcement."

"Alexia, I don't know what you said to the reporters last evening at the hospital, but the news reports which ran all night, I'm sure, affected the DA's quick interview this morning. Thank you. Yes, I'm certain about marrying your brother. You need to check with Roman about his commitment level. It is okay with me if you want to announce our engagement. You can do whatever you want after what you did for us last night. However, you want to do it."

◆ ◆ ◆

Alexia went up to her brother and Jimmy as they talked to the young deputies. "I saw you guys taking selfies. If you want to give me your email addresses, I'll take a professional photo of you."

She held up her camera, a Canon EOS 6D. The young deputies stammered and shifted their 'star-struck' look to Alexia. After all, she was a famous TV starlet who anchored the news every evening.

She took their photos, got their addresses, and walked away when the youngest deputy overcame his nervousness and asked for a photo with her. Jimmy grinned, and taking the camera, got the deputy's photos with Alexia.

Slipping an arm around the waist of Jimmy and Roman, she walked them away, "Okay, Roman. I love Julia. Now is the perfect time for an engagement announcement. Are you confident a wedding is in your future? I mean, it's a new definition of sudden."

Roman replied, "I'm certain. She is perfect for me. With her, I can be me again. Yes, we can announce the engagement. What is on your mind?"

"Let me track down, Stan."

Walking outside to the snapping of cameras taking her picture, Alexia thought, *"Interesting, so this is what it feels like. I'm always the one taking the photos and shouting the questions. I guess today I'm part of the story."*

Being 'camera-ready' was part of Alexia's DNA. Now twenty-seven, she started as an intern for a Portland TV station while still in college. Upon graduation, with her bachelor's degree in journalism, she moved in front of the camera. Everyone thought she was a natural, but her coworkers knew how hard she worked. She was 5'7" tall, with an eye-catching upper body and medium to short hair. She was a black-haired beauty with a bubbly personality, which caused strangers to talk to her like old friends in minutes.

The DA and the governor both fielded questions from the reporters like practiced politicians. Governor Anderson looked at Alexia as she stood next to them. She whispered, "I apologize for interrupting. Could I speak to Governor Anderson for one moment?"

She left the district attorney with a smile on his face, fielding questions, and isolated the governor from the crowd. Alexia stood in front of Stan with her back to the cameras. She did not want anyone to film her talking and have her lips read later.

She said, "Twice you've asked me to help massage public opinion. I'm not your press secretary, but I think now is the time to thank two people who helped us get the news coverage we wanted. Why don't you invite them for a glass of champagne as you announce your daughter's engagement?"

Stan replied, smiling, "You can quit your job and come to work as my press secretary any time you want. Why don't you invite whoever you want into the residence? I think the questions are winding down here."

Julia walked over to Carl and Rebecca, her two competitors, on the evening news in Portland.

She said, "I'd like to thank you for your station's coverage of what happened. Your broadcasts were fair and unbiased. You focused on the horror of the assassination attempt and not on the number of attempted assassins killed. As a thank you, the governor invites you into the residence as soon as this press conference ends."

With a questioning look, they both said they would be there.

Chapter 5

Mahonia Hall Dining Room

The staff iced champagne bottles and prepared lunch for Roman and Julia's families. The dining room was a beehive of activity by the Mahonia Hall staff.

With Jimmy at her side, Alexia escorted the reporters, Carl and Rebecca, into the dining room.

Rebecca was petite, twenty-five years old, with a brunette sex kitten look. Her round face, cute upturned nose, lushly curved body, and sweet voice caused men to watch her and not pay attention to the news stories. However, Rebecca didn't need to overplay her overt sexuality. It jumped through the television screen.

Carl anchored his stations broadcasting for twenty years. Over the years, he added thirty pounds to his waist, and his brown hair thinned. He always wore his suit coats buttoned to hide his waist and short ties. The unfortunate result showed up as a stretched coat across his stomach. His peers, however, still considered him an influential reporter in the area.

Alexia explained, "Governor Anderson appreciates your coverage of the assassination attempt. Over lunch, he will make a personal announcement. The statement won't qualify for the five o'clock news, but the governor is inviting you to the luncheon as a thank you. There will be personal, family-type conversations he trusts you'll not report, but you'll be free to use the announcement itself. Fair enough?" She asked as she looked at them both.

They both nodded in agreement.

Alexia said there could be additional announcements coming in the upcoming week. "I will notify you," she said with a grin, "Minutes after I notify my station."

With practiced ease, Rebecca sidled up to Jimmy and put out her hand, "I don't think you and I have met. I'm Rebecca. We're glad you were with the governor last evening. I think I heard the deputies referring to you as Smoke. Why do they call you that?"

Jimmy and Rebecca both grinned as Alexia answered for him.

"My brother said it's because he's elusive and difficult for the ladies to pin down."

She placed her hand on his arm and escorted the two of them to adjacent chairs at the dining room table.

Rebecca grinned and thought, *"Well, Meow to you too. But it's just what I thought. I just wanted to know for sure. I was right. She is staking Jimmy out as her territory."*

She pulled out a notepad and started taking notes of who the guests were. Governor Anderson settled into the head of the table and looked around. Already seated were both families, plus Governor Anderson's key staff. The defense lawyers from the morning's hearing were there, and surprisingly the governor invited the district attorney.

Stan cleared his throat as he stood, "I know everyone has heard the news. I want to announce my beautiful daughter's engagement to a man I look forward to welcoming into our family. Their initial meeting to the engagement may have only taken days, but I understand. The day I met Margaret, I knew she was the woman for me. Roman, I have spent more time with your mother and sister than you. I feel like I have known them forever, and Alexia, if there is ever a future for me in politics, I want you at my side for guidance."

Rebecca scribbled in her notepad.

"But Roman, you saved my daughter's life. Not once, but twice, which is more important than your saving both my life and Margo's. We will forever be grateful. I look forward to having you as part of our family."

He raised his glass in a toast, and everyone followed suit.

Alexia told Carl and Rebecca the luncheon announcement wouldn't be worthy of the five o'clock news, but it made bold headlines.

GOVERNOR ANNOUNCES HIS DAUGHTER'S ENGAGEMENT. SPECULATES ON HIS FUTURE IN POLITICS. OFFERS ALEXIA NELSON A JOB AS PRESS SECRETARY

Chapter 6

1991
Iraq
Post Desert Storm campaign

F ahim Zaman was in construction related to the oil fields, and his family contacts inside Saddam Hussein's government awarded him contracts for repair work on the pipelines. Fahim included sufficient padding for the bribes to his family contacts in his contracts. No one saw anything wrong with paying a bribe to get business, and over the years, Fahim became wealthy. Not as rich as the Saudi Princes, but wealthy by usual standards.

Following Saddam Hussein's invasion of Kuwait, Fahim became frantic to move his assets outside Iraq. Educated in England, Fahim knew what would happen when the impending war began. Whenever he could find a buyer, he sold off portions of his companies and all his property except for his home. He converted all assets into American dollars or British pounds. If a purchaser offered him gold, he took it and flew it to Switzerland without delay. He considered himself lucky when the American's 'Desert Storm' operation ended with his business assets intact.

Fahim was an educated man and a member of the Ba'ath Party, which promoted a Pan-Arabic view. He knew Saddam Hussein from both the mosque and party functions. Religion, business, and politics intermingled at these functions, each striving for dominance. Being educated in England and knowing Saddam Hussein, Fahim knew the inevitability of another war. Fahim feared the ensuing battle would destroy his assets and family.

Fahim did not know when the war he feared would occur, but started taking action to get his family out of Iraq. He began by sending his youngest brother, Khalil, to the military school he attended in England. People in Iraq considered it reasonable for well-to-do families to send their male children to England for schooling.

Khalil, however, questioned his need to go. "Why do I need to go to school in England? There is a great tutor at the mosque. I don't like England, it's cold and wet, and the girls are pasty white."

Fahim impressed upon him the danger he felt Iraq was in and the elevated risk for an individual like himself with ties through his construction business to government officials.

Fahim designated Khalil as the caretaker of Fahim's family. He set up regular business trips to Europe to visit his brother and deposit money into his Swiss accounts. What he couldn't do was take his wife or daughter with him. Saddam Hussein would permit business people to come and go, but Muslim women couldn't leave for any reason.

Khalil followed instructions. He became a model student at the military school, attended university, and continued his education with advanced degrees. His English was flawless and grammatically correct. Handsome and personable, the British girls loved him, and Khalil reaped the benefit of his exotic appearance in his bedroom.

He put on his flowing white robes at night and went to the mosque for lessons of another sort. His cleric was the exiled mullah, Abu Bakr al-Baghdadi.

Fahim continued selling off portions of his companies. Divesting himself of the ownership of his businesses, he then ran them on salary. Deep discounts on the value produced cash sales finalizing when purchasers placed the funds in his accounts in Switzerland or England.

He moved the bulk of his assets to England or Switzerland by the time Fahim's son Fathi turned twelve and Chawki ten. He enrolled his sons in military schools in England as soon as they were old enough. By now, everyone considered it a family tradition. In Fahim's mind, however, he was getting them to safety.

He refused the boys and his brother permission to return home. Instead, he met them in Europe on their holidays. He feared that if they returned to Iraq for vacation, it might be impossible to get them out again. He showed them photos of their mother and younger sister since neither could leave Iraq to visit them.

The western news channels began running stories about the development of weapons of mass destruction by Iraq. The belief that Saddam Hussein was developing nuclear, chemical, and biological weapons for terrorist attacks worldwide became established.

While the world watched with foreboding, the United States developed its coalition of thirty-five Allies. The alliance was the largest since World War ll. The coalition gave deadline after deadline for inspector access to the sites developing weapons. Saddam, again and again, denied having weapons of mass destruction. War's arrival seemed inevitable.

Fahim was confident there would be another war and that the United States wouldn't stop this time until Iraq unconditionally surrendered. Moreover, he knew the impending war would devastate his businesses.

People worldwide watched the unfolding of the military campaign of Shock and Awe. Tens of millions watched on television during Bagdad's initial nighttime bombing by stealth bombers and the tank blitz across the desert. Fahim fled across the desert with his wife and daughter while people worldwide stayed glued to their television sets.

Fahim and his family disappeared after speaking to an American army patrol.

Chapter 7

2003
Post "Shock and Awe" campaign
England

The United States and its coalition of Allies met with overwhelming initial success in their Iraq invasion and overthrowing of Saddam Hussein and the ruling Ba'ath Party. Pride filled the people of the United States and Britain at the public display of their power. National pride in the righteousness of stopping a tyrant from getting weapons of mass destruction filled the airwaves.

Fathi and Chawki followed their father's instructions when he took them to school and forecasted the war. During the day, they were dry-eyed and agreed with the overthrow of Saddam. At night, however, fearing the worst, they cried. They were now 15 and 13 and told no one of their parent's disappearance. A trust Fahim established continued to send the school its tuition each month.

Six months after the 'Shock and Awe' campaign, their father's brother, Khalil, visited Fathi and Chawki. Khalil was ten years older than Fathi and twelve years older than Chawki. Thus, he appeared as an elder brother figure instead of an uncle.

"It is six months since the Americans attacked our beloved country. Your father asked me to wait six months before telling you he and your entire family are dead. If they were alive, they would have arrived by now."

The boys burst into tears, protesting.

Unfazed, Khalil continued, "Here are his instructions for your life and what you must do to avenge your family. I'm now your banker and spiritual advisor. No one is to know I fill those roles. Are you prepared to follow your father's instructions?"

"Yes, Uncle," they sobbed.

"Let us begin."

Khalil said, "Your father's instruction is for you to always appear as a moderate Muslim who is 'westernized.' You should wear western clothing whenever appropriate. In addition, you are to master the English language and cultivate an upper-class British accent."

Khalil continued, "Your father instructs you to excel academically, participate in sports, and engage in physical activities. Above all, he commands you are to form no emotional attachments to western girls."

Khalil paced their dormitory room while reading from a document containing a list of instructions.

"This point is important. You must be discrete. Divulge no information about your family or friends I may introduce you to."

Then, ceasing his pacing, he looked each in their eyes as he asked, "Understood?"

"Yes, Uncle."

"When the time is correct, you must apply for college in the western United States. The preferred college will be in a small town in a rural area. You are always to fit in. When the summer holiday from military school or later college comes, you'll always say you are spending the holiday with family in Europe."

"But, Uncle Kahlil, our family is gone," Chawki muttered.

"This and all future summers, I will take you to meet your other family. I will introduce you to your family of faith and spirit, which is more important than your family of blood."

They went to the French or Italian Rivera when vacations began each summer. There, Khalil rented a yacht to cruise the Mediterranean. Khalil and the boys would make casual stops along the way, appearing as ordinary tourists. Afterwards, they would disembark in Libya and disappear for weeks of immersion training in their own culture in North Africa.

Chapter 8

September 2008
Oregon State University
Corvallis, Oregon

Khalil appeared in Corvallis, Oregon, in the spring of 2008, as he interviewed for a job as Professor of Mid-East Religions at Oregon State University. He specialized in the Comparative Studies of the Muslim Nations. Appearing for his interview in flowing robes but handing over his credentials as a graduate of Oxford, he made a striking impression with his clipped upper-crust British accent.

He visited a Realtor, "I'm going on staff at OSU. I want to purchase an apartment complex near the campus and walk to work. Do you handle that kind of property?"

The Realtor jumped at the opportunity to show him a 12-unit apartment complex near OSU. Khalil looked in each apartment before saying, "The units smell of spilled beer and years of college sex. Nevertheless, I will purchase it for cash if the property management company evicts the three largest unit's tenants and oversees renovating those units. I want the units stripped of carpeting and appliances, repainted, re-carpeted, and modern cabinets installed with granite countertops. I want the inside to feel brand new."

In September, Fathi and Chawki arrived to a renovated upscale apartment. Chawki completed his military school before leaving England. Fathi graduated two years earlier, spending the following two years in a secretive training camp in North Africa.

Kahlil said to Fathi and Chawki, "All is going according to your father's plan. Each of you can pursue a degree in a field that interests you at OSU. You should embed yourselves in university life and become a part of the community. Act like normal American college students. Each summer, we will continue your secret training in military skills, weapons, and explosives fields. I will continue your current religious studies, deepening your faith."

Under Kahlil's tutelage, both became radicalized in religion and politics.

All they needed was a target of opportunity.

♦ ♦ ♦

All three took private pilot lessons and became licensed to fly at the Corvallis Airport the following year. While they took classes, they professed an extreme passion for flying. Khalil seemed to always be at the airport. No one knew they had mastered flying years ago in North Africa because they never got licensed.

After the owner of a Beechcraft King Air 350 twin-engine turboprop plane parked at the airport unexpectedly died, his widow approached them to buy her husband's plane.

She said, "My husband was a doctor and loved to fly. With him gone, I can no longer afford the payments on the plane. Because of that, I could offer you a bargain if you purchased it."

No one suggested an autopsy to determine her husband's cause of death. The assumption was that he had suffered a heart attack, and no one considered a drug-induced heart attack. After a week of negotiating, Kahlil purchased the plane, receiving a substantial discount for cash.

Khalil and the boys then flew across the Cascades to Central and Eastern Oregon and started looking at ranches listed for sale. Kahlil wanted a minimum of 5,000 acres, he wanted it in an area with a sparse population, and he wanted a private airport on the ranch with at least a 3,500-foot grass runway.

He purchased a property bordering the Fremont National Forest in the mountains above Summer Lake and Paisley.

He explained to the Realtor, "I will use the ranch for elk hunting in the fall for friends from Europe. The existing ranch house will need modernizing and upgrading for the wealthy clientele. I will keep a permanent caretaker on the property for security and maintenance."

The Realtor nodded approval.

"During the summer," Khalil continued, "I will operate it as a rehabilitation camp for teenage delinquents. Instead of going to the expense of building dormitories, I think they should camp in large tents and rough it."

The Realtor said, "Tents are warm in the summer since we are near the Alvord Desert."

"It will be good for them to be uncomfortable. Most of the teenagers live pampered, spoiled lives. I think outdoor living, camping, and hiking will be a growing experience for young men. Learning how to ride, care for horses, and cook their food will teach them responsibility. They should learn respect for guns by learning how to shoot them."

He said, "I hope I can intervene in the lives of young men before they go bad."

He told his realtor, "Please let the neighbors know I will put in a state-of-the-art gun range. Then, undoubtedly, the young men in the summer and the elk hunters in the fall will benefit from a proper course in gun safety."

Khalil said, "The gun range will emphasize safety in its construction. If anyone hears firing, no one should worry."

Chapter 9

Present- Day
The parking lot
The governor's mansion
Salem, Oregon

Roman and Julia escaped the engagement luncheon. The reporter's cars were gone. As he opened the door on his bright red F250, she wrapped her arms around him and gave him a long hug.

She said, "I didn't think we would ever get out of there."

"It's an important day for everyone. You get cleared of any criminal charges on the would-be-rapist's deaths. The district attorney stands with the governor for a prolonged press conference, and the governor appears pleased with him, which will be valuable political capital next election cycle. And it appears Alexia is enchanted with my best friend, Jimmy. Even better, he seems just as attracted to her."

Julia poked him in the chest, and he drawled, "Oh yeah, and you and I got engaged. As I said, it was an important day."

She said, "There is a lot for us to discuss. I love you, but I know so little about you. I'm excited, but my practical side is screaming at me, asking me what I'm doing."

Roman responded, "My heart is pounding faster than during last night's attack. My experience is with nighttime actions, not getting engaged to a beautiful woman I barely know. Let's find a quiet place, get a cup of coffee, and talk for a while. Someplace peaceful where we can relax and get acquainted, but without a bedroom attached, which will keep me from plotting on how to get you into the bed."

"I agree. Let's go back to the restaurant overlooking the Oregon Gardens. It has wonderful memories for me. We don't need to get a room. Tonight, we can come back to my condo on the river. If we tire of drinking coffee, we can walk through the Gardens and continue talking."

They hugged as she climbed in the truck and headed for the Oregon Gardens.

They rode in silence, holding hands as he drove.

Julia commented, "Life has been hectic since we met. It has been non-stop activity. I don't feel like I've had a chance to be quiet, feel my emotions, and feel your presence."

"Time will expand to fit our needs."

"That was profound. Are you a philosopher by nature?"

He laughed, "I don't claim credit for being a deep thinker. No, a friend said that to me once, and it stuck. But doesn't it seem true? Haven't you experienced times when you were so busy you couldn't see daylight, and your appointments canceled or fell apart? So then, all at once, you have more time than you need."

"Yes, I suppose that's true," she answered. "While we're driving, and no one can eavesdrop, thank you. Thanks for saving my life last night and telling me to stab that guy, Hank Miller, again if I didn't want to deal with him in the future. They terrified me, with both of them holding me and trying to rip my clothes off. I screamed so much I couldn't catch my breath. My heart pounded out of my chest, and my vision closed in. I felt such relief when you ripped Charley off me, and I stabbed Hank. I knew torture and rape were minutes away."

Rubbing her face, she said, "When I stabbed him, I immediately felt a relief of that almost paralyzing fear. I felt my pulse drop and caught my breath. I felt safe. My next emotion was the shock that I stabbed him, followed by the fear of consequences for having stabbed someone who was now screaming. And then, the stark terror of, 'oh my God, he's still alive, he'll come after me again.'"

She took a deep breath, "When you said what you said, I knew you were right. I did not want to live my life with fear hanging over me. Even knowing he is dead; I am still an emotional wreck at the thought of his release on bail prior to trial or later from prison if they'd released him after serving his time. His future release was a ticking time bomb, ready to explode in my life. I couldn't live that way."

With tears streaming down her face, she said, "Your saying what you said validated my fear and released me to stab him again and again."

They were both quiet, and then she asked, "Does that make me a murderer?"

He pulled the truck into the parking lot at the Oregon Gardens Resort and, turning it off, looked her in the eyes and held her hands, "No, Sweetheart, you aren't a murderer. I have wondered for years if I am, but I can tell you with conviction that you are not."

Twisting in his seat to look at her, he said, "I know I told you I trained as a lawyer at Annapolis. I planned on entering the Judge Advocate General's office before the SEALS enticed me away. I have never taken the bar exam to practice, but I'm still a trained lawyer. If the DA knew a two or three-second pause existed between your first knife strike and subsequent strikes, I don't think it would make any difference."

"You don't think it mattered?"

"No, I don't. However, let's not tempt fate by volunteering information he didn't request. Let's suppose the DA would have charged you. The fancy attorney your dad hired for you, Mike McDuff, wasn't worried. His options included Option one, not guilty because of fear-based temporary insanity. Option two would be a valid case of self-defense, which is what the DA has decided. Option three, I don't know. Your attorney looked like he knew what he was doing and could come up with another dozen options. You aren't a murderer because you killed Hank while defending yourself. You are a beautiful young woman I'm proud to have as my fiancée."

Squeezing his hands, she said, "Thank you. Shall we go inside and get acquainted?"

Chapter 10

Roman slipped the hostess a $20 bill and requested a quiet table for coffee and a private conversation. She seated them at a distance from the handful of diners and left them alone after pouring the coffee. Occasionally, after that, she met Roman's eyes from a distance to see if he needed anything else. He didn't.

Julia continued the conversation, "If I'm not a murderer, how do I reconcile the moral issue of 'Thou shall not kill?'"

Frowning, Roman looked distressed as he answered, "Knowing the answer to that comes at a higher pay grade than mine. You know I have killed people. I always did so on the U.S. government's orders in an undeclared war, rescuing hostages, or perhaps protecting someone. An example is what just happened with your family."

Julia groaned as he said, "I have killed people in the desert, the jungle, and underwater. The killing is easy. Dealing with it later is not. I sat on my patio, built a fire, and watched the seasons change for an entire year as I contemplated that question."

Julia said, tears streaming down her cheeks, "I feel so guilty. Of course, it goes against my religious beliefs to kill someone, but it horrified me to hear Charlie and Hank talk about what they planned on doing to me. I don't know how you can stand what you have done. It would tear me apart."

She saw the tension around his eyes and his lips tightening as he spoke. "I believe God knows I may have killed, but not for enjoyment, and not for personal profit. Our country ordered my killings to protect others. Even in a quasi-undeclared war, the belief is that we're not just promoting our national best interest but protecting our country from the true evil I have seen around the world. And there is evil out there. My eternal future is in God's hands. If there is a judgment day, I hope I'm judged not on my actions but on my intentions. I intend always to protect and serve. But as for you, I cannot believe you've earned God's eternal damnation for protecting your life."

Julia held his hand and said, "It's important we talk about our faiths, what we believe in, church attendance, etc. But I think that's enough serious talk for today."

Shaking her head to shake off her mood, she asked, "I know you drink wine, but please tell me you aren't a heavy drinker."

"I'm not," Roman replied, "How about you?"

"No, I'm a cheap drunk." She laughed, "Two glasses of wine, and I'm tipsy. I will admit now and again to allowing myself to enjoy the moment, and it could be fun with you." As she stroked his hand, she said, "But I don't enjoy being hungover in the morning."

They were both quiet, holding hands before Roman asked, "Are you reclusive by nature, or do you enjoy the company of people? Do you like to entertain and perhaps have friends in for dinner?"

Grinning, she said, "Both, I can sit and read a book for hours, but I love to entertain. I like the give and take of conversation across a kitchen table. I would enjoy having three or four couples in for dinner and games, maybe board games, dominoes, or simple card games. What about you?"

"The same," he replied. "I grew up with Mom and Dad playing in card clubs with friends and relatives. There were and still are potlucks going on in her group constantly. I missed the connection with family and friends as I traveled worldwide."

"If you have missed it, Honey," Julia asked, "Would you like to have that as part of our lives? Would you like to start with dinner for a couple of our friends? We could see if they would like to get together every month or two?"

"Great idea," he said. "We could start introducing our friends and building our own connected support group. When would you want to start?"

Excitedly, she answered, "How about right away, maybe next weekend? The weather is perfect, and you have a magnificent place for a barbeque."

Roman nodded his agreement.

"I can't wait to 'Skype' my best friend Kathleen and tell her the news. Maybe she could fly out for our dinner. I'm eager for her to meet you."

"She must be a special friend if she would fly here for a barbeque." He asked, "Where would she be flying from?"

"Washington D.C., Kathleen and I are sorority sisters just like her dad, President Myers, was fraternity brothers with my dad at UCLA. Even though it's an honorary title, I call her dad Uncle Alex. He is my Godfather. It still seems strange that he is now the president, and my father is a governor. Uncle Alex met this beautiful girl from Texas in one of his classes and moved there when he graduated. Kathleen and I grew up thinking we were long-distance sisters. Our families vacationed together for years."

Pausing, she said, "I know you said you knew President Myers and played poker with him in the family quarters. Did you ever meet Kathleen?"

"No, it was always just him and some staff. Very informal. I could barely move with my wounds. He was always gracious."

"Uncle Alex is always comfortable to be around. Anyhow, when it came time for college, we didn't want to go to UCLA like our fathers. Instead, we decided on Arizona State in Tempe. The experience and time together were magical, and we bonded forever. Her mother's family owned a ranch outside Austin with thousands of acres. Her mother's family influence got Uncle Alex started in Texas politics. Unfortunately, she lost her mother in a car wreck when she was a teenager. It was a sad time. The ranch is in trust for her until she turns thirty. In the meantime, a management team runs it. Kathleen has functioned as her father's official hostess ever since her mother's death, which is why she is living in Washington."

"Well, her father won't be president forever."

"True, I wish Kathleen lived closer, so she could be a regular part of our dinner group. I want to invite a special childhood friend, Samantha. It's weird how life works out. She lived next door and was my friend when we were young. I remember her father as a great guy and a Portland Trailblazer. Charlie Miller's father killed him when a burglary went bad. Samantha lived with us for a while as her mother recovered from being shot in the burglary. We have remained friends forever."

With wide eyes, Julia got quiet, looking out the window. Then, looking back at Roman, she said, "I just realized Samantha's father's death started the chain of events which led to the Miller family trying to kill my father. I don't think I should tell her that if it weren't for her father's murder, I would never have met you, Roman."

"No, I wouldn't bring that up to her," he agreed. "The problem is, I have many friends I want you to meet. I don't want to alienate a friend by not inviting them. For certain, I want to invite Jimmy if he hasn't left on another assignment."

Julia jumped in, "Then you have to invite Alexia. If you invite her, he will stay."

With a grin, he agreed. "I think you are right. The heat between them almost crackled the air when they were close together. Which I think is great. I love my sister, but her taste in men is lacking. Jimmy is like the brother I never had. I'd love to see them get together."

Julia said, "If they haven't already, they soon will. I think for her, it was like me seeing you the first time. You were clear across the room, yet I knew you were for me. I think she connected with Jimmy in the same way. If I'm right, her mind is building walls, but her body is on fire. Just like mine is," she added with a grin.

Stroking her palm, he watched her squirm as he said, "I would like to invite some of my SEAL buddies who stayed in the area with me. You met Bridger. He's a lot of fun if he's sober, and it sounds like he will stay sober, hoping Cindy will marry him."

"Good."

"You met Andy Baker and his dog Brutus at the potluck. You'll love him. I want to invite Dink Lindsay so you can meet him. He'll up class the rest of us. Dink works as the maître d' at The Benson Hotel in Portland. I like him and would like to get to know him better myself. Dink, Andy, and Jimmy are all single."

Julia's emotions were transparent as her voice bubbled. "This is exciting. We're planning an event as a couple."

Just then, her phone vibrated with a series of text messages. She started laughing, "Listen to these. This one's from Dad, 'When's the wedding? Your Uncle Alex wants to officiate.' This one's from Uncle Alex, 'Congratulations, Sweetie, Roman is a great guy. Can I perform your wedding ceremony?' And this one's from Kathleen, 'What are you doing holding out on me? When do I meet him? What's the scoop? Is he a hunk? Dad says he a great guy.'"

"Are you serious?" Roman asked, "The president of the United States wants to perform our wedding?"

"Sounds like it," she answered, "I thought he and Dad would argue over who would give me away. I mean, he is my Godfather, which brings us to what we are avoiding. When shall we do this?"

"Guys would say the sooner, the better," he responded. "As for the perks of being married, I'd say tomorrow would be great for the wedding."

She gave him a playful smack, and he continued, "I think the real question is, what do you want to make of it? How many people are we inviting? Do we want small and intimate, or a fancy to do? What is your dream?"

She hesitated a moment, then said, "I hope you don't mind. I've always dreamed of a fairy tale wedding. You know, a white dress, an enormous crowd of people who love me, and my very own handsome prince."

Reaching across the table, she picked up both his hands, "If you are okay with it, I'd love the 'full meal deal,'" she grinned.

"It will take a lot of time for you to pull off." He continued, "But

I'll be okay with that if we don't wait on our relationship perks."

With a grin, she replied, "Perks can start tonight."

Rolling his eyes and shrugging his shoulders, Roman exaggerated an enormous sigh as he said, "Well, with that issue off the table, back to the question of the number of people you want to invite? What are you thinking, 50 people, 100 people, 200 people, 400 or more people? How many are we talking about? Do we need to rent the Portland Convention Center for 10,000?"

She laughed, "Stop it; I can't talk for laughing. I don't know. I'm sure my mom's reviewing the family lists, but Dad's thinking about his business associates and political cronies. Between them, they could come up with two to three hundred people with none of my girlfriends. But, from what I saw of your family and friends at the potluck last week in your boat store showroom, you could surpass that number. We were still out on the Santiam River doing river rescues, and your mom organized an impromptu potluck for when we got back. I swear there were 200 people in the building, and they all brought amazing food."

Grinning, he said, "I'll give you a hundred, maybe a hundred and twenty-five, but I don't think she hit 200. Give her enough time, though, and she could. She is a practiced potlucker."

Julia focused on his face and eyes. She could almost see him thinking. Then, he nodded, saying, "What I'm hearing are over 500 people. WOW, are you certain you don't want to fly to Vegas?"

As she shook her head, he continued, "Where do you want to do this? It will require a big place."

Squeezing his hand in hope, she asked, "How would you feel about the top of your mountain? Getting married on Hawkeye Ridge is beyond my wildest dreams. Is it possible?"

"Yeah," he replied after a pause, "Let's think about the logistics. On the positive side, there it has plenty of room and a magnificent setting." She squeezed his hand again.

He continued, "My cousin Darci' and her partner, Gwen, can do the catering. They're familiar with the logistics of serving up there. Depending on the weather forecast, we would need to rent a large tent or sunscreen, hundreds of chairs, etc. If we set up off to the side of the runway, the runway could remain operational. However, it will take days of grading and graveling of the road to the top. My chairlift can't handle that many guests. Currently, the logging road winds around three thousand acres of trees. My grandfather built it to get trucks close to the logging, not my home. Perhaps I can blade a straighter road, cut off some loops and make it shorter and not as steep. Even if I get the roadbed graded and graveled, it will be necessary to rent a fleet of SUVs and ferry people to the top in a shuttle service. And, if President Myers is officiating, we must coordinate with the Secret Service. I can see them requesting a metal screening setup like at an airport to ensure his safety."

Julia's smile diminished as she listened to him. A fleeting sadness crossed her face as she thought her fairytale wedding couldn't happen. Then her practical self reasserted itself, saying, "That is way too much work and expense to ask you to do for our wedding. I'd love to do it on Hawkeye Ridge, but it's okay if it's not possible. I want to marry you wherever we do it."

Roman shook his head, "I didn't say no. Redoing the road is a project I've put off. I've always known that it would be necessary to redo the logging road at some point. Now is the wrong time of the year for me to grade and gravel the road since we're about to hit the rainy season. I can get started on it now, but we can't get it done before the fall rain will stop the project. Grading the road in the mud isn't practical. If you want to see the view from the top at the wedding, you want the road graded, and you want your guests comfortable with the temperature at the 2000-foot elevation, we're talking about summer. I'd say the earliest would be Memorial Day, and the latest is in mid-September."

"That would be okay," she replied. "It would give both of our mother's time to freak out and time for me to do pre-wedding stuff with my girlfriends. Let's coordinate with our parents, but I think the end of summer would be great. The weather should be warm, and there shouldn't be any rain. That will allow you time to do what you need on the property. And, nobody will stress out over the time factor."

Chapter 11

Present-day
Dining Room
The Oregon Gardens Resort
Silverton, Oregon

Julia's phone rang with the tune 'Hail to the Chief,' and she said, "Oh my. Hello, Uncle Alex."

Roman heard a one-sided conversation.

"Thank you. I'm glad you approve."

"We're thinking about the end of next summer. Roman and I are discussing things right now."

"Yes, he's right here. Do you want me to put you on speakerphone?"

The president's voice came through the phone, "Roman, are you there?"

"Yes, Mr. President, I'm here," he replied.

"I want you to know how happy I am for you both. I think of Julia as my second daughter. She is my goddaughter, and I love her like she was my own. And Julia, God never gave me a son, but I would choose Roman if I could choose one. God moved in mysterious ways to unite two of my favorite people."

Julia squeezed Roman's hand as he said, "Thank you, Mr. President. I love Julia and will do my best to make you proud of me."

"Roman, I already am proud of you. It tickled me when I saw you on the recent newscasts. Stan sent me a complete copy of the video. I am happy to see you up and healthy. When you left the service, I knew you would be alright financially, but I wondered how well you would rehabilitate physically. I didn't know if you would walk without a cane ever again. How did you do it?"

"Well, Mr. President."

"Stop there. You are part of the family now. So, consider me an honorary uncle. Why don't you call me Uncle Alex like Julia does?"

Roman stammered his reply, "Thank you, sir. That will be hard for me to do. It's all I can do to sit here and talk to you. I want to stand at attention. How I rehabbed, sir, required a lot of painful work. In the beginning, I walked constantly, and when I could, I pushed through the pain and started jogging. Tai chi helped with my flexibility and focus. I pushed myself for hours each day before restarting my martial arts exercises. As soon as I could, I started working on our property. I did hard physical labor and kept moving from dawn to dark. Then, I would get out of bed and jog up the road in the dark for hours when the flashbacks hit."

Julia learned about Roman by listening to him talk to her Uncle Alex. She interrupted, "I've seen his scars, but didn't realize how bad his injuries were. He won't talk about it."

President Myers said, "It was grim, but he's not supposed to talk about anything because it's classified, and knowing Roman, he won't talk about it. So, as your Godfather, I'd suggest you don't press him for information, just love him, and count yourself lucky he entered your family's lives."

"I do, Uncle Alex."

"Roman, I'm sure there was more to your rehabbing."

"Yes, sir, several months ago, the SEAL team members in this area agreed to join me for a monthly Challenge Weekend. We start at 8 a.m. on Saturday and finish at 8 p.m. on Sunday. We do a lot of SEAL training, keeping our fighting and water skills sharp. It has helped us. We were getting soft, and we wanted to stay 'fit to fight.'"

President Myers said, "Incredible, you're still training as a unit? Aren't you in the mountains? How do you handle water training?"

Roman replied, "There is a local dam and reservoir, Detroit Lake, where we scuba dive. The civilian equipment isn't what we're used to, but it keeps our skill levels sharp. And no, we're not training to military standards. It's just a way to stay connected and challenge each other to stay fit."

Julia jumped in as the President hung up, "Tell Kathleen we are having a get acquainted barbeque not this weekend but the following one at Roman's house. I'd love it if she came."

♦ ♦ ♦

President Myers sat at The Resolute Desk in the Oval office, lost in thought as he stared at Frederic Remington's bronze, The Broncho Buster. Receiving no answer from the cowboy riding the broncho, he felt ill at ease after hanging up with Roman and Julia. He rang his Chief of Staff, "Is the Chairman of the Joint Chiefs, Admiral Seastrand, in the building?"

"Yes, sir."

"Would you ask him to stop in to see me before he leaves the building?"

Admiral Ronald Seastrand entered the Oval Office in minutes, "You wanted me, sir?"

"Do you remember Lieutenant Commander Roman Nelson?"

"The Ghost?" replied the Admiral, "How could I forget him? We scrubbed his file of classified data and now use his actions as a series of case studies at Annapolis. He's a legend in the SEALS in the Hand-to-Hand Combat classes. Each of the instructors tries to let the midshipmen think they were his coach. Have you heard from him? How's he doing?"

"He's doing great. He's going to marry my goddaughter. I'll send you a video file of his latest action. He's all over the news. Did you see the news on television about the assassination attempt on Governor Anderson in Oregon?"

Admiral Seastrand nodded.

"Well, it was Roman and Jimmy Stockade who saved his life. When I met Roman, he was a crippled wreck because of me. I felt a great sense of obligation to him for what he did for our country. A feeling came up inside me, making me want to know him. Call that feeling, instinct or intuition, or just a voice whispering to my emotions, whatever you want to call it. That voice inside me told me to stay connected to him. That's why I got him and Jimmy Stockade positions with the U.S. Marshals Service on special assignment to the president. Because I listened to the voice, they saved my best friend's life, and he is now marrying my goddaughter."

"Incredible, sir."

"That voice or intuition is talking to me again. Roman and his local SEAL team members are still training once a month as a unit. Just, he said, to stay 'fit to fight.'"

Admiral Seastrand nodded at the military terminology. "Very impressive. Hell, we ask our National Guard units to do one weekend a month, and we pay them."

"Exactly," the president continued. "A voice whispering in my head is telling me to outfit them like they were my personal SEAL team. Jimmy and Roman are marshals. Is there any way we could supply them with a pod of equipment? He mentioned the civilian scuba gear wasn't up to military standards, but mentioned nothing about weapons training."

Admiral Seastrand replied, "Sir, your hunches are good enough for me. If you want them supplied as though they were a SEAL squad, supplied they will be. The Navy has warehouses full of supplies. Commander Nelson would use it discreetly if he ever needed it."

Three weeks later, an 18-wheel flatbed semi-truck with Navy insignia pulled into the parking lot at *Nelson Boat and Tackle*. It contained a series of storage pods and a forklift for unloading them.

An individual in a Navy uniform walked into the store with a clipboard and approached Rose Nelson, "I am Petty Officer 3rd Class Shultz, with a delivery for Lieutenant Commander Nelson. He needs to sign for it. Do you know where he will want it delivered?"

Rose picked up the phone and called her son, "Roman, where are you, and what have you done? Wherever you are, you need to come to the store right away."

When the former SEALS opened the pods on the following Challenge Weekend, it felt like Christmas. One pod contained underwater gear. It held every piece of marine equipment they could ever need, with enough for each teammate. Parachutes and miles of rope for rappelling and camouflage gear appropriate for forest and desert environments filled another pod.

One container bulged with communication gear. Dink, the former communications specialist, was ecstatic. The pod contained radio gear for communication inside the squad while on a mission. Still, the mouth-dropping shock was the equipment that allowed them to communicate inside the military communication system worldwide.

Dink reviewed the binder containing connection frequencies and laughed, "Hey Skipper, guess what our password phrase is."

While the team listened, Dink said, "Casper the Friendly Ghost."

As the team roared in laughter, Jimmy said, "That's gotta be Admiral Seastrand's idea."

The final pod had them in disbelief. It contained weapons and explosives illegal for civilians to possess. Over and over, the team asked, "It just showed up? Didn't you know it was coming? Who shipped it to you, and why? Most of this shit is illegal for us as civilians to possess."

There was no paperwork or invoices, and there were no explanations.

Jimmy said, "Skipper, this is crazy. You'd think we were still active-duty SEALS, and these were the supplies for a mission."

Roman commented, "I know only one person who could authorize all this. Why he wants us to have it, I don't know."

Roman swore the team to secrecy and then moved the pods into his equipment warehouse with the logging equipment. Painting over the military insignia and labeling the containers as logging spare parts, he established around-the-clock video surveillance of the pods. The pod's ultimate defense layer was Bridger's booby-traps he installed for Roman.

Chapter 12

The parking lot
The governor's mansion
Salem, Oregon

Jimmy walked Alexia to her car as Roman and Julia left the governor's mansion for their get-acquainted conversation.

"Interesting," Alexia thought as he spoke, *"I've never seen him when he wasn't composed."*

Jimmy stammered, "I've enjoyed meeting you, Alexia. I've met no one like you. I wish we had the time to get acquainted."

"Uh oh," she thought, *"Balls in my court. Where do I want this to go?"*

With her pulse pounding in her ears, she hesitated before saying, "Do you have to leave right away? I agree. I'd like to get to know you better."

Unsure of himself, Jimmy struggled to say, "I could stick around until I get called for another assignment. How does your calendar look today? Do you have time to find a local park where we can walk and talk?"

They took their cars and went to nearby Minto Island Park, a 1,200-acre city park of meadows and woodlands bordered by the Willamette River. It contained miles of secluded trails winding through the deserted park on the quiet, beautiful, warm fall day. The falling leaves of the maple, sweetgum, and cottonwoods were mixtures of gold and red tones as they drifted to the ground.

Alexia wore slacks, but her running shoes were always in her car.

Jimmy went nowhere without his 'go bag,' which included running shoes. Looking around in the parking lot to verify that Alexia was his only observer, Jimmy took off his sports coat and tie and hung them on a hanger in his car. When he removed his jacket, his shoulder holster containing a Sig 9mm was visible.

Jimmy then removed additional weapons from his sports coat and placed them in a gun safe in the car. Next, he pulled a windbreaker from his 'go bag' and, putting it on, covered up his shoulder holster.

Alexia cracked a joke to lighten the moment, "Boy, you would surprise a mugger. You're a walking arsenal."

Watching his face, she saw him hesitate over his response, "The weapons became part of my clothing when I went into special operations with the Army Rangers. When my enlistment expired, I left the Army for the Navy, I liked the water, and the SEALS captured my heart."

Alexia matched his sober mood. "Thank you for sharing about yourself. I've wondered about you. Are you okay telling me more?"

"That depends," he joked, "Just like your brother, I'm classified."

"I would like to know about you," she said. "At the moment, I know you're handsome, polite, educated, and well dressed. I know you saved my brother's life, which is all I need to know. However, I would like to know the hidden details. What can you tell me about yourself?"

"For starters," he said as they walked along the tree-lined trails. "Your brother told you I saved his life, but he didn't tell you how many times he saved mine. Roman and I are both the same age, 31. I never attended a brick-and-mortar college, but I have enough online credits for my degree if they were all in the correct areas. Getting a degree didn't matter to me. I took the classes I thought would help me become a better, more-rounded person."

"Good for you. They appear to have worked."

"I hope so. I took communication and public speaking classes because I thought they would help my future career. Then, I took classes in Art History, knowing I would take shore leave in Italy and France. I spent days in the Sistine Chapel and the Louvre but took the classes before going. I wanted to educate my taste and raise my appreciation of what I would see."

"Now I'm filled with envy," she said with a half-smile. "I would love to see those places."

"You should see them. Just take some vacation and go."

"I know. I keep waiting in life to do things on my bucket list. Now for the scary questions," she said. "Please tell me you're not married?"

She continued with a playful laugh at his head shake, "Have you ever married? Do you have any kids? You know, tell me the personal stuff I'm dying to ask about."

Jimmy gave a half-laugh, "I guess I have an advantage. I know a lot about you. Roman loves you. He's shown me many photos of you, and I've seen portions of your emails. There were lots of newspaper gossip columns about you and your famous boyfriends. Buddies on shipboard share a lot, and Roman is proud of you. I feel like I got to know you before I ever met you. After I met you, your personality impressed me more than your beauty."

Alexia's head dropped as she looked at the ground and gave a slight head shake. Then, taking his hand, she said with a quivering voice, "I know Roman jokes about my tall, dark, and handsome flavors of the month."

Jimmy, observing her face and eyes, said, "I apologize. I didn't mean to upset you. To answer your question, no, I've never married or fathered children. No girlfriend has held my hand like you are doing now."

Alexia stopped him and, looking him full in the face, asked, "How can that be? As smooth, handsome, and for many women, as dangerous as you are, are you telling me you have never been with a woman?"

Jimmy's ears turned red as he looked at the ground and said, "Yup, not information you share with the guys, but never. As a young man, I was shy and insecure around girls. So if a girl spoke to me, I thought of what to say ten minutes too late."

He paused as they continued walking on the trail. He took a deep breath and said, "My mother raised me in Cleveland as a single mother. We were dirt poor, but she was proud. I never had new clothes until the Army gave me my first set. But, she kept the clothes from the Salvation Army Thrift Shop clean and pressed."

Holding Alexia's hand, he started walking again, "Mom raised me inside a strait-laced fundamentalist church. I started questioning her strict faith in junior high school, but I learned moral lessons that I value, including respect for women. When I left for the Army, I promised my mother to respect women, not become involved with the loose women around the Army camps, and not become a drunk. I've drunk too much a time or two, but I've tried to follow her advice."

He paused again before continuing, "My mother died six months after I went into the Army. I never knew she had ovarian cancer until her death. Perhaps that's why she encouraged me to enlist."

"I'm sorry. That sounds devastating."

"Yeah, it was," he sighed and shook his head sadly. Then, with a self-deprecating chuckle, he said, "I guess the answer is yes, I'm a 31-year-old male virgin. Unheard of, right?"

Alexia got up on her toes and kissed him on his cheek. "Thank you for telling me. Your story is safe with me. I respect you for telling me. You and I are the genuine 'odd couple.' Everyone looks at you and me and thinks we're sexually experienced and promiscuous, and we're not."

Alexia tried to tamp down her rising fear at his questioning look. With tears forming in her eyes, she asked herself, *"Do I tell him or not?"*

Jimmy waited before saying, "You know I want more information."

Alexia took a deep breath before beginning with hesitation, "I know the jokes about my bevy of men. People think I'm a tramp. I'm not. I'm terrified and don't know if I can ever become intimate with a man. Holding hands, flirting, and teasing are easy. I'm a practiced kisser, but my relationships end when the 'flavor of the month' wants to become intimate. I tense up, waiting on an anxiety attack as I think of what will happen."

Jimmy kept his face noncommittal and continued walking while he thought, *"Careful what you say now, Smoke, ol boy, that took a lot for her to say. Although, she still has more experience than me."*

She looked up as they walked to see his response.

"Do you prefer women?" he asked, hoping it wasn't true and looking straight ahead in case she said yes.

"Oh no," she laughed, "I dream about men, fantasize about the person I'm dating, and wonder if he's the one. Trashy romance novels late at night are my friends, and then I try to imagine myself doing those erotic things with the person I'm dating. Unfortunately, it's the action point I can't get to."

He stopped to look at her, but she shook her head and said, "Can we keep walking? It's easier to talk if I'm not looking at you."

As they started walking again, he asked, "Do you know what causes the anxiety attacks?"

Silent, Alexia walked, appreciating his silence before she said, "Yes, I know where it comes from."

Looking down at her profile as they walked, Jimmy saw tears streaming down her face. He handed her a linen handkerchief. She dabbed her eyes. After 100 yards of walking, he asked, "Did you ever discuss with the various members of the 'flavor of the month club' why you couldn't move forward?"

"No, no, I couldn't," she immediately responded.

"I learned from the counselors the military made us see prior to discharge," he said with concern in his voice, "You are better off talking about issues with an understanding person than keeping them locked up inside to fester."

Picking some ripe wild blackberries and handing them to her, he said, "Since I don't want to be another 'flavor of the month,' I promise to be understanding if you'd like to talk about it. Maybe we can figure out our mutual hang-ups together."

"It might take a while."

Jimmy drawled with a slow smile, "For the right woman, I could create awhile."

They continued walking, stopping now and again to pick the

sweet blackberries lining the back pathways. Hearing no response, Jimmy strolled quietly. It was a comfortable silence, with neither feeling the compulsion to talk.

◆ ◆ ◆

Alexia regained her composure as they walked. Looking up at him, she wondered, *"Is this the man I have been waiting for? He is smoking hot, I feel safe with him, and I like him. If I share with him what happened, will he run away? But, of course, if I don't let him know what happened, I will chase him away like everyone else."*

She said in a quiet, ragged voice, "I was raped."

Jimmy stopped and pulled her into his arms for a long, comforting hug. She resisted, tensing before putting her head on his chest and consciously relaxed.

Jimmy commented, "That was a conversation stopper I didn't expect. Would it help to tell me about it?"

"I don't know. I never have. I just bottled it up."

Alexia waited in his arms another moment and then started walking, "I was a freshman in college at Oregon State. My sorority sisters invited me to go to a pool party with them. Every weekend, there was a standing pool party at an apartment complex near OSU. A professor from the Middle East owned the apartment. I didn't know if he was Iraqi, Iranian, or Saudi. I just knew he was wealthy. The pool party started every Saturday and every Sunday at noon. You were welcome if you were female and showed up in a bikini. The sororities kept the pool packed with beautiful young women in bikinis. There was an open bar of alcohol and munchies. My understanding was that Muslims didn't drink. Boy, was I wrong. I met the professor, the oldest of the three guys, hosting the party. He and I started drinking and making out."

Alexia struggled to talk. Her voice came out in broken spurts as she gasped for air between sobs. Jimmy listened in silence. "I got drunk on champagne, but I felt he was out of control and told him to stop. My struggling seemed to fuel him. He got aggressive and physical, raping me repeatedly throughout the night. When he let me leave in the morning, he told me to keep my mouth shut if I knew what was good for me. If I told anyone, he said his friends would kill me."

Sobbing, with her shoulders shaking, Alexia said, "I believed him, dropped out of OSU and my sorority. I went to Portland and registered at Portland State University, which is how I wound up with an internship at the TV station. His threat worked. I've said nothing to anyone until now about what happened."

Jimmy's voice was like ice as he said, "I'd be happy to go chat with him about what he did, maybe explain to him the error he made."

Alexia looked at Jimmy and retook his hand, "That's sweet, but no. If he backtalked you at all, you'd kill him. It's why I never told Roman, but if the gentleman in question ever surfaces in my life again, I may give you his name for a midnight call."

Jimmy answered, "I wouldn't kill him unless I felt it was necessary, but he'd never rape another woman."

Alexia knew she held hands with Jimmy, but it sounded like the voice of the man she'd heard referred to as 'Smoke' who spoke. His voice was ice cold and edged like a razor blade. While walking and holding his hand, she looked at his face and clenched jaw. She knew he would do as he said if she gave the go-ahead. She shivered.

Smoke walked in silence, remembering another time, and thinking, "It wouldn't be the first time I've 'de-nutted' a rapist."

He put the memory aside. He did not need to start another string of flashbacks.

Chapter 13

Alexia and Jimmy continued walking through the park for hours with the leaves crunching beneath their feet. Just like Roman and Julia, they were asking questions and getting acquainted. The migrating geese landed in the open fields near the river, their raucous calls loud in the distance.

A primary topic of conversation became Jimmy's desire to stay close to Alexia. He said, "Correct me if I'm wrong, but it feels like we're talking about taking the time to develop a solid relationship? It's what I want. Is it what you want?"

She replied with a trembling voice, "It's scary, but yes. I like you, I respect you, and I trust you. I've already told you something I've told no one else about myself, and you're still here. Hopefully, in time, I will become comfortable with you. I hope when I am, I can fall in love with you and make love to you."

Jimmy asked, "Do you want to do that?"

"What do you think I've been thinking about all afternoon?"

"Same here," he responded. "I don't think a cold shower will help. You need to let me know when you think you are ready."

"I will."

The afternoon got late as they walked. Not wanting to stop talking, Jimmy invited her to go out for dinner later in the evening.

Alexia said, "I need to go by my condo in Portland, clean up, and change before going anywhere. Crying has wrecked my face. I can't go to dinner with puffy eyes and smeared makeup."

"I hope it's been good crying."

Squeezing his arm, she said, "It has."

"I'll close my Salem hotel room and get one in Portland for the evening. That way, I'll be closer to you until it's time for me to leave."

At 6:30, he rang the bell on her condo dressed in a camel-colored Italian cashmere sports coat with darker brown wool-blend slacks. In addition, he wore an open collar silk polo shirt of an ivory color.

She answered the door with a mid-calf, red sheath-style sleeveless dress. It was high-necked but slit up the side to mid-thigh. She wore heels, bringing her closer to Jimmy's height.

Jimmy gave her an appraising look, "You look stunning. You are a beautiful woman."

She returned the compliment, "I told you I couldn't be a one-night stand, but I wish I could be the way you look."

Jimmy smiled, took her hand as they walked to the car, and said, "Let's take our time and work on multiple nights."

At her smile, he continued, "I hope it's all right if we go to dinner at The Benson? One of my friends works there. Since his discharge from the service, I haven't seen him and want to say hello to him."

He saw her flinch for a moment, and then she explained, "I haven't eaten there in a few years. It's where I met Roman the night he returned from the SEALS. I was with a member of my tall, dark, and handsome flavor of the month club. It was an unpleasant experience, but I would be proud to return with you."

As they drove to The Benson and left the car at valet parking, Jimmy told her he was thinking about resigning from the marshal's office and staying in Portland.

She said, "That puts a lot of pressure on me. I hope I'm worth the risk."

"You are," he added, smiling.

He said, "I've thought about opening a security firm for years.

There is an enormous market in the corporate world for personal security for upper executives. My projects for President Myers involved high-level bodyguard work for corporate CEOs or political officials. They were all friends of the president. My job was to keep people safe while the FBI figured out who and what the threat was and neutralized it. It was stuff similar to what I did for Governor Anderson, but it gave me great training."

Walking into The Benson, he continued, "I think there are a lot of wealthy individuals and corporations who would like not just a bodyguard service but a total security package. And they would like to do it without government or press involvement. I have the resources, connections, and experience to pull it off."

From across the room in the staid Benson came a loud, welcoming voice, "Smoke, is that you?"

Hurrying towards them from across the room came the maître d', Dink Lindsay. Dink and Jimmy hugged like long-lost friends, "Chief, it's great to see you."

"And you, what say we forgo the Petty Officer and Chief and make it Dink and Jimmy?" Jimmy suggested.

"Agreed, you call me Dink, and I will try to call you Jimmy, but you'll always be The Chief or Smoke in my thinking," said Dink

Dink then looked at Alexia. "I apologize for ignoring you, Miss Nelson. Welcome back. We have missed seeing you."

"I don't know if I am surprised you remember me or if I'm embarrassed you do."

"Nonsense, you are a memorable woman, and may I add, one who looks stunning this evening. You are always welcome here. The problem that evening wasn't with you," he replied with a smooth baritone voice.

Dink continued, "Let me escort you to our private dining room." As he led them to an alcove, Jimmy asked when he would be off duty, explaining, "There is something important I need your advice on, and perhaps your participation."

Dink raised a questioning eyebrow as he looked at Alexia. Jimmy answered the look, "It's nothing she can't hear. She's part of it."

Dink said, "Why don't you enjoy a relaxing dinner? I'll stop back when dinner is over."

He warned them, "Two former Rangers work here. When he returned home, they got the Skipper's autograph, and both got the signatures framed for their walls. Is it ok if they stop by? I know they would love to get your autograph, Chief."

Surprised, Jimmy nodded his head.

Returning over dessert, Dink introduced Mark and Kelly, two clean-cut buff young men in their late 20s. They stood at attention near the table. "Chief Stockade, we're honored to meet you. You are a legend in special operation conversations. Would you autograph a menu for each of us? We may need to prove we met you to our friends."

Alexia remembered watching the two young men when they asked Roman for his autograph when he arrived back from active duty. She commented on how much they had matured in their sophistication and confidence levels. Polished in their bearing and conversation, they exuded charm.

Kelly said, shifting his attention to her, "Thank you, Miss Nelson. Mentoring by Mr. Lindsay helped a lot. You would do us a great honor if you also autographed the menu for us."

She signed the menu just below Jimmy's signature. She couldn't help but see how he signed. He personalized each autograph with their name and signed it as Chief Warrant Officer James Stockade. Below his signature, with quotation marks, he signed it "Smoke."

Jimmy asked them about their careers in the Rangers and told them he started as a Ranger before switching to the SEALS.

Mark said, "We know, sir, the Rangers still talk about you rescuing those girls in North Africa."

Jimmy said, "I hope they're not talking too much. That rescue is still classified."

Kelly laughed, "It's becomes much less classified after a pitcher of beer. I think every new troop gets told the story."

Jimmy changed the subject, "With the skill sets you both have, why are you part of the wait staff here at The Benson?"

They gave him the standard answers of meeting and working with friendly people, a pleasant place to work, a significant benefits package, etc. After the surface answers, what it came down to was the pay. Upon returning home, there were no jobs for their skills other than as a 'mall rent a cop' or a local security firm for minimum wage. They made more working at The Benson than they could in their military career fields. Both functioned as either a bartender or a server. The salary provided an adequate base wage, but the tips were exceptional.

Jimmy asked them, "If you could make money using the skills you learned as a Ranger, would you prefer to do that?"

"Absolutely."

Jimmy said, "I enjoyed meeting you both. If I hear of an opportunity I think you would be interested in, would you like me to call you?"

They both gave him their cell phone numbers and told him to call day or night.

◆ ◆ ◆

Later that evening, Alexia sipped her Crème Sherry and commented, "I thought your buddy Dink was smooth, but you give the word a new definition. Those guys were eating out of your hands. Where did you learn that?"

"Watching guys like Dink, who was always the epitome of sophistication. I told you I've planned on opening a security firm for years. It was always my exit plan for getting out of the service. When we got discharged, I had the money I needed to start my business, but little motivation. Now I do. I can't go traipsing all over the country for President Myers and expect to have time to get acquainted with you. So, I think now's the time to open my business."

Twirling the Oregon Cabernet in his wineglass, he looked at Alexia. "Remember I told you about my shyness. It didn't take a rocket scientist to know that wouldn't take me where I wanted to go.

I don't consider myself smooth, but I invested a lot of time, effort, and money to develop the skills I thought would eventually further my business. So, if the Navy offered a class that would advance my special operations skills or the soft skills I would need in business, I took it. Knowing I lacked people skills, I took classes on communication, conflict resolution, or sales, along with the basic business courses."

Nodding her head, she said, "You are a driven personality, aren't you?"

"I don't think driven is correct. Focused is perhaps a better word. Before I jump into business, I want advice from you and Roman and to hear Dink's ideas. Do you think Roman could free up time tomorrow?"

"I expect it depends on what Julia has in mind," she said with a knowing grin. "Why don't you text him and find out?"

Digging out his phone, he texted Roman, "Ghost ol' buddy, I need your serious advice. Hoping I can meet up with you and Julia, Alexia, and maybe Dink tomorrow, about noonish? I could spring for lunch?"

His phone chirped with, "Sure, where at and what time? We'd love to get together. Lots of news on our end."

A minute later, the phone chirped again. "Julia wants to know if this is business advice or personal advice. She knows her dad would let us use the conference room at the governor's mansion if it is business. She also said if it is business advice, she could ask him to sit in if you wanted."

Reading it out loud, Jimmy hesitated. Alexia, however, jumped at the idea. "What a great idea. Tell her yes, you would value her father's advice."

For a short while, the phones chirped back and forth non-stop. By the time Dink showed up, Jimmy told him of the change in plans, "Instead of picking your brains tonight, could you free up lunchtime tomorrow?"

At Dink's agreement, Jimmy continued, "I would like your input on an idea. The Skipper and his fiancée will be there, Alexia and I, and Governor and Mrs. Anderson."

"No way. I'd love to see the Skipper, but I don't belong in the same room as the governor. Not if you want me to say anything. He's a frequent guest for dinner. He and Mrs. Anderson are wonderful people, but nothing I say would be relevant in his company."

Jimmy convinced him otherwise.

Chapter 14

Flashback
Boko Haram camp
Nigeria, Africa

Later, lying in his strange hotel room, Jimmy forced his mind to stop thinking of Alexia. With no conscious thought, it rolled back to his first tour of duty in the military. He was a sergeant in the Army Rangers. He and his squad were advisors to the Nigerian Rangers attempting to locate the female students kidnapped by the Boko Haram. The Nigerian Army recaptured a handful of the young girls held as sex slaves, but over one hundred were still missing.

The Nigerian Rangers and their American advisors followed the Boko Haram deep into mountainous terrain in a stealth operation. Finding the hidden enclave, the Nigerian Rangers did as their American counterparts advised. Waiting until the darkest part of the night, they infiltrated the encampment wearing night-vision goggles. The Rangers knifed the sentries without warning.

With the sentries eliminated, the Rangers silently entered each hut and waited until a shot rang out, awakening the camp. The terrorists raised their hands as they saw guns pointed at their heads.

Morning found Jimmy lining up the captives for the march back. Each prisoner had the young girl he claimed as his sex slave standing by his side. Pregnant bellies frequently stretched their clothing. The Nigerian sergeant stopped and spoke to the pregnant girls. Several received a fatherly hug from him. Tears formed in his eyes, and anger vibrated in his voice when he came to Jimmy.

He told Jimmy, "Those pregnant girls are my daughter's classmates. Fortunately, my daughter was home for her mother's birthday at the time of the kidnapping. Last night, we did matters your way, and it worked. We are in my country, so today we'll do matters my way, and it will also work."

The Nigerian sergeant never heard of the Stockholm syndrome in which captives bonded with their captors, but he saw it in action over the years. Lining up the girls, he walked them down the line of their captors one at a time.

The sergeant took each young woman down the line of captives. Then, in front of each man, he asked, "Did this man rape you?"

Multiple men frequently raped the women before an individual claimed one for his own. At least one woman identified each of the men as a rapist. However, a captive seldom acknowledged as a rapist, the man who claimed her as his permanent sex slave.

The sergeant told Jimmy, "These men will die today for what they did. We are not wasting our time taking them back for a trial. We'll line them up and shoot them. Last night, we followed your orders not to kill. Today you may give each of the rapists the gift of life."

The Nigerian sergeant continued, looking Jimmy in the eyes, "However, actions must have consequences. There is a price for each life. They are guilty of raping and impregnating these young girls. We are not returning them for a trial. I will bring these men to you one at a time, and everyone can watch as you offer them their life. But, the price for their life is you geld them, and they become the lifetime slave of the one they impregnated. They can then support the child they fathered but do no additional harm to the mother. If they think the price is too high, we can shoot them. Life must have consequences."

Jimmy grimly sharpened his knife as they brought captive after captive to him. Finally, the sergeant asked each rapist, "Do you wish to live your life gelded as the slave of your forced child bride, or do you choose death?"

It was a gory spectacle as each prisoner walked naked to Jimmy, lifted his penis high, and watched Jimmy toss his testicles in a bucket.

Then, with Nigerian Rangers holding each arm, another Ranger cauterized the wound with a hot iron and, in one motion, lifted the iron rod and branded their chest as a rapist.

The men's screams and the women's wailing seared into Jimmy's subconscious.

With an audible gasp, Jimmy's eyes popped open. He turned his head from side to side and, taking a deep breath to slow his heartbeat, recognized his hotel room.

Sliding out of the sweat-drenched bedclothes, he went to the bathroom and washed his face.

Chapter 15

Shortly before noon, cars arrived at Governor Stan and Margo Anderson's home. Margo sat Julia down to discuss wedding plans while Roman and Stan chit-chatted, getting acquainted.

Dink Lindsay arrived with Jimmy, bringing boxes of various pizzas, bags of chips, and soft drinks. Alexia showed up with vegetable trays and dips for the health conscious.

They skipped the conference room and went to the kitchen and family dining area. After plates of food surrounded the table, Jimmy began. First, he thanked the governor for allowing them to meet at his home and agreeing to sit in on the conversation. Next, he told the governor how much he enjoyed working with him on his security detail but was glad the need appeared over.

Jimmy then got into the purpose of the visit. "For years, I have dreamed of opening a security firm after getting out of the Navy. I have invested years of training and classes preparing for this venture."

Roman watched his friend with a grin that went ear to ear and nodded his head. Jimmy's strange mixture of classes now made sense.

Jimmy continued, "Upon discharge, the opportunity to work out of the U.S. Marshals Service doing what I wanted to do was the only remaining piece of training I felt I needed. I'm ready. I have decided I want to stay here in Oregon. It's time for me to get my business going. I want to tell you what I'm planning because I value your advice. Please point out any pitfalls you see and give me your recommendations to help me succeed."

Dink piped up with a question, "Let's start with the hard issue. Smoke, ol buddy, what kind of security firm are you talking about opening? The term 'security firm' covers a lot of ground. Lots of former SEALS go into 'security work.' All too often, they're just working as a paid contractor or mercenary doing what we did when we were in the service. Our government hires thousands, but the security firm eventually works for the highest bidder. Is that what you are talking about?"

Jimmy shook his head as he replied, "No. You are correct in saying many former military employees turn to work as private contractors upon discharge. They provide essential security services overseas, protect our bases and embassies, or tackle assignments that are off-limits for our armed forces. It's one way the government has provided necessary services with a shrinking military. The various governments, ours included, 'outsource' and hire the former military to continue doing their former jobs under private contracts. So, the leaders may shrink the military budget but pay for the same services out of a different pocket. Sneaky."

Jimmy paced the room, eating pizza and talking. The food disappeared as his friends ate and followed his rapid movements around the room with their eyes.

"I've slept in enough tents, eaten enough sand, and killed enough people. I don't want to do that anymore, regardless of the pay. Another type of security would fall into the realm of corporate espionage or protection against corporate espionage. In today's world, that requires high technology computer hacking skills. I know people with those skills I can hire, but that isn't my interest."

Picking up another slice of pizza, Jimmy paced with a contagious grin. Catching Roman's eyes, he said, "I'm not interested in protecting a corporation from corporate malfeasance. I can't help them if an accountant is 'cooking the books' or employees steal secrets. I'm talking about a firm that would do what I did for Governor Anderson.

"The firm I envision will provide personal, private, high-end security for high-net-worth individuals. We will get called when an individual needs protection against a specific threat until someone else identifies and resolves the risk."

Roman returned Jimmy's look and winked, as Jimmy, looking at the governor, said, "Think of what we did for you, Governor Anderson. One team, I suspect you never saw. It surrounded this house 24 hours a day while the Millers were a threat. Another team provided a car in front of you, and behind you everywhere you traveled, with a series of rotating cars. That way, no one could become familiar with your entourage. If you remember, I always wanted to know your schedule a day in advance?"

Stan nodded.

Jimmy continued, "We scheduled a moving team of undercover people going where you were going, but we got there and secured the area before you arrived. The last layer of defense was me. As your driver and personal assistant, I inserted myself up close and into your life. My job required me to be close to you at all times. That's the service I want to provide. It will be expensive and discrete. But, I think some people need protection and may not want local police involvement."

Taking a breath, he asked, "Comments?"

Governor Anderson started the conversation, "I know there is a need. There are plenty of high-income earners who receive threats. Think about it; corporate CEOs receive threats from disgruntled people about how their firm does business. Many celebrities and professional athletes can afford your services and receive threats. Politicians are always receiving threats. I don't know if they could afford your services, but many were wealthy before they got into politics."

The governor nodded, "Yes, I think there is a market need."

It was Roman's turn to talk, "My mind turned to the business side. You'll need an excellent lawyer to help set up the proper corporate structure. You want to incorporate so that you shield your assets from liability."

Jimmy nodded, and Stan said, "I can refer you to an excellent lawyer."

Roman continued, "You'll need an insurance broker who can handle the liability insurance for you and your employees. You must protect your corporation, yourself, and your employees from lawsuits or damage claims."

Jimmy nodded, and again, Stan said with a grin, "I can also refer you to a business insurance broker."

Dink asked, "What about the laws? What happens if one of your guys is carrying a gun and gets involved in a shooting?"

Jimmy answered, "I need a conversation with Stan's lawyer friend to answer that. We want to operate inside the law and have concealed carry permits for whatever state we're in. The issue is, what happens if we shoot someone, and we're no longer members of the military or the marshal's office?"

Jimmy stopped pacing and frowning and said, "I need a long conversation with Governor Anderson's lawyer about those issues. However, I plan to hire former Special Operations guys, SEALS, Delta Force, Rangers, etc. I presume that those guy's hand-to-hand combat skills make them deadly. I know Roman and I are lethal in close contact situations. So, if the threat is up close, weapons aren't necessary. My experience with the marshal's office makes me think situations seldom wind up in a gunfight."

Dink rejoined the conversation, "Where do all of us fit into your thinking? We love you, Smoke, but it appears your plans include everything we're talking about."

Jimmy took a breath before answering. Looking at everyone, he said, "I want you on my Board of Directors. All of you. Roman, I want you to help me develop our agent's training program in hand-to-hand combat. Dink, I want you to train our team members on class and sophistication. I want them to have the skills to fit into any situation. Do with my team what you did with those two servers at The Benson. They are former Rangers, yet they could serve or be guests in any high-brow setting. They are what I want our representatives to look and act like."

Looking at Alexia and Julia, he said, "I'd like you both to sit in on hiring interviews. I'm not looking just for combat skills but for a well-rounded, polished person. Your 'woman's intuition' in hiring will be valuable in eliminating the aggressive male macho types. I want people who are polite because it's in their nature. Dink can teach them what fork or wine glass to use, but you can't teach human nature."

Looking at the governor, he said, "Governor Anderson, I never expected to know an individual of your stature, but I would always value your input, knowledge, and wisdom. I don't know if ethics laws allow you to sit on a for-profit board, but if you can, I'd love to have you."

The conversation flowed back and forth for the rest of the afternoon. By the time the afternoon came to a close, Jimmy knew his plan.

Jimmy said, "I'll contact the lawyer, business insurance broker, and CPA Stan recommended tomorrow. Alexia, would you reach out to your realtor friend right away? Let her know I need help locating an office in an exclusive complex. I don't need a large office, but I want it to exude class and be in a private setting."

"I'll send her a text right now, but I know she is busy."

"You might also tell her I want to find a comfortable home on acreage. I want to be south of Portland, perhaps in the Wilsonville, Canby, or Aurora farmlands. I'm hoping to find a property with a barn or warehouse, maybe a former horse property, where I can use the barn to train my 'special agents.' Please let her know if she can find the right office and home for me, I'm prepared to submit purchase offers tomorrow. If she is like most Realtors, she will cancel conflicting appointments and make herself available if she thinks she will make two big sales in one day."

Alexia and Julia gasped out loud. Dink and Roman, however, grinned and nodded their heads. The action-oriented Smoke they knew was back.

Jimmy said, "What I'm reluctant to do is contact President Myers and resign my position as a marshal."

With conflict in his voice, he said, "I don't know why I dread telling him I want to quit. Maybe it's because I like him as a person, or maybe it's because when the chips were down, he did right by our team."

Dink questioned, "I don't know how you all seem to know the president. How did that happen?"

Alexia and Julia shared a look and said, "We know the answer to that, 'it's classified.'"

Everyone laughed.

◆ ◆ ◆

As they wrapped up, Stan reminded Roman and Julia of a previous week's conversation.

"The day after the two of you did the river rescues, I told you I would award you a medal, The Governor's Hero's Medal. The presentation is scheduled for Thursday at 10 a.m., at my office. Jimmy, I want you there. I intend to give you the same medal for the action on Hawkeye Ridge. The three of you saved many lives last week, including mine and your mothers. So, you can damn well receive a medal."

Roman shook his head.

"Now, Roman, quit shaking your head. I want to take advantage of the press coverage at the medal presentation and announce that you accepted an appointment as Statewide Director of Natural Disaster Preparedness. Your state needs you. Please tell me you'll help us out?"

After a bit more arm twisting, Roman said he would do it.

◆ ◆ ◆

Julia watched Alexia across the table during the meal and Jimmy's presentation to his friends. She thought, *There's a woman watching her man with pride in her eyes. Jimmy may not know it, but she has his single days numbered.*

As the conversation wrapped up, the topic became a discussion about a barbeque the following weekend at Hawkeye Ridge. Stan said prior appointments kept him from attending, but everyone else agreed to bring a 'potluck' dish.

Chapter 16

Present-day
Corvallis, OR

Khalil, Fathi, and Chawki were back in Corvallis to start the next term at Oregon State University. Khalil made an impressive sight striding around OSU in his flowing white robes as he went to teach his classes on Comparative Studies of the Muslim Nations. Students striving to understand the constant chaos in the Mideast filled his lecture halls.

Khalil did not go to Libya this year. Instead, he hosted rotating contingents of visitors at the ranch outside Paisley. None of the visitors wore robes, but they did wear cowboy hats that shielded their Mideast heritage from the sky. Their concern was shielding their faces from satellite cameras, not sunburn.

Most of the visitors were from the United States or Western Europe and looked like regular summer camp participants. They developed their confidence by sleeping on the ground in tents, cooking their food, riding horses in the mountains, and playing games on the obstacle course. They fired weapons at the new rifle range by the hour. Khalil constructed the rifle range to baffle the sound.

No visitors saw the hours of classes conducted under cover of the large tents on explosive handling and creating IEDs, improvised explosive devices. When it was time for a 'live fire' exercise of the bombs they made, they used an abandoned quarry next to the rifle range. Khalil planned to explain the explosions as blasts to create rock for landscape retaining walls if anyone asked about the noise.

There were also classes on computer hacking and phone cloning. Rashid, who lived in Khalil's apartment complex in Corvallis, became the acknowledged expert. They spent hours learning to pass near an individual using their phone and clone the password. They focused on learning how to access an individual's social media accounts and listen in on private conversations. No one knew what they were looking for, but Khalil told them, "You'll know what you are looking for when you find it. Until then, keep looking."

Fathi and Chawki hosted the Saturday bikini parties at the pool. Over time, the apartment complex filled with young Muslim men, but the pool party continued as an established event with the young sorority girls. Those men sharing the apartment were disciples of Khalil and held radicalized viewpoints. They were trained jihadists looking for a challenge worthy of their developing skills.

Rashid spent the summer working on a maintenance crew for cell phone towers. In the evening, he pinpointed the towers in the Willamette Valley and the towers crossing the Cascades on a map. With his interest in technology, he paid attention to the fragility of the towers.

He asked his coworkers, "What would keep them from working?"

Or, "How long would it take to fix the tower if 'X' happened?"

Rashid appeared concerned the entire network would go down. "How do we protect against a catastrophic failure," he asked each new supervisor.

Fathi worked all summer for the Oregon Department of Transportation in the Santiam Canyon, and Chawki worked for the U.S. Department of Forestry, fighting fires in the Cascades. Fathi learned how to drive a dump truck and road grading equipment. His job paid him to get a CDL, a commercial driver's license, endorsement on his license.

Chawki went through training to fight forest fires. It was a multicultural experience. Many young men were Caucasian, but a significant portion was Hispanic. He was the sole Muslim.

Chawki worked alongside young men who were grateful for a well-paying job. The hard physical work provided enough income for the immigrants to support extended family members. Without fail, the immigrants possessed a positive spirit and an attitude of gratitude. They loved the United States and went through hardships to get here.

Chawki felt a sense of pride in defeating a fire but was certain what his coworkers would think if they knew what he and his uncle were planning. He questioned the knot in his stomach as he worried about their future actions.

◆ ◆ ◆

Both Fathi and Chawki complained to their uncle about doing such strenuous jobs all summer. They'd looked forward to cruising the Mediterranean again on a yacht, not fighting forest fires and driving trucks.

Khalil explained, "You must blend in and appear like normal college students who need a job in the summer. You'll not know until later if the skills you are learning now in the summer jobs will have value in your mission."

He reminded them, "We're waiting on a target of great opportunity to appear. When it does, it is possible that what you learn in your summer jobs will be useful."

Chawki disobeyed his uncle, Khalil, in one way. Khalil ordered his nephews to form no emotional attachments with western girls. Chawki rationalized, in his mind, that he hadn't.

He was dating a girl of Iranian descent whose grandfather emigrated when the Shah of Iran fell from power. Her father was born in the United States, making her a second-generation American. She looked Iranian and was beautiful, slender-faced, and intelligent. Medium tall, her most frequent campus look was skin-tight jeans, a form-fitting tank top, and black hair falling around her shoulders. Her name was Ablah, which means perfectly formed. Chawki thought her name appropriate.

Chawki didn't know Ablah's difficulty in focusing on her classes. He appeared in both her daytime fantasies and nighttime dreams. Her heart said he was perfect based on what she knew of him. She thought he was a moderate Muslim, speaking impeccable English with a slight

British accent. He appeared to embrace the western lifestyle. She was not interested in a man who would require her to wear a burqa, but she would wear a hijab to the mosque. She limited her mosque attendance to religious holidays.

However, Chawki saw Ablah believed she was an American of Iranian descent. She didn't see herself as an Iranian living in America. Chawki knew his uncle would consider her a Western woman, even if her religion was nominally Muslim. He knew Khalil would demand he sever the relationship. So, like young men before him, Chawki solved the problem by not telling his uncle about his girlfriend.

Arriving back at OSU, Kahlil called his disciples together. Inside a building near OSU, which Kahlil used as a mosque, he urged them to stay vigilant for an opportunity and continue practicing the skills they learned over the summer.

Holding a clipboard, he reviewed a spreadsheet with their names on it. He explained, "Our goal is to free our country of the infidels. There is a plan to accomplish this, but we need a great leverage point. To keep our skills sharp, I have an assignment for you. I want each of you to target a person in the public eye. You are to get near them and clone their phones. When you have their passwords, you can monitor their social media."

Tapping his spreadsheet, he said, "Choose anyone you want who is a public person. Let me know who your target is. But Rashid, I want you to access a Portland newscaster, Alexia Nelson. Start tracking her."

Rashid nodded, "That shouldn't be too hard. But Iman, why are we doing this?"

Kahlil answered, "Mathematics proves fewer than five connections separate each person on earth. You know someone who knows someone who knows someone, etc. If we monitor the social media of prominent public figures, we'll be able to eavesdrop on their conversations with other prominent people. We don't know yet who we'll be listening to, but it could be they will share information we can use."

♦ ♦ ♦

Rashid set his plans and went to Portland. He discovered Alexia's schedule in the newsroom. He drank coffee on a park bench, watching for her arrival, and when she arrived, he followed her into the lobby and up the elevator. Like most people her age, Alexia looked at her phone, text messaging as she entered the building and went up the elevator. She overlooked Rashid. Rashid, following her, did the same. By the time the elevator arrived at her floor, Rashid had cloned her phone and could pull up her contacts and passwords. He accessed her email and social media accounts and paid rapt attention to what he found.

Chapter 17

Roman's home
Hawkeye Ridge
Gates, Oregon

J ulia took over organizing her dinner party at Roman's house with a smile on her face. After discussing the parameters of the BBQ potluck, Roman left it to her to start "nesting" and, climbing on his grandfather's old Caterpillar D8 bulldozer, began grading his driveway.

Julia sent out a group email that all could see and respond to. She invited Smoke, Alexia, Dink, Thomas and Samantha Jefferson, Andy Baker, Bridger and Cindy, and the Bluebonnet Princess.

Sitting on his deck in the evening, Roman filled in Julia with the day's progress of grading the road. He said, "If the weather stays dry, I think I can get the road graded in a week to ten days. The challenge is that we must put in culverts to keep it from washing out over the winter. I've got the crew working on the road instead of our logging projects. If we can get the water flowing into the drainpipes before the winter rainy season, we can lay the first layer of rock to gravel the road. There are many 'ifs' in the conversation, but getting a layer of rock down and the culverts in will make graveling and compacting the road easier next summer."

Julia and Roman chatted, and then he looked at her email. Finally, he laughed, "Who is Thomas Jefferson?"

Julia replied with a grin, "Thomas is the sweetest man, I know you'll like him. He's Samantha's husband and is a handsome, articulate black man. He's proud his DNA shows he's descended from Thomas Jefferson. According to him, that was always the family myth, but he got himself tested, and it's true. He's perfect for Samantha. Maybe she has the same security issues as me, which drew her to Thomas. I know she feels safe in his presence. He's a former Army Ranger."

Roman replied, "Great, I look forward to meeting him. Who is the Bluebonnet Princess?"

Julia explained, "My best friend, Kathleen, uses an alias for emailing her friends. The Secret Service wants her to use an official White House phone and email accounts for texting and emailing. Because she doesn't like the White House staff reading her communication, she keeps a private phone and email account to use with her friends."

Roman frowned, "You mean she is bypassing the established security system?"

Julia repositioned herself on the patio furniture. Curling her legs under herself, she laughed at him, "Now, don't be a party pooper. You don't want me texting and emailing her the private girl conversations about you and me, do you, on a secure server? Knowing a security agent is reading my description of you and me? I mean, she wants to know everything about you."

Roman shook his head and said, "I guess not."

Julia continued, "I invited her to the BBQ. She wants to come out early and spend time with me on pre-wedding planning. It will be the perfect opportunity for us to catch up. She's almost as excited about our engagement as I am."

With an exaggerated pout on her face, Julia said, "I can spend tonight here with you, but tomorrow I've got to go back to my condo. I need to ensure it's clean enough for Kathleen to stay with me and throw out any sour milk in the refrigerator. I also need to go to the school where I volunteer. They need to know that my schedule will be uncertain from now on. Is it silly to worry about quitting a volunteer job?"

While Julia spoke, Roman's phone rang to a ringtone of Hail to the Chief. Raising his eyebrows to Julia, he answered, "This is Roman, sir."

The phone conveyed a booming voice, "Hello Roman, this is Uncle Alex." They chatted, and then President Myers got to the point. "I understand my daughter is flying out to spend time with Julia. I have a favor to ask of you."

Roman replied, "Of course, anything, sir."

Uncle Alex continued, "The Secret Service is concerned about Kathleen staying with Julia at her condo. Would it be possible for her and a group of Secret Service to stay at your home? The Secret Service says it is safer than her condo."

Roman said, "Of course, sir, I have the room. How many agents would accompany her?"

Uncle Alex said, "That depends on you. How secure is your home? I understand it's isolated."

Roman answered, "I can make it secure, sir. Do you know of any actual threats? If there are, our old team could help provide security."

"That's what I hoped, Roman. There are no actual threats, but the FBI keeps its eyes on a few crazies in Corvallis. They have done nothing illegal on American soil, and we can't touch them until they do. The Secret Service also wants to chat with you about the wedding and the security necessary to perform the wedding on Hawkeye Ridge. Perhaps you could have a preliminary conversation with them."

After talking, Roman looked at Julia and asked, "Did you get that? It looks like you and Kathleen will stay here. I need to call in a favor from the guys."

◆ ◆ ◆

Two days later, Jimmy took the president's armored SUV, which was still at the governor's mansion, to the Portland Airport to pick up Kathleen.

While driving to the airport, he thought about his previous conversation with President Myers. Jimmy started the day by resigning from the U.S. Marshals Service by emailing his supervisor with a copy to the president.

Within the hour, he received a reply to his email. The stamp, NOT ACCEPTED, was in red letters across the face of the email. With it was a message to please call President Myers and a phone number.

Jimmy called. They put him through to the president in minutes. The president thanked him for his prior service and said, "As a personal favor, I'd like to ask you not to resign from the marshal's service but from active duty. Instead, please accept a reserve appointment similar to Roman's. If I need you, I want to know you are available to me. I promise not to abuse the privilege."

Jimmy said, "I could do that, sir, but won't there be a conflict of interest in my owning a security firm?"

President Myers said, "I don't care. Nobody will know unless something comes up, and I need to activate you."

"If you're sure it's ok, sir."

President Myers said, "Jimmy, I don't know how much you believe in hunches and premonitions. I don't base my life on them, but I get powerful feelings occasionally. When you and Roman mustered out of the service a few years ago, something told me to keep you both close to me. My stomach was in a knot until you both agreed to stay in the marshals' service. Because I did, you and he were on hand to save my best friend's life. That same hunch resurfaced awhile back after chatting with Roman. I expect you know I sent some pods of excess equipment to him. My instincts are kicking me in the stomach again. Don't ask me why I want to keep you and Roman close to me, but I do. When I met you and Roman, I felt a connection to both of you."

There was silence as Jimmy heard the president take a breath. "Humor me, Jimmy. Keep a reserve appointment as a U.S. marshal. I do not know why I feel you need to remain a marshal. On the other hand, your status as a marshal may be important in the future. I can't explain my feelings, but will you honor them?"

"Yes, sir."

President Myers breathed a sigh of relief as the knot in his stomach slowly subsided.

Chapter 18

Hesitating before opening the mosque door, Ablah thought, *"Momma would be happy to see me entering a mosque, even if it is to see an Iraqi."*

Ablah came to observe Chawki. Dressed in modest clothing and wearing a hijab, she paused momentarily before entering.

Chawki showed up on her arm and escorted her to the classroom. It was the first time she saw him in his white robes. Paying more attention to Chawki than the subject, she thought Chawki did an excellent job with the introductory religious course. She didn't know the moderate classes were the 'feeder' classes, out of which the Iman, the mosque's spiritual leader, handpicked those of a less tolerant nature for personal training.

Midway through the lesson, a young man waving an iPad shouted across the room, "Chawki, good, you're here. Is the Iman here? Where is he?"

Chawki pointed to the rear of the building.

Following Rashid with her eyes, Ablah watched him enter a room at the rear. Turning back to Chawki, she thought, *"What has happened?"*

Chawki continued to teach, but his friendly manner evaporated. With a frozen smile, he stumbled over his words and watched the back room. He appeared rattled and nervous.

Chawki cut class short, explaining he didn't feel well, and asked everyone to leave. Then, cold and distant with Ablah, he thanked her for attending the course.

Confused, Ablah asked, "When will I see you again?"

Chawki's eyes flickered to those chatting near them who may have overheard her question. He then searched the room itself. Finally comfortable that no one was observing, he relaxed, took her arm by the elbow, and walked her to the street. Then, in an undertone masked by the traffic, he said, "I will be in touch with you."

◆ ◆ ◆

After escorting everyone from the mosque classroom, Chawki walked into the back room. Khalil was excited, "We have it. We have found our mission. We're rejoining the war to free our homeland."

When questioned, Khalil was secretive. He swore Rashid to secrecy and told Chawki he needed time to think. He asked Chawki to bring the entire team to his apartment tonight at 8 p.m., saying, "Do not allow anyone to interrupt me until then. I need to contact a friend overseas."

◆ ◆ ◆

Entering his disciple's gathering later in the evening, Khalil paced back and forth while complimenting Rashid for his find. Finally, Rashid said, "No, Iman, it was you. I am just the worker bee. How did you know to follow the newscaster, Alexia Nelson?"

Khalil said, "She and I have a history. I thought with her job as a broadcaster, she could have important connections. Please tell everyone here what you found."

"I captured her contact information yesterday. When I accessed her information, I could see her texts and emails. She has a boyfriend. There were pages of just trash conversations between the two of them. Disgusting."

Holding his iPad up and pointing to it, he said, "She is invited to a barbeque this coming weekend at her brother's home. His name is Roman, and Roman's fiancée is Julia. She's the daughter of the governor. You'll never guess who Julia invited to the barbeque."

When everyone conceded defeat, he said, "The president's

daughter, Kathleen, will be there. The Iman was correct in saying everyone is five distance points of connection or less from everyone else on earth. Think about the beauty of mathematics, which led us to this point. The Iman knows Alexia, which is one. Alexia knows Roman, that's two. Roman knows Julia, which is three. Julia knows Kathleen Myers, that's four, and Kathleen knows her father, the president, that's five distance points."

Khalil said, "Now there is a great lever for a project worthy of our training. We do not yet have a plan of what to do with this information, but we know we'll find our fulcrum. As the ancient Greek, the father of mathematics, Archimedes said, 'Give me a lever long enough and a fulcrum on which to place it, and I shall move the world.'"

Talking and walking around the room, he appeared unable to stay still. He said, "We shall devise a plan. Over the upcoming Christmas break, I shall travel to our brothers overseas. We must coordinate with them for an act as significant as I envision. In the meantime, keep the connection points under surveillance. I want someone to monitor the text, email, and social media of Alexia, Roman, Julia, Kathleen, and their online connections. We do not know what we'll find, but we'll find our fulcrum."

Chapter 19

The week of the BBQ

Smoke drove the SUV to the 142nd Fighter Wing of the Oregon Air National Guard, adjacent to the Portland International Airport.

He presented his credentials. One security officer checked his paperwork, and another watched his every move. After a meticulous inspection of his documents, a security officer admitted Jimmy and led him to a hangar sitting off to the side.

After a brief wait, an executive jet with White House insignia landed and pulled into the hangar. The first people out of the plane were the Secret Service. Their inspection of Jimmy's credentials against the paperwork they brought was even more meticulous than the original guards. Upon satisfying themselves that he was, in fact, James Stockade, the president's daughter, exited the plane.

Jimmy thought, *"Holy crap, here's another one. Do beautiful women only know beautiful women? First, there's Julia, next came Alexia, and now, this one. There must be a nest of them somewhere."*

Kathleen was 5'7", slender, with luxurious, thick, dark blonde hair, set off by a thin nose and a firm jaw. A grin always appeared contagiously on her face. Her slight but definite Texas twang was highlighted by her full but well-shaped eyebrows and a cheerful personality.

One Secret Service agent climbed in the passenger seat beside Jimmy, and two got into the bench seat. Kathleen sat between the two Secret Service agents in the middle of the bench seat, watching

Jimmy in the driver's mirror. His driving was erratic, but fast. First, he sped up, and then he slowed down and did the speed limit. He, however, always watched his mirrors.

Enthralled with looking at the beautiful scenery as they sped down Interstate-5, the Secret Service agents paid no attention to his driving.

◆ ◆ ◆

Watching Jimmy in the rearview mirror, Kathleen thought, *"It's too bad Julia told me to keep my hands off him. He's handsome. Daddy told me about him and Roman. He doesn't look dangerous to me, but why's he so focused on his mirrors?"*

His intensity caused her to ask, "What's going on? You haven't said a word and look tense while driving. What's up?"

Jimmy asked, "Did anyone know you were coming to visit Julia today?"

The Secret Service agents went on full alert.

She answered, "Just Julia, perhaps she told her friends. I didn't tell anyone about the trip. I wanted to stay out of the limelight."

Jimmy commented, "I think there is a car following us. Whoever it is, they're not that skilled at tailing."

The Secret Service agent in charge ripped a phone out of his pocket and requested a local police escort for the SUV. As Jimmy sped past the next on-ramp, a county deputy sheriff's car accelerated in front of them, and another sheriff's car dropped in behind them.

The car Jimmy was paying attention to took an exit ramp and disappeared.

Jimmy couldn't help asking, "Wouldn't it be smarter to get a license plate number for the car?"

The agent-in-charge said, "No, we're concerned with Kathleen's safety. The FBI can determine who was following and if they were a threat. Our job is to keep Kathleen safe."

The rest of the drive was uneventful. As the caravan pulled into Gates, Jimmy told the Secret Service agent in charge to release the sheriff's deputies. The agents argued with him until he said, "At least,

80

let us go through the gate first. Then, you can call a tow truck to get them off the logging road when they get stuck. I guarantee that any regular car in front of us will get stuck. I don't want to sit here for two hours as you try to move those cars."

Passing the deputy's car, he stopped, opened a gate, and waved the police cars off. Then, he shut the gate, shifted into four-wheel drive, and started up the hill. The vehicle access to Hawkeye Ridge was a steep, rutted, dirt track of a logging road. Sheer cliffs with no guardrails and 90-degree turns caused careful driving.

Jimmy commented, "It looks like Roman's been out here with a road grader. It's in a lot better shape than I expected."

The agent bouncing in the back seat said, "If this is good, I would hate to see bad. I need a window down, or I'll be sick in the car." Grinning, Jimmy rolled the agent's window down.

Roman walked the Secret Service agents around the property, showing them the security features. Then, they discussed their security concerns about the president's visit for the wedding and how to resolve those concerns. Later in the afternoon, Jimmy left with the Secret Service.

Jimmy left the SUV locked inside Roman's logging equipment garage at the bottom of the hill. He took Roman's spare car and returned the agents to Portland.

♦ ♦ ♦

Julia and Kathleen sat on the back deck with a blaze in the firepit. They'd caught up on 'girl talk' and were now visiting. Kathleen looked down the hill and rose to her feet.

She said, "That is a beautiful German Shepherd. Is he yours?"

Julia replied, "No, I wish he were. His name is Brutus. Andy must be around checking the property."

Kathleen got up and went into the yard without another word, calling for Brutus. Brutus looked back into the forest and wagged his tail, standing still. Fearlessly, Kathleen walked up to him. She sweet-talked him the entire time as she approached.

Brutus waited on her with his ears pricked forward, watching her approach. When she got close, she said in a commanding voice, "Brutus, sit," and he sat.

Andy Baker, watching from the woods, froze in shock. Kathleen knelt directly in front of Brutus and continued to sweet-talk him. She asked him if he knew how to shake. Brutus stuck out his paw. Without standing, Kathleen shook his paw and picked up a branch lying nearby. She continued talking to him, asked him if he knew how to fetch, and threw the stick. Brutus looked into the forest and bounded after the branch. When he brought it back to her, she commanded him to drop it, and he did.

Kathleen wrapped her arms around Brutus's neck and hugged him. Brutus acted like a puppy, rolling on his back and kicking his legs for a belly rub. His tail wagged as he sat up and attempted to lick her face. Laughing, she pulled back and told him he wouldn't like the taste of makeup.

A deep voice said, "That was amazing. Dangerous but amazing."

Brutus pulled back and went to his master, and Kathleen looked up into the most vivid blue eyes imaginable. Andy Baker measured 6'3" in his socks, had wavy Black Irish hair, and the classic 1940s movie star's chiseled rugged face. A small cleft dimpled the point of his chin, and he weighed a muscular 195 pounds. Andy wore green and tan camouflage fatigues and carried a sidearm on his belt and another in a shoulder holster under his left arm.

"You must be Kathleen?" He asked. She agreed, and as he put out a hand to help her to her feet, he introduced himself.

When she got to her feet, he commented, "You know what you were doing with Brutus was dangerous."

"Brutus isn't dangerous. He's a pussycat and in his heart thinks he's a lapdog."

Andy looked at her before laughing, "That's what I always tell people, and nobody believes me."

Andy walked Kathleen back up to the fire pit. Then, saying his goodbyes, he asked if the Secret Service were gone. Roman explained that the Secret Service leader said his orders from the president were to get Kathleen to Roman's and leave her alone until she was ready to go home.

He added, "The president told him our security clearance level is higher than the agents, and we can protect her better than the Secret Service."

Andy laughed, "Well, he would know, wouldn't he?"

Julia asked, "Do you want to stay for dinner with us? We're not having anything fancy, just a simple steak barbeque."

Andy looked at Brutus, who sat nuzzling Kathleen's hand for an ear rub, and agreed, saying, "I would love some steak."

Later, as the fire burned down and the sunset tinged the sky orange, Julia said to Andy, "Roman tells me you are a gifted singer. He wouldn't say where, but claims you sang every evening to the team. How about singing for us tonight?"

Andy first minimized his skill and declined, but she asked again. Finally, Andy reached into a shirt pocket and pulled out a small beat-up harmonica.

He played a couple of bars of an old American classic like 'Home on the Range' and then sang the song. He played songs made famous by Gene Autry, Roy Rogers, or Johnny Cash, old-time country music. Not the new romp and stomp, but the classic ballads.

He mesmerized Kathleen. She sat near Andy, watching the emotions play on his face as he sang. Brutus's conflict was apparent. He lay with his head in Andy's lap like he always did, but then kept turning until he moved his head under Kathleen's hand to get his ears rubbed. Kathleen appeased him by moving closer. Whenever she stopped scratching, Brutus would poke his head under her hands. Kathleen placed her phone on a stand and filmed Andy singing. Julia watched Kathleen with a slight smile and a twinkle in her eyes.

The conversation between friends was comfortable and casual, with the wedding plans the primary topic. Roman contributed the information about the Secret Service's requirements for the wedding.

"I showed them everything, the house, the workshop and hangar, the chairlift, etc. They saw the electronic surveillance at the gate, but what impressed them was a retired SEAL team with Brutus on guard duty. They want all gifts dropped off at the bottom of the hill and sent through a detector like at an airport's baggage shipping. I told them I planned on having a series of SUV shuttles pick people up at the bottom of the hill and bring them up. The agent said he would want to install another detector prior to people loading onto the shuttle, similar to the body scanner at an airport."

Andy got to his feet when the conversation lagged and said, "It's time for me to take Brutus and go home. It will be an early morning tomorrow in the governor's office for the awards ceremony."

Kathleen walked Brutus and Andy to the chairlift to say goodnight. When she came back, she looked distracted.

Julia asked, "What's up?"

Kathleen said, "He's special."

Oblivious, Roman asked, "Brutus?"

To which Kathleen replied, "Him too."

Chapter 20

Awards ceremony
The Capitol Rotunda
Salem, Oregon

The following day, the number of people who showed up forced the ceremony's move from the governor's office to the Oregon State Capitol's rotunda. Roman and Jimmy wore dark blue suits with white shirts and red ties. Their black shoes shone, and they both stood in the military posture of 'at ease,' which didn't look at ease or relaxed.

Anyone remotely connected to Roman or Julia, arrived early and stood quietly visiting. Margo and Stan's large group of friends and family members packed the vast Rotunda. The curved marble stairwell provided the best view.

The local reporters, and Carl and Rebecca, who came down from their Portland stations, were shocked to find the president's daughter at the awards ceremony.

Governor Stan Anderson, with his wife Margaret by his side, talked about what an honor it was for him to present the day's awards. "We are proud parents. We always knew our daughter embodied greatness inside herself, but it took a special event and a special person to bring her greatness to the surface."

He described the nail-biting terror of a parent realizing his daughter was on live television for hours, rescuing rafters from a flooded river with an unknown man. Stan talked about being glued to the TV like everyone else and seeing this man's incredible skill in saving lives.

"I didn't know if I should pray for the people on the rafts or my daughter. I was horror stricken by the risks she took. Then I realized I should pray for this man I didn't know. I realized my daughter's life was in his hands, as were the lives of the river rafters. I frantically tried to find out his name."

Looking around the dome, Governor Anderson said, "Everyone watching on television realized this man coached my daughter on what to do. And, in full confidence, she did what he told her."

He talked about the stress, fear, and anxiety he and Margo felt when the Miller family attempted to kill him and the relief when James Stockade entered their lives and took over security. The crowd held its breath, listening to his description of the recent assassination attempt by the Miller family. The group gathered in the rotunda could hear the bullets pinging off the bulletproof glass in their mind's ears. In their mind's eyes, they saw the flash of the weapons firing in the dark and felt the fear as he described hearing his daughter screaming at the top of the hill as their chairlift continued to the bottom.

Stan articulately and lavishly praised Julia, Jimmy, and Roman. He finished by saying the term 'hero' had become overused and watered down in daily life.

Placing The Governor's Hero's Medal around each of their necks, he said, "I want to hold up to the children of Oregon, these three-outstanding people, as an example of what a genuine hero is."

After the applause, Stan asked for quiet and continued in a somber tone. "My most important responsibility as governor is to protect the people of Oregon. I'm proud to appoint Roman Nelson as the first-ever Statewide Director of Natural Disaster Preparedness. He has agreed to act as the liaison between the state government and the municipalities. I want him to help the local communities prepare for future catastrophes."

Stan then asked Kathleen if she wished to make any comments. She did, "My father couldn't be here today. He asked me to represent him at this special award ceremony. Before I left Washington, he told me former Lieutenant Commander Roman Nelson and retired Chief Warrant Officer James Stockade are two of his all-time favorite people. He asked me to tell Julia, Commander Nelson, and Chief Stockade how proud he is of them. My father asked me to convey to the people of Oregon how fortunate you are to have these two retired SEALS here, in positions of responsibility."

She looked at Roman and Jimmy, then pointed at men scattered around the room. "I'm not at liberty to tell you what they did for the awards they received. But, I can tell you they provided a vital service to our nation, and all the former SEALS in this room received a Unit Citation in the Oval Office. Those wounded in action received Purple Hearts. Chief Stockade received a Silver Star, and Commander Nelson received the Presidential Medal of Honor."

A gasp rippled throughout the room.

She continued, "The Ghost" and "Smoke," as I understand their teammates call them, are legends in Special Operations. I'm excited to get to know them. I hope they will allow me to become a member of what I see as a tight extended family."

When Kathleen called them "The Ghost" and "Smoke," Roman and Jimmy locked eyes in a look of distress. Roman muttered, "Crap," under his breath. Until now, close team members knew those names and what they meant. They now feared the nicknames could create an adverse public reaction.

Rebecca and Carl approached Alexia and thanked her for her text, alerting them to bring a film crew to the Rotunda. Rebecca expanded on her previous expression of gratitude. "I am so thankful for the courtesy you have shown Carl and me. It's just the past few days I've gotten to know you. Until now, I have perceived you as my cool, aloof, successful competition. This is my third year working in Portland. I moved here for the job three years ago. My station loves my work ethic, but I've made no friends. My job's interstation rivalry and competitive atmosphere made me think about getting out of journalism and going home. However, your actions are causing me to change my viewpoint and think I may be hasty if I quit."

It wasn't a place conducive to talking with the people milling around, but they embraced. Alexia said, "I'm sorry you perceived me as cold and aloof. Each of us has our issues. Cool and aloof is my self-protection mode. Please forgive me and know the image is about me, not you. You're good at what you do. I hope you don't quit."

They chatted, getting acquainted, and then Alexia said, "I have a scoop for you. There's a story I would like on the air, but because of my connection to the person involved, I shouldn't break the story."

Rebecca raised her eyebrows and looked across the room at Jimmy. Alexia nodded, "Yes, why don't you ask him about his career plans? Is he leaving Oregon? What's in his future? Those are natural questions for you to ask. Be a reporter. Probe if he's reluctant. You may find a story."

She continued, "As a friend, what is on your schedule for tomorrow, tomorrow night, and Saturday?"

Rebecca responded with sarcasm as she rolled her eyes. "Nothing. Sitting at home and pretending I'm on a date."

Alexia asked, "Can you separate reporting from personal?"

"Absolutely," Rebecca said.

Alexia suggested, "Why don't you keep your schedule open? It isn't my place to invite you, but I will try to get you included in a girl's get-together this weekend. I think you would enjoy it and fit right in. But, everything you see and hear and everyone you meet will be off the record."

Agreeing, Rebecca rushed off to interview Jimmy about his future.

On the 6 p.m. news, Rebecca's station's lead story was about a recipient of the Hero's Award quitting his job with the U.S. Marshal's Service to stay in Oregon. Rebecca reported that Jimmy planned to open a high-end security firm and hire former Special Operations members. She mentioned he was looking for a location for his business and would soon accept resumes.

Within minutes, former Special Ops agents across the state were trying to track down a phone number for "Smoke."

Chapter 21

The Awards Ceremony

The rest of the day was chaos for the three award recipients. There was a luncheon for those involved in the ceremony, but everywhere they went, reporters followed them. As a result, they became practiced at brief responses useable as TV sound bites.

Roman said, "Soon, I will invite a representative from the various cities, towns, and counties to attend a short program. The program will be in a month. I want their input as we develop a plan of how I can support our communities on disaster preparedness issues."

Roman acknowledged that the larger municipalities had programs in place, but many smaller or unincorporated rural areas didn't. He said he wanted to set systems in place where each region could determine the most significant risks facing their locations and prepare their residents for those risks.

Alexia watched with amusement. Today she wasn't there as a reporter. Instead, her understudy at the studio was the reporter on camera today. Alexia grinned and nodded encouragement to Jimmy as Rebecca pigeonholed him with a microphone in his mouth. At Alexia's nod, he relaxed and answered Rebecca's leading questions.

During the luncheon, Alexia chatted with Julia and Kathleen. Kathleen and Alexia bonded as kindred spirits. While discussing the upcoming activities, they agreed to invite Rebecca.

The young women had more to do and share than time to do it.

So, they agreed to sneak away the following day and go to a day spa in Sisters.

Kathleen was unfamiliar with Sisters. Julia described it to her, "Sisters is a quaint western town just over the top of the Cascades in Oregon's High Desert country. It's a trendy tourist-oriented town about an hour and a half from Roman's home on Hawkeye Ridge. It's fun with nice places to eat and cute boutiques for shopping."

Kathleen said, "It sounds like fun if we can be back in time to hear Andy Baker. He invited me to come to hear him. Do you know where he is singing?"

Alexia explained to Julia and Kathleen. "Once a month, Andy performs at The Fishing Hole, a country bar near Gates in Mill City. It sits on the cliff's edge overlooking the most famous salmon fishing hole on the Santiam River. It's a hole-in-the-wall place serving burgers, fries, and beer."

She added, "The bar struggled to do enough business to stay open until Andy volunteered to sing there once a month. On whatever night he's singing, the seating in the bar area is standing room only."

Alexia texted Rebecca. "Would you like to join a couple of girlfriends and me tomorrow? We are going over the mountains to a day spa in the little town of Sisters and returning to watch a friend sing in a local bar tomorrow night? You could even stay over for a barbeque on Saturday."

She received an excited text back. Rebecca filled it with emojis, expressing joy and thanks.

In it, Rebecca asked, "What can I bring? Is it a potluck? What should I wear?"

Her subsequent text said, "I couldn't find a motel on the internet. Is there a local hotel where I can stay?"

Alexia responded with her clothing suggestions, saying, "Don't worry about a motel. There are none. Why don't you bring your sleeping bag and pillow? You can stay in the 'bunkhouse.'"

Alexia suggested she show up at *Nelson Bait and Tackle* at 8 a.m. and park her car in the secure parking area with the boats across the street. Then she said she'd meet her inside the store.

Roman showed up at breakfast in the morning with his work clothes on. He planned to get on his grandfather's D8 bulldozer and work on the road. Minutes later, Julia and Kathleen showed up in casual but cute clothing.

When Roman asked, "What's up? You look like you're heading out."

Julia said, "We are. We thought we'd have a girl's day in Sisters. There won't be any guys looking over our shoulders, watching us get our nails done, and eavesdropping on our gossip. Nobody knows Kathleen is here. We'll be back in time to hear Andy sing."

Shocked and appalled at their plans to sneak out in Julia's Mercedes AMG for a fun day without security, he said, "You mean you planned to leave without telling me you were going or where you were going? I can't let you do that. I'm responsible for Kathleen's safety."

Julia's issues with controlling men erupted, "What do you mean you can't let us? You're not in charge of our lives."

Their first domestic disagreement erupted spontaneously. Roman said, "I'm sorry, I can't let you run off without security. Kathleen, you know that. President Myers may be your father. Julia, he may be your honorary uncle, but he is my president. I promised the president I'd take care of Kathleen's security. I need to change clothes, call Smoke and find some team members to go with us, and we can be on our way."

The back-and-forth wrangling ended with Julia saying in a huff, "We need to leave if we want to make our appointment at the salon. If you think you must crash our party, you can catch up to us in Sisters, but we need to go."

Roman started changing clothes in a frenzy and gathering up weapons. Then, racing to the garage, he got into the Argo and sped to the logging equipment warehouse where he stored the Ducati. While doing so, he called Jimmy.

When Jimmy answered, Roman started talking, "Smoke, we got troubles. The girls just took off on their own, headed for Sisters."

"WHAT?" exploded through the phone.

"You heard me." Roman continued, "I'm about to get on the Ducati. It's the fastest ride I've got for the mountain curves. But, unfortunately, I'm about 20 minutes behind them. Can you join me as fast as possible, but before you do, please call Bridger and those two Rangers, who work for Dink, to see if you can get them up to guard the house until we get back?"

The angry voice of Smoke replied, "What were they thinking? That is an out-of-control action for the president's daughter. Well, it's a good thing I started settling down and spending money this week. I bought a matching Ducati, in blue. It'll take me five minutes to get on the road and start playing catch up. So, you run point until I get there."

Jimmy changed into his leather riding suit with the Kevlar reinforcements and body armoring pads while they conversed. Putting on his helmet, hooking up the Bluetooth to his phone, and connecting to his voice-activated speed dialing system took a minute. He spoke to Dink as he reached into the cargo container of the Ducati 1098S. He took a blue flashing police light from it and attached it to the bike's front.

Jimmy explained the situation to Dink, who agreed to call Bridger. Dink volunteered to head to Roman's home if he couldn't reach Bridger because he thought Bridger was on the coast fishing. Dink started by calling his two Ranger buddies, Kelly and Mark, to patrol the grounds. Dink took it upon himself to reach out for additional support from Roger Harper, Roman's CFO of *Boy Toys & Her Toys Too*, and Andy Baker. Unfortunately, he couldn't reach Bridger, Roger, or Andy.

Jimmy hit I-5 south of Wilsonville. He ignored the speed limit signs with blue lights flashing and siren blaring.

Already on Highway 22, Roman flew through the winding curves. Both rode Ducati's with blue lights flashing identical except for color. Roman's was a deep red, and Jimmy's was blue. Roman hugged the center line and passed everything in sight. Whenever a car appeared in front of him, he turned on his siren.

Tight-lipped and jaw clenched, Julia took out her anger at

Roman in speed. Driving her AMG straight into the wall of an upcoming curve at 20 mph over the posted curve speed, she would crank the wheel at the last second and accelerate coming out of the turn. The sound system rocked the passengers, inhibiting conversation. A squeal of fear came from the backseat, causing Julia to slow her speed and turn down the radio. She said, "I don't know who I'm mad at, Roman, myself, or my overcontrolling ex-boyfriends. I hate having a man try to control me."

Rebecca kept quiet, glad she was a guest with no part in planning the day's outing. She squeezed into the tiny backseat with Alexia and focused on not falling over as the car rocketed through the curves.

Kathleen and Alexia were apologetic. They knew their part in the decision, which caused the fight between Roman and Julia. Kathleen felt incredibly guilt-ridden.

Kathleen said, "I'm so sorry, Julia. I shouldn't have agreed to the plan to run off without Roman. We both know he's right. It's just that I've dealt with such smothering security since Dad's election as president. The idea of a carefree day with just girlfriends was so tempting."

Inside her head, she replayed the frequent lectures given by the Secret Service about her need for security. Her carefree day disappeared. She now felt nervous and vulnerable.

Chapter 22

Security Breach
On the Road to Sister's

On the day of the Hero's awards, Rashid knocked on Khalil's apartment door. When Khalil answered, Rashid said, "Iman, I monitored the reporter as you asked. I know her schedule and the schedule for everyone else this weekend."

As they read the series of texts and emails, Rashid said, "It looks like they're sneaking away from security tomorrow. Shall we try to intercept them?"

Khalil thought about it and said, "No, our plans are not advanced far enough. For now, monitor their communications and perhaps practice following them."

The following day, Chawki watched from down the road as Julia pulled out of *Nelson Boat and Tackle*. He called Fathi and Rashid and let them know what kind of car Julia drove.

Fathi and Rashid sipped tea while overlooking the river. They were in the restaurant at Marion Forks. It was a beautiful fall setting with the sweet trills and flute-like notes of water ouzels filling the air. With the ouzel's heads and bodies dipping, they sang their songs and walked into a large creek, although people called it a river. The songbirds dove and walked on the creek bottom, looking for food before surfacing downstream. As the songbirds exited the river, their singing restarted without missing a note. Fathi and Rashid were oblivious to the birds.

When Chawki called, they paid their bill and waited in the

parking lot for her to drive by. They were unremarkable in the older minivan's dull appearance, effortlessly blending in with the traffic. Unfortunately, the parking lot was below road level, and Rashid pulled the van's nose up to the road's edge for a quick parking lot exit.

As Julia came speeding into Marion Forks, she slowed down. Rebecca asked, "What are the chances of a bathroom stop at the restaurant?"

Alexia said, "Yeah, let's stop for a minute. This backseat is almost nonexistent. I need to stretch and get another latte."

They did not hear the cursing in the minivan, "Now what do we do? We can't sit here and wait for them. They've seen us."

Fathi and Rashid pulled onto the highway towards Sisters and Bend and went a quarter of a mile before turning into the fish hatchery. Then, they turned around and watched the passing traffic for the bright blue Mercedes.

Minutes later, the girls were back on the highway. As they went past the fish hatchery and picked up speed, Julia looked to her left and saw the van sitting at the entrance. Curious, she paid attention to her mirrors as it pulled in behind her.

She thought, *"That's odd,"* and began watching it.

In the van, Fathi and Rashid argued. Rashid advocated stopping the car and kidnapping the girls. He argued, "They're alone. The two of us can overpower four girls."

Fathi, however, kept saying, "Then what? If we capture them, what do we do with them, where do we go, what result do we get which helps in the struggle for our homeland?"

"But Fathi, they're alone. This opportunity may never occur again."

♦ ♦ ♦

No matter how well Julia's AMG handled the mountain curves or how fast she drove, Roman's Ducati raced through the bends at a higher speed.

She did not have the aggressive driver training taught by the SEALS or Roman and Jimmy's experience racing on Germany's autobahn. While stationed in the Mediterranean, they rented Ducati's for weekends of high-speed cruising of Europe.

Today, he flew past Big Cliff Reservoir, Detroit Dam, and Detroit Lake. He did not slow down for the crossroads town of Detroit. Turning on his siren to alert people he was coming, he sped through the town.

Roman focused on controlling his anger. Still angry at Julia, Kathleen, and Alexia, his primary emotion now was fear. He didn't even know Rebecca was in the car. But, subconsciously, Roman was panic-stricken. With white knuckles clenched on the Ducati's handlebars and his neck and jaw muscles tied in knots, his eyes searched the road ahead for danger at his aggressive speed.

As Roman approached Marion Forks, he turned on his siren and kept the blue lights flashing. Julia stopped for ten minutes at Marion Forks and, re-entering the highway, slowed to a sedate 60 mph. Roman rapidly closed on her.

As Julia passed the Junction of Highway 22 and Highway 126, Highway 22 developed a passing lane for the steep final upgrade to the top of the pass. She commented, "It looks like a van is following us."

Kathleen exclaimed, "WHAT?"

"Yes," Julia said. "When we stopped at the restaurant for bathrooms and coffee, I saw a van waiting to pull onto the highway. Then, I noticed it pulling out of the fish hatchery behind us when we left the restaurant. Since then, no matter how fast I go or what I slow to, it maintains the same distance."

They got worried after Kathleen explained that someone had followed her on her way from the airport. Alexia called Jimmy or Roman, saying, "I guess it's time to apologize and eat humble pie, although they couldn't do anything from where they are."

However, no cell phone coverage existed in the mountains.

On the steep climb to the top, Julia said, "Oh no, what do I do?"

The van sped up and closed the distance between them as the sheer cliffs slowed her comfort with speed. As they crested the summit, the undulating wailing of a police siren penetrated the car.

In her rearview mirror, Julia saw a flaming red Ducati scream past the van with lights and sirens blaring. It slowed and fell in behind her car, turning off its lights and siren. The minivan dropped back and took the turnoff into Hoodoo Ski Resort.

Kathleen and Alexia waved at the motorcycle, hoping it was Roman. But with the helmet masking his face, they couldn't be sure.

Julia said, "That's him. I'd know his Ducati anywhere. What I'm worried about is the reception I'll get from Roman when we stop."

Kathleen said, "Easy, we get out and surround him, with all of us talking at once and apologizing. If we tell him how glad we are he didn't listen to us, maybe he won't be too mad. We could even kiss him."

Julia added, "On his cheek."

They did that when they reached the spa in Sisters, which short-circuited the angry lecture Roman rehearsed in his head for the entire trip. With Kathleen and Rebecca hugging his arms, Julia wrapped her arms around Roman and gave him an intense hug. She told him she loved him, was sorry they fought, and how scared everyone was until he showed up. Hearing that, he pulled back and started asking questions.

While Julia explained about the van following them, a loud siren and flashing lights pulled onto the sidewalk near Roman. Alexia looked at the blue Ducati and said, "Oh no, not Jimmy."

He ripped off his helmet with fire in his eyes, "Who's hair-brained idea was it to run off with no security?"

Kathleen tried to take the blame, "I'm so tired of the Secret Service. I was just excited to act like a normal person."

Shocked, Alexia watched Jimmy ferociously ream Kathleen out. She knew this was a Chief Warrant Officer chewing out a troop for screwing up. Jimmy made them feel like chastised grade-schoolers as the school principal disciplined them.

He continued looking at Kathleen and Julia, "Both of you are acting like the spoiled, pampered, rich girls you are."

Finishing, he looked at Kathleen, "You are lucky your father is our friend. If you were my client, I'd quit on the spot. You don't deserve our security."

Shaking his head in disgust, he put on his helmet and stepped onto his Ducati when Roman said, "Smoke, wait, we need to talk."

Turning to the four women, he suggested they get their massages. However, before they could go in, he pulled out his U.S. marshal's badge and asked the salon owner if he could walk through the facility before their appointments started.

When Roman exited the salon, he and Jimmy talked. Finally, Jimmy agreed to stay on guard duty while Roman returned to seek answers. Jimmy tried to position himself to see both the front and back door.

Half an hour later, Dink Lindsay's deep maroon Nissan Murano pulled into the parking area with loud music, causing turned heads a block away.

Dink explained to Smoke that his two former Rangers, the servers from The Benson, were patrolling the skipper's home. The responsibility of guarding the perimeter of Roman's home thrilled Mark and Kelly. Unable to access the house, buildings, or electronic surveillance systems, they patrolled below the house to the gate. Dink opened up the logging equipment shed and, out of a POD, got them each a Christini Technologies, Inc. AWD motorcycle to use running around the property.

He said, "They're like kids in a candy store driving up and down the logging road and taking the all-wheel-drive bikes up the mountain under the chairlift line."

Dink explained, "Bridger, Roger, and Andy were unreachable. However, I got ahold of Bridger's girlfriend, Cindy. She told me the three of them spent the night on the coast. They were there for an early morning check-in for a salmon fishing charter out of Depoe Bay."

Dink didn't know when they would return, but he knew Andy sang tonight in Mill City.

Chapter 23

Roman's trip back to Hawkeye Ridge was slower. The trip gave him time to process what happened. When he got into his home office, he called the White House switchboard and left a message for Admiral Seastrand, Chairman of the Joint Chiefs of Staff, to call him. Within 15 minutes, his phone rang.

The Chairman said, "Commander Nelson, it was good to hear you called. President Myers tells me you are doing well. I'm glad to hear that. What can I do for you today?"

Roman replied, "Intel, Admiral. I need intelligence. Something is going on out here, and I don't know what it is. I thought my results would be better talking to you than the Secret Service."

Admiral Seastrand replied, "What's going on? What kind of intel do you need? Is Kathleen safe?"

Roman explained everything. "Smoke says a car followed them from the airport on the way home. Today, Kathleen, my fiancée, my sister, and a girlfriend skipped out on security for a trip to a spa. A van followed them until I showed up. I'm afraid someone has hacked Kathleen's schedule. Somebody knew in advance where she would be and when. I need to know who it is."

The Admiral replied, "I understand the problem. Is Kathleen secure?"

"Yes, sir."

"It will take some discrete digging on my part. As you know, the military can't conduct surveillance inside the U.S., but if there's a will, there's a way. It will require caution in accessing the information. I'll check with the CIA to see if anyone they have surveilled overseas is in your area, then I'll sic the computer experts on this. It sounds to me like Kathleen got hacked. Give me time to poke around in the shadows. Tell Kathleen I'll recommend to her father she extend her stay with you. Can you keep her safe?"

"Yes, sir."

"I will talk to the president and explain everything to him," Admiral Seastrand said as he hung up.

◆ ◆ ◆

Inside the day spa, the four girls chatted. They planned a relaxing morning, but now felt ashamed and embarrassed.

Rebecca, who wasn't involved in the decision to ditch security, commented, "I knew Jimmy wasn't directing his tirade at me, but I felt like my hair got singed as he flamed everyone. I've never in my life heard anything like that."

The subject switched to tonight's attendance at the local restaurant and bar to hear Andy sing. Earlier, Alexia texted Rebecca about what clothes to bring. No clothing issues existed for Alexia, with her full closet of clothes at her mother's. However, Kathleen and Julia's plans included finishing the trip to Sisters with a shopping spree to buy clothing to wear tonight.

Kathleen commented, "I hate to bring up the shopping trip. If I suggest it to Smoke, it will validate his comments about my being a pampered, spoiled, rich girl. What hurts is to know he is right."

Alexia finished paying for her salon services, "Let me talk to him."

She walked outside to Jimmy and waved at Dink. Holding Jimmy's hand, she said, "Everyone knows we were wrong, sweetheart. We feel terrible about what we did. Kathleen will promise never again to duck security. I know Julia, and I will promise never to be a party to it again. Can we get past it? Can we finish the day as planned now that we're here?"

He asked, "What were you planning?"

She said, "Lunch in a fancy outdoor eating area, and then shopping for clothes and boots. Kathleen wants to look hot for Andy tonight."

Jimmy grinned and said, "Now that's interesting. When did Andy come into the picture? I guess it doesn't matter. I am hungry and missed breakfast."

Alexia motioned for the remaining three girls to join them. Julia and Kathleen both held their hands up and, with a grin, swore they would never again ditch security.

Kathleen said, "You were right about everything you said. I learned my lesson."

Jimmy introduced Dink to those who didn't know him and explained he would take Roman's place. Dink commented to Kathleen how glad he was to meet her and then, turning to Rebecca, reached out his hand. "It's nice to see you again, Rebecca."

Rebecca shook his hand while looking over his immaculate grooming and fashionable clothes with interest. Then, she said, "I know I have met you, but I don't remember where."

Dink responded, "That's not surprising. It's common for people to not recognize me outside of The Benson."

Realizing she still held his hand, and it felt natural to do so, she reluctantly let it go. Rebecca apologized for not recognizing Dink but questioned why he was part of the security detail.

Alexia answered for him, "Do you remember my former boyfriend, John Dunn, the actor?"

When Rebecca nodded, she continued, "Do you remember when he got thrown out of The Benson Hotel with a broken nose, black eye, and a broken arm?"

Again, Rebecca nodded, and Alexia continued, "Dink is the man who did the honors and thrilled me. He is a former SEAL, just like the rest of these guys, and will sit on the board of Jimmy's security firm. He will try to teach everyone some class. Jimmy wants his team comfortable in highbrow situations."

Dink grinned and said, "We'll just be trying to wrap a feather pillow of sophistication around the brass knuckles and knives."

The conversation went back and forth around the lunch table. Dink and Smoke were eyeing any of the public who came near them. Alexia noticed Dink and Smoke sat on opposite sides of the table so that each could watch the other's back. She wondered if Kathleen, Julia, or Rebecca noticed how alert Dink and Smoke were. After lunch, everyone disappeared into a series of clothing and shoe boutiques. It shocked the women, but both men's comments proved valuable in their purchases.

Chapter 24

That evening, Roman drove Kathleen, Julia, and Rebecca off Hawkeye Ridge and down the logging road in his 4x4 pickup. They stopped at *Nelson Bait and Tackle* to pick up Alexia and crowded three in the truck's rear seat as they headed to The Fishing Hole.

All four young women wore tight jeans, boots, fancy blouses, and neck scarves. Rebecca wore an embroidered vest that hugged and emphasized her bosom, which Dink picked out for her in a boutique. He told her it fit perfectly, and that she looked terrific in it.

She agreed and bought it, telling Alexia, "I've never heard of a man helping a woman pick out clothes, and yet here are both these dangerous men helping us clothes shop."

Alexia wore a stylish jacket that coordinated with her jeans. Julia and Kathleen sported elegant leather jackets, which oozed money, and Kathleen also wore a cowboy hat. She wore a cowboy hat, giving the appearance of knowing how to wear it. However, she incessantly fiddled with the brim to get the crease she wanted.

Roman wore better quality Wranglers, but they showed wear. His cowboy boots showed the scuffs and scratches of heavy use but shone with polish. His Pendleton wool shirt, soft with years of wear, looked comfortable. He appeared at home in a working-class bar with his Carhartt vest and silver belt buckle.

Seeing the packed parking lot, Roman commented, "It looks like everyone in town is here. Andy is the best thing that ever happened to The Fishing Hole."

Most of the vehicles were pickups and SUVs. However, an entire section held motorcycles, most of which were Harleys.

As they walked past Andy's Lincoln Navigator, Brutus stuck his nose out the window for Kathleen to pet. The windows were down, but none over two inches. Andy didn't want Brutus to take off someone's fingers.

The bar reverberated with loud conversation and smelled of burgers, fries, and beer. The grill in the kitchen was visible to everyone walking through the front door. Flames flared up as the burgers dripped grease and sent out volumes of smoke. No one claimed the bar was politically correct, with the bartenders all being young women with curve-revealing jeans, cowboy hats, and bare midriffs. They carried trays holding pitchers of beer and glasses.

Andy sat on stage, warming up, with three tables reserved in front of the stage for his friends. He looked comfortable on stage with his brown high top, lace-up work boots, relaxed-fit Wranglers with a big buckle on his belt, and a long-sleeved camouflage shirt. His wavy black hair fell full over the ears and covered his shirt collar in the back.

Andy's stage equipment was simple: an acoustic guitar and a twelve-string guitar with a microphone stand for himself and his harmonica. He didn't use a keyboard.

Andy waved them to the three empty tables and came off the stage to say hello. He hugged Roman and said, "Sorry, Skipper, I didn't get the message you needed me until I got back from the coast, but I brought you a salmon for the barbeque."

He and Roman chatted for another minute as he hugged Alexia and Julia. Dink had Rebecca on his arm and introduced her. Andy reached Kathleen, who said, "Don't I get a hug? Everybody else got one."

Andy hugged her and said, "I hear you caught hell from Smoke today."

"I'm sorry. I thought I'd apologized to everybody already. I promised I would never try to ditch security again. It's a game I've played with the Secret Service. I never expected it to turn into a big deal."

With the loud background noise, Andy held her close and put his mouth close to her ear. He explained, "There's a bunch of us here who love your dad. We put our lives on the line at his orders in the past. Not everyone made it back. When the chips were down, he stood up for us. We love him for it and would all give our lives defending him. Our lives were on the line, not just when we went on a mission, but even when we were training. It was hazardous work. We know we're lucky to come home in one piece. We have no patience for someone who risks their life for fun or requires us to risk ours. That is why what you did today triggered everyone's anger."

As her eyes filled with tears, Andy held Kathleen, "I'm sorry; I never heard it explained in those terms. That is a perspective I never considered. Thank you. I've never felt in danger before, but today I felt vulnerable, and it was my fault. That will never happen again."

Letting her go and waving a server over for everyone's orders, he grinned and said, "I recommend the burgers and fries, since that's the extent of the menu. The beer comes in three flavors: Bud, Coors, and Millers. It comes in two sizes, a glass or a pitcher."

He told the server to put everyone's ticket on his. When Kathleen protested, Andy laughed, "The owners are friends of mine. The deal is that I sing for free to help them get established. My pay is that my friends and I get to eat and drink for free. It seems fair to me, I get to look like a generous guy, and it doesn't cost me anything."

Andy climbed on stage, strummed chords on his guitar, tuning it, and began singing. The background noise got quieter as people quit talking and started listening to him sing old ballad after old ballad. He sang the famous songs of Gene Autry, Roy Rogers, Hank Williams, and Johnny Cash.

Andy and his music were a big deal in the small town. The combination bar and restaurant tables were jammed full of local people who knew everyone and accepted Andy as one of their own. Andy recognized everyone in the room, at least by sight.

Partway through the evening, it surprised him to look out at the audience and see a table of strangers. The locals kept glaring at them, and the strangers looked uncomfortable and out of place.

Fathi, Chawki, and Rashid sat at a table with Ablah. Andy knew none of them. Andy observed three men of Middle Eastern heritage and a beautiful young woman he suspected was of Iranian descent. The young woman looked happy and excited, but the men appeared nervous.

Andy couldn't hear Ablah talking as she thanked Chawki for bringing her. "I don't know how you found this place, but the singer is wonderful, and so are the burgers."

Andy observed them from the stage and passed a SEAL hand signal to his former teammates. "Alert at your 6 o'clock."

Within seconds, the men surrounding Julia, Kathleen, Rebecca, and Alexia casually shifted position. Sitting at the table were Roman, Jimmy, Roger, and Dink, with Bridger just arriving with Cindy.

Roman leaned forward and whispered into Julia's ear, "Pass the word. Nobody goes to the bathroom alone. Everybody goes together with one of us as a guard."

Julia bristled at receiving an order but agreed, thinking of the day.

Julia passed the message to Kathleen, who asked why before looking at Andy on stage, who gave her a stern stare. Kathleen shrugged, nodded her head, and, once again, passed the message forward.

As the evening went on, the crowd hollered requests. Andy accommodated if he knew the song. Then, he began singing songs he wrote at the audience's request. The room got silent in anticipation. Many of the veterans in the room wept as he sang melancholy songs about lonely nights at sea, desert nights with sentries surrounding you, and the doing of deeds that violated your religious beliefs. He sang of friends who didn't come home alive and those who did but were physically or emotionally damaged. He also sang of the difficulty of loved ones and relatives accepting the now 'wounded warriors.'

But his songs held forth a message of hope with a girl always waiting and a future which still called. The songs focused on a vision of a brighter future.

Andy wrapped up his singing, saying, "We have celebrities in the audience tonight. Sitting up front are three individuals who just received the Governor's Hero's Medal. Please give a shout-out to Roman, Julia, and Jimmy."

A crescendo of shouting filled the room before he continued, "If you haven't heard, Roman just got engaged to Julia." With that, another set of wild yelling rocked the room.

"Also, sitting up front is someone I have just gotten to know. I would be proud to hope I can become a friend of hers. Give a big Oregon welcome to Kathleen Myers." The crowd went crazy when they realized who was in the room.

"As I wrap up for the evening, I want to dedicate a song to Kathleen. It's a song written by heroes of mine, Roy Rogers and Dale Evans. This song is how they ended every television show and many of their movies. So, Kathleen, this is for you."

Roy Rogers and Dale Evans appeared on the televisions scattered around the room, which generally showed sporting events. Roy rode his famous palomino, Trigger, and Dale was on her horse, Buttercup.

Roy strummed his guitar, looked in the camera, and launched into 'Happy Trails.'

Andy stood next to Roy on a television, strummed his guitar, and, looking at Kathleen, sang along with Roy.

♦ ♦ ♦

The room went crazy. Rashid, Fathi, and Chawki tried to leave, but Ablah refused. "I must meet those women. I want to shake their hands. They inspire me. They show me what is possible here in the United States. I will meet you outside."

She eagerly pressed forward and bumped up against a solid wall of men. They stood in front of the women she wished to see. Looking at Roman, she said, "Please, may I shake hands with the young women? They inspire me. They show me what is possible."

Roman and Jimmy scrutinized her before Roman said, "Honey, I think you have a friend who wants to meet you."

All the women came forward, introduced themselves, and shook hands with her. Roman said if she wanted a photo, he would take it and email or text it to her. Ablah gave him both her email and phone number so he could send the pictures.

Ablah kept repeating what an honor it was to meet the president's daughter, the governor's daughter, and two famous television newscasters. She said, "This could never happen in the Middle East. I could never be in public like this, talking to both men and women. I'm so happy I'm an American."

The girls agreed to stay in touch with Ablah on social media and exchanged contact information.

Outside, Fathi and Rashid gave Chawki hell, "Who is this girl? Where did you meet her, and why did you bring her?"

Rashid slammed Chawki up against an SUV. The car erupted with loud barking and growling. Someone coming out of the bar hollered for them to take their fight elsewhere. The tensions were intense as they waited silently for an exuberant Ablah to come out.

Chapter 25

Roman spoke to Jimmy, "I think Ablah was sincere."

Jimmy replied, "It was strange. I wish I knew if the car following the girls to Sisters was related to Ablah. But you are right. My read is that Ablah is on the level. I'm suspicious, though, about the guys at her table."

Jimmy continued, "Is it ok if I spend the night in the bunkhouse?"

"Sure, everybody else is. You may as well join them."

◆ ◆ ◆

Roman's truck seemed roomier going home. Alexia rode back to her place with Jimmy. Andy invited Kathleen to ride up the hill with him and Brutus. As part of the team, he said he'd be spending the night in the bunkhouse and roaming the property later while on guard duty. Her heart pounded as she said yes.

Dink offered a ride to Rebecca, an offer she eagerly accepted. Today and tonight were the most fun she'd experienced since arriving in Oregon. She thought Dink exuded class and was excited to be alone with him. She couldn't help hoping for a goodnight kiss.

Bridger returned to Cindy's with her, and Roger planned to spend the night in the bunkhouse.

Rebecca asked Dink, "What is the bunkhouse, and where is it? My bag is in my car at the Tackle Shop."

Dink answered, "As we go by, we can stop and get your bag. Roman's got a building he calls his bunkhouse. It's a hangar for his plane, a workshop for his tinkering and woodworking, and includes a garage for cars. It has two large rooms set up with bunk beds and bathrooms. One room is for men and one for women. Each room has six bunk beds, so each will hold twelve people. That works out well for a guy's weekend or training exercise. It also works if someone has too much to drink and needs to spend the night or if Roman has multiple guests like tonight. The problem is there is no privacy for couples."

♦ ♦ ♦

Alone with Roman, Julia rode back to what she already thought of as home. She said, "I love Alexia and Kathleen, but I'm happy to be alone with you."

"Same here," he smiled.

When they arrived home, Julia said, "Why don't you give me a minute to get my makeup off before you come to bed? Kathleen knows we won't lock the door. There's no need to wait up for her. She may be occupied with Andy for a while."

Roman laughed and agreed.

A short while later, he walked into the bedroom. The lights were dim, and music played softly in the background. Julia wore one of Roman's starched dress shirts and nothing else. Unbuttoned, the shirt draped to the top of her thighs.

She said, "I know I apologized earlier for attempting to elude security with Kathleen. It was a dumb thing to do and caused you a lot of work and emotional distress. I didn't enjoy fighting with you. So, I want to make amends." She started removing his clothes. He reached for her, and she said, "Oh no, I got my massage this morning. Tonight, I get to give you a massage."

She pushed him onto the bed, face down, and straddling him, began rubbing massage oil into his back and kneading his muscles. "I didn't just buy clothes in Sisters. I got a bottle of special massage oil."

Turning him over, she rubbed the oil on his chest and, inches at a time, rubbed it lower. He moaned, "Wow, that burns."

"Is it an enjoyable burn?"

They broke into a long kiss when he reached to pull her closer.

She moved away from his hands and continued to massage him. She asked as she moved lower. "Did I tell you it's flavored?"

"No, you didn't." He groaned again as she teased him with a soft touch.

"It is. I bought another bottle for you to use when you need to apologize for something."

"I can't wait."

"Neither can I."

Chapter 26

Andy opened the door of his Lincoln Navigator, and Brutus went crazy when he saw Kathleen. She hugged him and rubbed his head and shoulders.

After a moment, Andy told him to get in the back seat, and he did. As they left the tavern and headed for Hawkeye Ridge, he asked her, "How did you get so good with dogs? Brutus is a trained killer. Yet, he loves you. How did you manage that? Where did you learn how to command dogs?"

"I'll give you the long answer. My mother's parents owned a vast ranch in West Texas. When they died, my mother inherited it. Dad and Mom were married then, and I was just a baby. We lived on the ranch already, and Dad had gotten started in politics and was in Austin a lot. He tried to fly home on the weekends.

"Mom's parents raised her on the ranch. She left for college and returned after graduation. Mom wanted the same experience for me. Dad knew nothing about ranching, so Mom hired a ranch management company to run the operation, and we just lived there in the ranch headquarters. To make up for Dad's absence, Mom got me a puppy. I don't know what breed Socks was. I think he had Golden Retriever and perhaps Collie in him. He was a blonde color with thick fur and a loving personality. There was a white spot on his nose and four white feet, so we called him Socks.

"Most of the dogs on the ranch were Australian Cattle Dogs, red heelers. Heelers are working cattle dogs on ranches and were a tremendous help in moving the cattle from one pasture to another. They do, however, require structured training and firm control."

Andy interjected, "Yeah, they would."

"Mom got me involved in a local 4H program. Most 4H programs in farm country involve raising animals, pigs, cattle, or sheep for the market, or perhaps in an equestrian program. Instead, she got me into a class for dog training, which I think was her program for raising me.

"I think my mother trained me by having me train Socks. I worked with the healers, too. They are magnificent dogs and always want to be working for you. But, Socks was my love. We 4H'd together for years. He was smart and my best friend. When I thought the world was being mean, I'd talk to Socks. We'd sneak off somewhere, and I'd hug him and, hiding my face in his fur, cry into his neck. He'd lick the tears off my face and make me feel like everything would be ok. I still miss him. He loved me unconditionally."

Andy said, "That's how Brutus is for me. He's my best friend."

"I know, I can tell. Brutus would give his life for you."

"He almost has." Andy paused in reflection before saying, "Do you still own the ranch? I thought you lived in Washington, D.C.?"

"My mother died in a car wreck when I was sixteen. Her will stipulated the ranch would go into a trust for me until I turned thirty. Until then, the ranch management team will continue to run it. They invest the income from the ranch in a blind trust since Dad is president. The monthly check I get to live on is bigger than I need. I don't know how they invest the rest of the money or how much there is."

Andy nodded, "Makes sense with your dad in politics."

"When Mom died, I was too young to live alone on the ranch. So, I moved to Austin to be with Dad. By then, Dad was governor of Texas. Dad hired private tutors to 'homeschool' me so I could finish high school. I think Dad enjoyed having me around. Even though I was finishing school, Dad asked me to function as his escort for state functions. Part of the 'homeschooling' included training in manners, style, class, etiquette, etc. He scheduled dance instructors, public speaking instructors, anyone who could help make me comfortable on his arm in high-profile situations."

"That's amazing. Everyone has seen you in news clips. You always look so poised. Now I know why."

"Maybe, I grew up being in television sound bites. While still a teenager, I acted the role of hostess for functions my father would host. I fulfilled the duties of the first lady of Texas and, later, the same position at the White House. Everyone knows I'm his daughter, and no one expects me to know anything about politics or state affairs, but Dad talks to me about the people he's dealing with and the non-classified situations. I'm his sounding board. I help him understand the personalities involved in whatever is going on."

Shaking her head, she said, "I would love to see my father date or perhaps get remarried. I know he loved my mother with all his heart, but he's been alone for years. Whenever I broach the subject with him, he tells me he can't have a personal life until he's out of the White House. He's cautious about the women seen in his presence. I think he feels safe with me performing as his hostess."

Andy asked as they exited his car on Hawkeye Ridge, "What about you? I've seen photos of you on the evening news. Do you have a social life? Is there anyone waiting in the wings?"

Surprising herself, Kathleen took his hand and said, "No, I'm my father's daughter. I'm conscious of who is on my arm. I could never hold your hand in Washington. The people waiting in the wings for me are the Secret Service. Maybe that's why I was so excited about coming to tomorrow's BBQ. Dad told me Roman, and your team would provide the security. I didn't think of the danger in eluding security this morning. I just wanted to feel like a normal young woman that could go to the spa with her girlfriends."

They approached the house. Andy said, "It's getting late. Shall I let you go in, or would you like to sit out and listen to the wind in the trees?"

Kathleen said, "If it's all right, I would love to keep talking. I'm enjoying myself. I never expected a handsome man like you to hold my hand or serenade me in public. At least not until Dad's out of politics. If we did this in Washington, there would be a dozen photographers snapping shots of my every facial expression."

Shivering, she added, "If it were just warmer, it would be perfect. It's getting cool."

Andy wrapped his arms around her, led her to the patio where he turned on the propane space heater, and, pulling a blanket out of a chest, seated them on the sofa.

Kathleen started questioning Andy about his life, dreams, and aspirations.

Feeling warmer from the heater and snuggling under the blanket, she said, "You're terrific. Have you ever thought about a career in music?"

Andy laughed, "Yeah, me and every school kid with a guitar who thinks he can sing. I've known dozens of guys who tried to break into music. It's challenging without the right connections. Would I love to perform? Sure. Am I willing to invest my life chasing an improbable dream? No, I'm not. My life is good right now. I expect you know; I came out of the service with money. It wasn't a fortune, but it was enough to buy a beautiful house and ten acres across the canyon. I've got full retirement pay. It's more than enough."

"I'm glad. So many of our vets are struggling."

"Don't get me started on that subject. It's wrong what this country allows to happen to its vets."

"I agree."

"Getting back on the subject, the local Humane Society convinced me to volunteer a couple of days a week, helping socialize dogs for adoption. I also run a part-time business teaching people how to train their dogs."

"Oh, you'd make a great instructor."

"Brutus and I volunteer for search and rescue work for lost hikers, and I do free handyman work if someone needs something done and can't afford a contractor. I just try to give back to people the blessings I've received. My schedule is busy but low-key. Life is good. I'm not willing to give up my life to beg someone I've never met to give me a shot in the music industry. It's too big of a long shot."

Hours later, Dink discovered them on the patio while doing a perimeter check. They were stretched out on the sofa with a blanket.

Brutus's head came up, watching Dink as he returned to the bunkhouse and getting his own sleeping bag, and Andy's returned to the patio. With Brutus watching his every move, he gently covered Andy and Kathleen with both sleeping bags and watched as Kathleen turned to Andy and laid her head on his shoulder.

As the sun began shining and the birds chirping in the morning, Roman's bedside phone rang. It was Smoke. "Hey Skipper, time to rise and shine. We have a situation down here at the gate. Rouse everyone out of Slumberland and send them down. I think I may need Brutus, and we should call in the guys I hired this week."

Roman went from a sound sleep to wide awake at the phone ring. "What's going on, and how urgent?"

"Alexia and I sat up talking until the wee hours, and then instead of coming up to the bunkhouse, I crashed in your apartment over the boat showroom. As the sun came up, I heard cars arriving and filling up the parking lot. Checking it out, I found people from every news organization in the state, plus a bunch of paparazzi who flew in. There's a crowd of photographers in front of the gate hollering to get in."

Roman again questioned why they were there, but the sinking feeling in his stomach told him he knew.

Jimmy just said, "Check your Facebook and your social media apps. I'll get reinforcements down here for today and tonight. Get showered and cleaned up. The odds are good that you'll wind up on a news clip. Mark and Kelly are at the gate, and Roger is visible in the trees, so there's no immediate urgency, but I think we need all hands on deck."

Chapter 27

Roman jumped into the shower and started dressing as Julia pulled up her Facebook page on her phone. She looked at her phone and groaned as he put on khaki slacks, a shirt, and a leather jacket. His appearance was upscale casual. Julia knew no one would suspect he carried an arsenal of weapons.

She answered his question, "You remember Andy introducing Kathleen and then dedicating 'Happy Trails' to her?"

At his nod, she continued, "There were about a dozen different people who videoed him singing and posted it on their Facebook pages. The best and most touching post came from Ablah, which has already gone viral. There are over three hundred thousand views already."

Julia started fixing breakfast while Roman called the bunkhouse. Dink answered and told Roman that Andy was asleep on the patio. He said they agreed to split Andy's guard shift between them and allow him to sleep.

Roman walked onto the patio and grinned. He motioned for Julia to look. Brutus sat near the couch with his eyes on Roman and his ears alert. Andy slept soundly with Kathleen in his arms. She lay half on her side and half on Andy and snored lightly.

Julia said, "I'd love to take a picture, but I know I shouldn't."

Andy's eyes flashed open as she spoke, and he looked around. Comprehension flowed into him, and he asked, "What's up?"

Kathleen groaned as she moved and sat up. Julia explained, "Ablah posted your 'Happy Trails' to her Facebook. It's gone viral. There's a horde of paparazzi at the gate."

Roman said, "Yeah, Smoke wants you and Brutus down there ASAP to put respect into everyone. But, I'd suggest you get cleaned up before you go, in case you wind up on video."

Swearing, Andy jogged to the bunkhouse to shower, shave, and change clothes. Julia took Kathleen by the hand, and they ran for showers.

Later, everyone was back for a quick breakfast. Rebecca and Dink joined them. The women were in the kitchen comparing notes on last evening, and Roman and Dink were on the patio waiting for Andy to return.

Kathleen and Rebecca discussed the two handsome men's unexpected arrival in their lives, Andy and Dink. Coming for a weekend of 'girl time' and the BBQ with Roman and Julia's friends, they were both surprised at the emotions they were feeling.

Rebecca said, "My heart melted when Andy sang to you, Kathleen. Andy is such a hunk. I think half the women in the room were crying, and half were dying to go home with him."

Kathleen commented on Dink, "Well, you captured Dink's attention from his first hello in Sisters. Andy appeals to me more, but I have never seen a man exude class and sophistication like Dink. I know more from my father than I should about these guys. He couldn't stop bragging about them. They're dangerous but dependable men. I'm not in a situation where I can let a man into my life, but if I could, Andy was pulling the right strings."

Moments later, Andy, Dink, and Roman walked in the door. The ladies expected the retired SEALs to wear camouflage clothing. Instead, they wore sturdy khakis, Danner desert boots for the mountain terrain, and casual shirts. They looked like an advertisement for business casual in the outdoor world.

Over breakfast, they discussed what to do. Kathleen volunteered to speak to the paparazzi.

Roman said, "No. The paparazzi are on my property, and I promised your father security. I need to establish limits now and not wait until our wedding."

The men climbed into the Argo and went downhill. While still out of sight of the gate, they stopped and let Andy and Brutus out of the rig. Roman called his Uncle Russ for backup support from the Marion County Sheriff's office.

Stopping at the gate, Roman and Dink got out. The reporters began shouting questions, which Roman ignored. Instead, he shook hands with Mark and Kelly, who were guarding the entrance. Jimmy and Alexia came out of the tackle shop, and Roman motioned them through the gate. When Alexia went through, a howl of protest rose from the reporters. Roman held up his hand for quiet.

Speaking into a bullhorn, he said, "I'm Roman Nelson. *Nelson Timber* owns the forest behind me, which includes my home. *Nelson Bait and Tackle* owns the store and the parking lot you are standing in. What's important to you is my family, and I own those companies. You are on private property. There are no trespassing signs posted every fifty feet. I have no comment regarding my guests and will never comment on these or any future guests. You need to know I'm a private person and will be aggressive in defending my privacy and property."

As he paused for a breath, the paparazzi shouted questions. Ignoring their questions, he continued. "I will prosecute anyone ever found trespassing on my property. After the hospital releases them, they will be charged with criminal mischief and trespass. I've already called the sheriff's office and an ambulance. You parked and are standing in the parking lot of *Nelson Boat and Tackle*. If you read the parking lot's signs, we permit people to park here for 30 minutes if they patronize the business. Your cars arrived more than 30 minutes ago, and you aren't inside the store. Therefore, you are trespassing. The tow trucks are on their way. You should leave now."

He paused for another breath as they shouted questions. Continuing to ignore them, he said, "This is James Stockade, owner of *SOS Inc.*, which is *Special Operators Security, Inc.* I hired him and his firm to provide security for my property."

Jimmy stepped forward, took the bullhorn, and said, "Andy, please introduce Brutus."

Andy stepped out of the trees with Brutus on a leash. Videos rolled as they recognized Andy.

Still speaking into the bullhorn, Jimmy commanded everyone's attention. The reporters were too busy shouting questions to observe behind them every tow truck within ten miles showing up and towing away the news trucks.

Jimmy said into the bullhorn, "Those of you who crossed the fence are guilty of criminal trespass. You have ten seconds to identify yourself and return across the fence. Beyond that time, a military-trained search and attack dog will find you. You should expect that your dog bites will require hospital treatment; they typically do. Please remove yourself from your hiding spot."

Jimmy then began counting down from ten. Focused on Jimmy and his count, the reporters ignored any noise behind them. Finally, at number one, Jimmy said, "Andy, release Brutus to Search."

During the entire conversation, Brutus was alerting and focused on a spot up the hill. He quivered with excitement and barely sat still. Then, Andy slipped off the leash at Jimmy's order, and Brutus bolted into the brush and trees. Andy, Mark, and Kelly followed him up the mountain. Snarling and screams came from up the hill. Andy did not call Brutus off until he caught up with him.

An ambulance arrived, and Jimmy sent two medics up the hill with a stretcher. Andy and Brutus returned and remained at a distance from the gate.

The message was unmistakable. Brutus's excited appearance shouted, *"That was fun! Who's next?"*

The Marion County Sheriff's car arrived, and the reporters turned to discover the parking lot was empty of news trucks.

Amidst the reporter's outcry, Roman raised his bullhorn again, "If you are a local reporter, I appreciate what you do and hope to establish a good relationship with you. I invite you to a webinar I will conduct next week on the State of Oregon emergency preparedness programs. But if you aren't a local reporter or are paparazzi, you have no business here. Everyone must know I value my guest's privacy and my own, and I never give a second warning. I gave you notice when I arrived that you and your vehicles were trespassing. The gentleman on the hill received his notice. We towed your trucks because they violated our parking regulations. As much as I wish to remain on favorable terms with everyone, you have just three minutes to get off our property and onto the public highway. Or, you may go inside our store and start spending money, which permits you to park while shopping."

Looking at the deputy, he said, "Deputy, please charge the person coming down the hill on a stretcher with criminal trespass and any additional charges which apply. Tell the district attorney I will press charges and expect him to pursue the maximum charges and sentences. Please let the district attorney know. I expect him to prosecute the trespassers and not offer them a plea bargain."

Looking at the crowd of reporters and paparazzi, he added, "Any of these people who aren't inside our store in three minutes, please charge them with trespassing."

A reporter yelled a question about what happened to their news trucks. Roman's response was classic, "That's not my problem. It's your problem. My problem was people trespassing on my property and harassing my guests. I've dealt with my problem. *SOS Inc.* will handle the problem from now on. If you haven't noticed, they're competent and play rough."

Each station featured clips of Roman's talk throughout the day, while showing Brutus taking down the hiding paparazzi. The local reporters were incensed over their truck's towing, but they had no use for the out-of-area paparazzi.

Roman was becoming known as someone who made the news.

Chapter 28

It was a morning for conflict. While Roman dealt with the paparazzi, Khalil and Fathi grilled Chawki about Ablah.

It wasn't a pleasant conversation. Khalil reminded Chawki of his father's instructions to avoid emotional entanglements with western girls. Chawki protested that Ablah was Muslim.

Fathi disagreed, "Didn't you hear her telling everyone how excited she was to meet those girls? Proclaiming for everyone to hear how proud she was to be an American. She doesn't care about kicking the American Satan out of our homeland."

While Chawki strove to defend Ablah, he knew his relationship with her was doomed. Rashid entered with his Ipad and turned to Ablah's Facebook page. "Look at this and these text messages," he said.

Everyone looked at the post of Andy serenading Kathleen. Rashid then showed them the previous month's text messages from Ablah's phone. Many of the texts were between Chawki and Ablah.

Rashid read them out loud. Embarrassed, Chawki knew how silly the messages sounded. Chawki knew Rashid cloned Ablah's phone to access the texts. Thinking about it, Chawki thought, *"I'll bet the bastard cloned my phone too."*

Khalil was furious. He ordered Chawki to stop seeing Ablah. Chawki submitted to his uncle's request. He requested permission to meet with Ablah one last time to break up in person. He explained he wished to return the gifts she gave him.

Khalil agreed.

With everyone watching, Chawki texted Ablah and made a date

to meet her later in the day. He chose a public place, knowing someone would watch.

He asked permission to leave, saying, "I need to gather up her gifts to return, and I need to go shopping."

Leaving his cell phone at home for fear Rashid would use it to track him, he wandered with no apparent purpose around the campus. His random walk, appearing aimless and depressed, allowed him to see if anyone followed him. When he was certain no one followed, he went into the closest phone store and purchased two prepaid cell phones.

Meeting Ablah later, he held a grocery bag that contained the gifts she gave him. It included the presents and a prepaid cell phone buried in the bottom.

Not knowing there was a problem, Ablah gave him a full-body hug. Then Chawki, thinking he might never see her again, returned her embrace and kissed her. Chawki started by complimenting her on her Facebook post. She was excited about the post going viral. Chawki commented on her mentioning her pride in being an American in her post.

She said, "I am."

He replied, "I understand how you can feel that way. Fathi and I left Iraq when I was ten years old, and I spent eight years in England going to school. We arrived in Oregon right after I finished. I left Iraq long ago, so Iraq no longer feels like home to me. I would consider England, where I grew up, my home. But Oregon feels like home since you came into my life."

"That's so sweet."

Chawki replied in anguish, "No, that's the problem. You can no longer be a part of my life. I've told you I'm a moderate Muslim, which is not true. I'm Muslim by birth, but I'm not by nature religious. My family, however, isn't moderate. They're extreme in their beliefs while professing reasonable beliefs. We must not see each other again for your safety and mine."

When she cried, Chawki turned her so the man from the mosque following in the distance could see her cry. Holding her in his arms, he didn't look into her eyes. That was too hard to do. Instead, he said, "I love you, but we must end this now."

Chawki held her as she shook her head and continued crying. However, he said, "Do you see the man in the robes behind us?"

When she said yes, Chawki continued, "Please continue to cry, he is watching us, and I must talk to you for a minute."

She continued to sob. Chawki said, "My uncle, my brother, and the people surrounding them aren't nice. If they thought you or I were a risk to them, they would take us to our ranch, cut off our heads, and bury us in the quarry. We wouldn't be the first people they've killed that way. My uncle's friends initiated them into that practice in North Africa. Rashid has cloned your phone, hacked your email, and monitored your text messages and emails. From now on, say nothing to anyone you do not want them to read or hear."

Ablah sobbed and shook her head as she said, "You are paranoid. That can't be. This is America."

He said, "It is true. Your life is too important for me to take a chance that I'm wrong. Look in this bag and pull out the shirt, but nothing else."

She did so, and he said, "Yes, this is the shirt you gave me. I fear they may have cameras in my apartment. Put the shirt back in the bag, in the bottom, under the other gifts you gave me, is a prepaid phone. I will text you every day at 5 p.m. to let you know I love you. I programmed the phone with my prepaid cell phone number. Never contact my old phone number and never call the new phone. Send me a text if you wish. If you text me, never send one, which will take you longer than one minute to enter and send. Rashid is an expert at cloning phones. Never turn the phone on if anyone else is within a hundred feet. "

She asked, "If you aren't making this up to get rid of me, why are they doing this, and why don't you report them?"

Chawki answered, "I'm not making this up. There is nothing to report, there are no plans, and there is nothing in motion. But they're looking for a target. A target that will help them re-ignite the fight for our homeland. The problem is, even though they're not friendly people, they're my family, and I love them."

Chawki kissed her again and strolled away, expecting never to see her again. His shoulders slumped as he looked at the ground and walked off to join the man in the white robe.

Ablah, watching his back disappear into the crowd, sobbing in disbelief.

Chapter 29

The BBQ guests arrived on Hawkeye Ridge. Jimmy, Alexia, Dink, Rebecca, Thomas and Samantha Jefferson, Andy Baker, Bridger and Cindy, and Kathleen were there. None experienced a problem getting past gate security, and there were no crowds at the gate.

Everyone laughed at the news coverage they saw of the morning's activities. Finally, Andy said, "Doesn't Brutus look pleased with himself? I swear he thought it was like old times." The former SEAL team members treated Brutus like another guy. Everyone else moved carefully around him. Brutus, however, appeared conflicted. His usual spot was within arm's reach of Andy. Today, however, he went back and forth between Andy and Kathleen.

Within minutes, everyone acted like long-time friends. It was a comfortable group, with Julia and Roman filling everyone in on the current wedding plans.

Roman said, "We're hoping to host the wedding here on Hawkeye Ridge. There is enough room at the side of the runway to set up everything there. We're thinking about late August or early September."

Julia said, "I know I want Samantha as my Matron of Honor and Kathleen as my Maid of Honor."

Roman said, "My best man has gotta be Jimmy. Beyond that, I don't have a clue about wedding protocol."

The women thought, "Typical male."

Thomas Jefferson fit right in with the SEALS. Everyone wanted Jimmy to talk about his venture, and Thomas asked if he would need his own skill sets. When Jimmy asked what those were, he joked, "Like the rest of you, controlled violence and mayhem, and the ability to move unseen. Since I expect there are limited needs for those skills, how about Human Resources, computer hacking, electronic eavesdropping, and computer monitoring?"

Jimmy said, "You're hired! We can talk about the details later. I've gotten phone calls and text messages all day from former military guys. I think I'll rent a room next week, do an overview of what I need, and then collect resumes for interviews. It doesn't look like hiring qualified people will be an issue."

About then, Julia's cell phone rang. Frowning, she said, "For heaven's sake, caller ID says it's a payphone," but she answered.

It was Ablah, in tears. She repeatedly apologized for calling after just meeting Julia, but said, "I think it may be important."

Ablah asked if there was any way she could meet with Julia and Mr. Nelson, perhaps tonight. She said, "You are the most important people I know. I do not know if there is a danger or not, but I want to tell you what I know."

Julia put her phone on speaker so that Roman could hear.

Roman stepped in, "Ablah, this is Roman. No need to apologize. If you think there is a danger, we can meet tonight. Let me give you the address of our store. When you pull into the parking lot, drive your car to the back of the lot. You'll see a gate. Leave your vehicle there, and two guards will meet you and send you up. If you are in Corvallis, you are about an hour away. Why don't you plan on having dinner with us and perhaps spending the night if you are in danger?"

"Thank you. I'm in Stayton, about twenty minutes away, and have been crying and driving all afternoon before I called you. I was afraid you would think I am crazy."

The conversation on the patio turned to what she wanted and what danger existed.

Andy asked, "Do you want me to meet her at the gate with Brutus. He can check her for weapons and explosives, and she won't even know we did it?"

Roman nodded yes, and Andy and Brutus walked to the chairlift.

Kathleen accompanied them and gave Andy a fearful hug. "Be careful."

Andy made a joke of it and said, "Always," but thought to himself, *"I haven't had a woman tell me to be careful since my mother when I left for the service."*

A short while later, Andy came back with Ablah. He told Roman a guard at the gate took Ablah's car out of sight and parked it in the logging equipment shed.

Ablah apologized excessively and repetitively for interrupting the party, but her face was tear-streaked, and her eyes swollen.

The women who met her the night before took over. Julia said, "Wait until after we've eaten to talk about what's happening. Let's get you freshened up. You'll feel better able to talk after washing your face and having a bite to eat."

Everyone went in to 'freshen up' as Roman put the steaks on the grill.

After the potluck dinner, Julia broke out cards and various board games. She explained that she and Roman hoped to form a group of friends who would get together monthly for dinner and games. She urged everyone to get started while she, Kathleen, Roman, and Jimmy visited with Ablah.

Taking Ablah, who felt less stressed, they sat down to talk in Roman's office. Ablah explained about her boyfriend, Chawki, breaking up with her. She repeated his explanations and mentioned his promise to send her a message daily at 5 p.m.

Roman looked at his watch. It was six o'clock. "Did he?"

She pulled out the prepaid phone and handed it to Roman. He turned it on, looked at the emoji text of a broken heart, and turned the phone back off.

Ablah questioned if Roman and Jimmy thought the danger was real and what they thought she should do about it. Then, she asked, "Do you believe Chawki is in real danger?"

Jimmy asked, "Do you know the names of Chawki's brother, his uncle, and the others close to him?" His question appeared casual, even though he took notes on a small pad.

At Khalil's name, Jimmy stiffened and glanced at Roman. His jaw clenched, and his voice turned as cold as cracked ice. No emotion was in his flat voice, which came out with precise knife-edged words.

Roman knew Jimmy was no longer the Chief Warrant Officer of the nation's preeminent Navy SEAL hostage recovery team, but the glacial voice he heard was a voice Roman knew from the past. It always came before a hostage recovery mission, in which orders included killing all captors. It was the voice of the man his teammates nicknamed 'Smoke' for his ability to move unseen in dangerous situations and kill quietly.

The icy voice of Smoke said, "Yes, the danger for Chawki is real. You can do nothing for him without placing him at risk. Do not contact him. If you must respond to his five o'clock messages, do nothing but send him emojis. Do not communicate with anyone here tonight with your phone or email. Do not talk about anything you don't want Chawki's 'not nice relatives' to see."

Looking at Roman, he said, "Skipper, I think she needs an encrypted phone to reach us on."

Wondering what Jimmy knew, Roman agreed, "Ablah, I'm starting a series of statewide meetings. I will look for volunteers in lots of cities. There will be an opportunity to join a volunteer disaster preparedness group at a meeting I'm holding in Corvallis in about two weeks. Watch the newspaper for where and when. When you come, see Julia for a binder of information. Inside the binder will be an encrypted satellite phone. Since everyone knows we met you, acknowledge us, but do not act like a close friend. Keep the phone with you always, since you must assume they can search your place at will. Also, let's check out your apartment if it's alright. We can find out if cameras and recording devices are inside it."

At the mention of cameras in her apartment, Ablah's eyes widened, and her face became pale.

Breathing rapidly, she asked, "Please, if you find them, can you remove them?"

Roman said, "We could, but if we find any, I think you should leave them in place. Just be boring in the area where the cameras or recording devices are."

Ablah agreed, and Roman discussed who should search for the cameras with Jimmy.

Jimmy said, "It might be time to try out Thomas Jefferson. Of course, we know it would be a cakewalk for Dink. But, since we're no longer on the government payroll, who do you think we should bill for this?"

Roman laughed and agreed with asking Thomas to tackle Ablah's apartment. "It's a funny situation. We never worried before about billing someone for our time. However, I think you should do the job and submit an invoice to Admiral Seastrand. I bet he gets you paid so you can pay Thomas."

Stepping out of the room for a moment, Jimmy returned with Thomas. He explained what they needed and asked him if he could handle it.

"Sure, no problem. I need to gather the right equipment, but I can handle it."

Talking to Ablah, he asked her questions about her apartment. He explained to her, "I think we should assume they bugged your place with audio and video. The issue is to find the stuff without being seen finding it. Even if I turn off the power to your apartment, I assume the bugs are battery-operated. They might even utilize night vision if those guys are as good as your boyfriend said."

Thomas continued, "Let's do this tomorrow. I will show up and act like I'm your cousin's husband. You act surprised that I'm there. I'll explain that I heard through the family grapevine you got dumped, and I just came by to console you. You cry and put on an act about breaking up with a guy you loved but ask me to fix your internet while I'm there. Maybe say your wireless router is giving you problems, anything to give me an excuse to walk throughout your apartment. I want to go into every room, even the bathroom. When I leave, walk me out to my car. When you do, leave your electronics behind. I'll let you know what I find."

With everything arranged, Julia invited Ablah to stay, saying,

"We have tables of cards, backgammon, and dominos. Afterward, you can spend the night in 'the bunkhouse.'"

Delighted with not returning to a 'bugged' apartment, Ablah agreed.

Roman asked for everybody's attention and said, "I've spoken to Admiral Seastrand, the Chairman of the Joint Chiefs of Staff. Because of the two incidents of someone following Kathleen's vehicle, we think someone has hacked some of our phones. Perhaps all of them. I suggest everyone get another phone or do a factory reset on your current one. I recommend changing your passwords on your phone, social media, and email accounts."

Everyone talked about being hacked as they played games.

As the evening wound down, they again sat around the fire pit. Kathleen said, "This has been an incredible several days for me. Julia is my sister from different parents, and I'm so excited for her. Roman, I love the way you make her happy. Julia has never seemed so relaxed and fulfilled. All of you touch my heart. Ablah, I have such respect for you and compassion for what you are going through. Coming out here, I knew I would meet new people, but I didn't know how much you would mean to me in such a short time."

Tearing up, she said, "Meeting someone like Andy and his amazing dog, Brutus, was unexpected. The two of you are special. I'm so glad I met you. This may seem like a strange request. Christmas is a special holiday for me, and I would love to hear Andy sing some Christmas songs. Andy, could you play some Christmas songs for us? We can all pretend there is snow on the ground."

Kathleen propped her phone up for recording, and Andy picked up a guitar. He played song after song. He played secular songs like 'Frosty the Snowman' and played the traditional Christmas music he heard as a child. Everyone sat silent and respectful, with the wind whistling through the trees.

As he played, Kathleen became pensive. She listened while lost in her thoughts. As Andy finished with Silent Night, tears drifted down her cheeks.

When he finished, everyone was quiet.

Kathleen gathered her nerve, "Andy, would you do me a favor?"

He replied, "Anything."

She said, "Every Christmas, Dad and I have local children from the D.C. schools come in and decorate a tree in the family area of the White House. Would you come back for the event? While the children are decorating, I'd like to have you walking around among them, playing Christmas carols. It would create a memory those children would cherish forever. I know I would."

Chapter 30

When Kathleen left for home, Smoke showed up with three vehicles. Kathleen got into the Navigator with Andy and Brutus and left Gates as the caravan's middle car. Smoke took no chances.

Roman started his series of statewide community 'town hall' meetings that evening. He'd emailed the elected leaders of every small town in Oregon. He offered to come to their city and hold a 'town hall' type meeting to discuss disaster preparedness.

Unsure of himself, he thought he would start with the nearby towns. His natural choice was Gates, where a local church volunteered its facilities. Roman and Julia showed up an hour early. He hoped someone else would come. As the start time approached, people started straggling in, with a sizeable crowd arriving as he began the program.

He told Julia, "I know we talked about what to say. I've got my slides ready, but it still seems like I should have a detailed point-by-point presentation. Maybe I'm just nervous."

She said, "Tell people that."

She added, "I've watched my dad and his cronies make political speeches all my life. Nothing is more effective than what you planned. Tell them about yourself, share your experiences, and what led you to your preparedness beliefs. When you have their attention, offer to help and ask them to help you make the program work."

Still nervous, Roman did that. Thanking everyone for attending, he started by giving everyone a brief biography of himself. Then, Roman shared his experiences since leaving home for Annapolis. He spoke of exotic places and things he saw, which affected him. Alert for his talk, many in the audience knew him and wondered about his time in the Navy.

Roman said, "Not everything the Navy does is war-related. More than once, our ship was the initial relief aid to arrive after a major earthquake, tsunami, or typhoon. I've seen the heart-wrenching devastation of many families' lives. Often, we would be the first help to arrive on the scene. Our primary responsibility was restoring stability and providing food, water, and medical help."

As he talked about those circumstances, he projected photos from his iPad onto the screen with a projector.

"At heart, I'm an incurable optimist, but I understand tragedies happen. So, while I hope for good to happen, I want to do everything possible to mitigate any disasters that may strike. I strive to always hope for the best and prepare for the worst. Many of you are familiar with my home, and I know you questioned what I built into it. Here is your explanation. I buried the house halfway up its sides, and there are no trees nearby because of the fire risk. That's why I'm doing the property clearing in our forests the way we do. I'm attempting to fireproof my forest against a catastrophic wildfire."

Looking around the room, he saw people nodding their heads. "The chairlift is convenient, but it's primarily a fast evacuation route for my mother if there's a dam failure."

"Do you think either of those is possible?"

"Yes. Enough of a risk that I live on a mountaintop and want an immediate escape plan for my mother."

Looking around the room, he saw people he knew well shaking their heads. One of his distant relatives said, "Naah, Roman, Detroit, and Big Cliff are two big ass'ed dams. They ain't coming down, and forest fires occur every year. We know there's always time to escape."

"I hope you're right. But, are you ready to bet your family's lives on that fact?"

There was a moment's silence before the response, "That's a hellova heavy bet. What you're doing in your forests is extreme. Do you think we could have that big of a fire, and how could the dams come down?"

"Yes, I think we are due for a significant fire. Our forests are bone dry with the drought conditions caused by climate change. Filled with fallen trees and underbrush as fuel, all it would take for us to have a raging rim-to-rim fire is a prolonged east wind in the summer with a spark occurring on the east side of the mountains. The canyon could be an inferno."

As wives looked at husbands, the distant relative said, "Ok, I'll give you the possibility of a fire, but what would cause the dams to come down?"

"They are prime targets for terrorists. A rogue nation like North Korea, or perhaps Iran or Iraq, wanting to show off their missile capability, is another. I think the Cascadia Subduction Zone Earthquake is the most likely possibility outside of an act of war. My new job is to get the various Oregon communities involved in determining what natural disasters could occur in their local area. Once we know what can happen, each community can prepare in advance for those eventualities."

Once again, looking around the room, he saw people shaking their heads.

Roman continued, "The state has created many top-down committees that examined various disaster scenarios. But, to a large extent, the committees historically are unsuccessful in getting local communities to accept the disaster realities or develop local action plans if the disaster occurs. Part of their lack of success was resistance to the state as big brother applying top-down management and direction. As a result, no one believed the disaster possibilities the state committees discussed were real or felt the threats were large enough that they needed to prepare. Just like you live in a forest and downstream from a dam, yet don't believe a fire or dam collapse is possible."

People in the room looked at the floor in embarrassment.

"I want to help each community develop a list of risks in their area with which they're concerned. What do the people in a community feel could happen? Not what the state says could happen. Once each community has established its list of risks, then the question is, how can they prepare for those risks in advance?"

Heads were nodding in the crowd.

"I need your help. The governor has appointed me to do a job I've never done. I know it's an important job, and I'm afraid I may fall flat on my face. I'm asking you to help me build a template, a system that the communities can use in their localities. Hopefully, several of you will join me on a committee investigating potential risks facing our town and the local canyon. We can bring the list back to another 'town hall' in two weeks. At that meeting, I'm hoping the audience will get involved in brainstorming a wide range of steps for each of the risks you identify. We can then design actual action steps that will get something done. Advance preparation can make a significant difference in a disaster."

Scanning the room, Roman saw understanding and agreement on many faces.

"A recommendation I'll have is that each community should get involved in promoting the CERT program. CERT stands for Community Emergency Response Team. FEMA sponsors the program. FEMA's classes train volunteers to prepare for the disasters their community may face. It's preparing in advance because when a disaster strikes, it is always unexpected. If it strikes, how do you act? It's not about preventing the tragedy. It's about surviving it. The training is free, and they provide the instructors. We need someone local to organize and coordinate the training. Someone who can convince their friends and neighbors to attend the training."

Roman then opened the meeting for questions. After answering those questions, he asked for committee volunteers.

Cindy volunteered first. She said, "I'll be the CERT contact person and connect with the county director in establishing a program. I can even promote attendance in my beauty shop. Everyone who comes in for a cut will get a sales pitch on attending the program."

When she said that, the women in the room groaned.

All the former SEALS living in Gates, Bridger, Roger, and Andy volunteered. Roman accepted them but kept talking about wanting the old-time residents on the committee. At last, Uncle Russ and two of his buddies agreed to serve on the committee with a bit of crowd encouragement.

Uncle Russ asked, "Is it ok to hold our meeting over beer and burgers when Andy's singing?"

Roman laughed with them and said, "Of course, if drinking and driving are on the list of potential disasters."

Roman now had a template for getting local communities engaged in disaster planning. He thought if he could get the communities involved in step one, disaster planning, step two, brainstorming, and step three, action planning would move forward.

Oregon is a large state with communities in remote areas. Some of those communities had never received a visit from someone they viewed as a politician. Roman sent out emails to the towns, inviting them to call for a meeting. Getting no response, he started calling the community leaders.

He told them he was scheduling a series of road trips for meetings throughout the state. He said, "I want to ensure we get your community involved, since disaster planning is critical for your area. I kept the time open for you, but you need to guarantee fifteen people in the room for this to work for your community."

Roman went from a casual lifestyle to one which was frenetic overnight. His position included an office in the Capitol Building with access to the governor, a secretary, an expense account, and a regular paycheck with benefits.

Chapter 31

After putting Kathleen in the Secret Service's hands and onboard her plane, Jimmy hurried to meet Alexia and her realtor friend. He wanted to look for an upscale home with a large barn or warehouse. Jimmy wanted a secluded five to ten acres with the house. First, though, he needed office space for his business.

He didn't need a large office, but he wanted it posh. The Realtor showed him a three-room suite in Wilsonville, which Jimmy loved. He told Alexia, "I like the layout of the rooms. The room off the hall would be the receptionist's area. I like that the receptionist can escort people into the waiting area through one door or enter my large office without going into the waiting area."

He continued, "I like that, what would be my office has an outside entrance so I can come and go without being seen. The door from my office into the hallway is a huge plus."

Alexia said, "Why?"

"It will allow a guest to enter through the receptionist area, sit in a secluded waiting area, and leave my office unseen by anyone who has arrived and may be in the waiting area."

Jimmy knew the clientele he sought would want absolute privacy.

Jimmy didn't quibble over the rent but demanded new carpet he would choose, fresh paint with him selecting the paint color, and unique lighting fixtures. He wanted everything to exude class and money. He wanted everything completed and occupancy in seven days. It excited Alexia to think of helping him decorate.

Jimmy signed the lease on the office by noon. An hour later, he wanted to look at houses.

The Realtor and Alexia were both surprised at Jimmy's pace. Alexia thought, *"He's just like my brother and the pace at which he tackled my mother's renovation. Is it part of SEAL training, full-speed attack mode on everything?"*

Talking to the Realtor, Jimmy said, "I've previewed the properties listed on your area-wide multiple listing service. Are there any high-end properties that aren't in your multiple listing service?"

At her denial, he said, "Then, this is the one I want to see. Can we view it now?"

He handed her his iPad and showed her the photo of a home on the realtor's multiple listing service. The Realtor said, "This client requests 48 hours advance notice to view the home."

Jimmy said, "People in hell can ask for ice water too. Call them and tell them you are with a well-qualified cash buyer who wants to buy a home today. I don't care how clean it is or if everything is staged for appearance. Those aren't the factors that will concern me."

Ten minutes later, they were on their way to look at the home.

Alexia didn't see the photo of the property. Jimmy said when she asked about it, "It's in the country outside Canby and Aurora and will be a quick commute into the office in Wilsonville. Driving time for commuting to your office in downtown Portland would increase. It has ten acres. The home is 4400 square feet on one level, with a big wrap-around porch. It has four bedrooms and five bathrooms, and the listing says it has a three-car attached garage and a separate seven-car garage. The listing photos are beautiful, but I want to see the barn and indoor riding arena."

As they pulled into the driveway, Alexia tried to keep herself from gasping at the property. The ten acres were fenced and cross-fenced in white vinyl rail fencing. The house sat on a slight rise, with a wrap-around porch that invited you to sit in the rocking chairs, which lined it to watch the sunset.

Jimmy held Alexia's hand as the Realtor gave them the grand tour. Alexia felt warm, knowing the Realtor thought she and Jimmy were a couple.

She couldn't help oohing and aahing over the house. It exuded class and style.

As they walked to the garage and then the barn, Jimmy asked why the owners were selling such a magnificent property. The Realtor said, "I believe they want to downsize and move to the Palm Springs area."

Alexia, reading Jimmy's expression, thought, *"He loves it. My God, how much money did he and Roman walk away with?"*

Jimmy told the Realtor he wanted to talk with Alexia. When they were alone, he asked, "What do you think, Honey, if we get to that point, would you want to live here?"

She smiled, "If we get to that point, I will live with you anywhere, but I would love to live here."

He kissed her briefly and said, "OK, talk to me about the house's furniture. What furniture would you like to have them leave?"

She thought for a minute and said, "The wooden furniture. The home office furniture is incredible. The dining room set, the rockers on the porch, and the outdoor furniture are magnificent. The end tables, buffet tables, and sofa tables are classic. They're all top end, but I don't see the sofas and chairs as your style or mine. I'd expect you would want to replace the bed, which is rather personal, but the armoire is nice."

Jimmy asked her, "What about the sofas or chairs? Could they work in my office? Perhaps in the waiting area?"

She thought about it for a minute and said, "They would work, and they are the right style."

Jimmy called the Realtor over and told her, "I'd like to submit an offer. Write it up for the full price. But, I want them to include all the home furniture except the beds. I need no financing since I will pay cash, but I want title and possession in fourteen days."

The Realtor hedged, "I doubt if they can be out in fourteen days."

Jimmy said, "Sure they can. They can move into the big motor home in the second garage. All they need to pack is their clothes and dishes. I'm asking them to leave all the furniture except the beds. Tell them that whatever they leave beyond what I'm asking for is fine. I'll either use it or donate it to charity. Give them the phone number for

Bekins Van Lines. Bekins could be out here, pack, and load the sellers within two days. If they wanted, they could be on the road to Palm Springs by this weekend."

He paused and said, "The listing info shows the time on the market is over a year. So, you might ask them how many other offers they've received."

By six o'clock, the signatures of the electronic documents were complete. Jimmy was about to become a homeowner.

Still operating in high gear, he was ready to go look at office furniture when Alexia said, "Time out. There's always tomorrow. I need food. Do you want to grab something somewhere or come to my place? I'll whip up a bite to eat."

Jimmy answered, "No question. If you're cooking, I'll be there."

A short while later, Jimmy showed up on her doorstep with a bottle of chilled Riesling. He was still in the clothes he wore all day. However, Alexia wore a casual lounge outfit with bare feet and a pale rose toenail polish.

Candles lit an intimate setting on the dining room table, and soft music played.

She looked stunning to Jimmy, and he thought, *"She went into warp drive when she left me."*

The salad bowls were already on the table. Water boiled for fettuccini noodles, Alfredo sauce bubbled in a saucepan, and he could smell garlic baked chicken in the oven.

Alexia came into his arms for a full-body hug and a sensual kiss, "I was proud of you today and couldn't be happier for you. I'm intimidated by the choices and changes you have made to stay near me, knowing my issues. Neither of us knows if I will ever be able to resolve my intimacy issues and be able to make love to you. Yet you quit your job, moved to Oregon, and bought a home to stay near me."

She gave him another slow kiss and said, "We better eat dinner. I think it's ready."

Later, they lay on the couch, kissing. Jimmy started rubbing her nipples through the sheer blouse. She started moaning with desire as they came erect and then froze. Her entire body stiffened, and she gasped for air.

"No, stop, please stop." She heard her voice telling Jimmy to stop when everything in her wanted him to continue.

Aroused, Jimmy held her against him and stroked her back until her breathing slowed and the panic went out of her eyes.

"I'm so sorry. I'm such damaged goods. You'd be better off with someone else. I can find you someone. Lots of my girlfriends, including Rebecca, are or would be interested in you."

"Don't be silly. You and I are perfect together."

Rubbing his erection through his trousers with her hand, she said, "But it's not fair to you to get you turned on and then stop."

He groaned, taking her hand away, "Doing that is what's not fair."

Jimmy got up. She asked, "Where are you going?"

"Back to my motel room for another cold shower," he answered.

Chapter 32

The following day, while she ate, Alexia sat at her breakfast table, drank coffee, and stared at her phone as though the screen contained teeth. Then, knowing now was the time to face her demons, she picked it up and, with shaking fingers, dialed a phone number her doctor gave her during her last annual exam.

The number was for a female psychologist who specialized in sexual issues related to rape. When the receptionist answered, Alexia's voice broke as she requested the soonest appointment.

Two weeks later, Alexia helped Jimmy shop for items for his home. Much of the furniture stayed, but he needed dishes, pots and pans, blankets, and the decorator items which make it a home. Jimmy often deferred to her design opinions, but he held definite ideas about style.

As they drove from store to store, she gathered her nerve and told him she saw a counselor.

Jimmy asked, "Do you want to tell me about it?"

"No, it's embarrassing, but I think I should tell you about it, even if I don't want to talk about it."

"I see," he said, "I'm all ears."

Alexia continued, "She helped me identify my buried emotions related to the rape. It's a long list. Shame I didn't fight harder, and embarrassment over a sexual attraction to the man who raped me was easy to identify. She pointed out that I have a lot of guilt over showing up at a pool party in a bikini and getting drunk with an older man. Part of me feels like I invited the rape, and there's a tremendous amount of fear to this day that he will kill me like he threatened if I tell anyone what happened."

"I'm glad you are talking to a counselor. Just know if that character ever shows up in your life, your brother, and I will make sure he doesn't harm you."

"Well, it wouldn't help me if the two guys I love both went to prison for murder."

"Not to worry, they'd never find the body," he said confidently.

Alexia gave him a long look and said, "When you talk like that, I don't know if you are kidding or serious. The counselor says I have months of therapy ahead of me, dealing with those emotions and putting them into the proper perspective. But, I know what you want to know is, are you forever relegated to cold showers, or can you hope to turn on the hot water in your house?"

Jimmy laughed, "And the answer is?"

Alexia said, "There's hope. She gave me a homework assignment. I'm supposed to sleep at night thinking about explicit X-rated sexual scenes with you. The therapist said I should visualize the scenes in such graphic detail I can feel you enter me."

Jimmy asked, "Wouldn't it be easier if I did the deed?"

She smacked his arm and said, "No, I'm supposed to imagine us in such detail that it triggers another panic attack when I'm alone. She gave me a series of biofeedback exercises to use if I can trigger a panic attack. Learning to control my emotions will give me the confidence to short circuit the panic attack. After I've learned to control the attack, I hope the subsequent steps will be enjoyable for both of us."

Chapter 33

As planned, Thomas showed up at Ablah's apartment. After acting surprised he was there, she played out the routine they discussed.

She said, "You work for Comcast as an installer. Since you are here, could you check out my router? My Wi-Fi connections are messed up. I'm not getting the signal I should be getting."

Thomas started checking her electronics. He looked at her television, desktop, laptops, tablet, phone, and music devices.

Acting confused, he told her, "I'm not sure. Something is interfering with your signal. These apartments are so close together. I would bet a neighbor has cracked the password on your router and is piggybacking his internet connection off yours. There is no way of knowing who it is. I'll make you a trade. I'll pick up a device at work, which will interfere with his ability to steal your signal, which should increase your streaming speeds. I can bring it back tomorrow after work."

She asked, "What's the trade?"

Thomas said, "You let me take you out for pizza tomorrow night, ok?"

She hesitated and then said, "Ok."

Thomas said, "The doors on these college apartments are flimsy, and you own a lot of expensive electronics. So, I'd suggest you get a locksmith to put on a deadbolt."

She agreed and walked him out to his car to say goodbye. As soon as she got in his vehicle, Thomas quit acting.

"Yes, you've got bugs. Whoever is watching you has cameras

everywhere in your living room, dining room, and kitchen. I saw nothing in your bathroom or bedroom. I recommend you change in the bathroom and wear sweats to bed until I get back with the scrambler. You get the deadbolt changed tomorrow, so Rashid can't come back and figure out how to override my device. You should have me come back every couple of weeks to recheck that he hasn't overridden my scrambler."

Ablah put off going to bed until exhaustion overcame her, and then she carried baggy sweats and a full robe into her bathroom. Closing the door, she scoped out the tiny room, then pulled her bathrobe on, overtop her clothes. She did her best to change out of her clothes and into her sweats while wearing the robe. Still freaked out, she moved a chest in front of her bedroom door before falling asleep.

The next day, Thomas briefed Jimmy and Roman on his findings. "The guy is good. He used sophisticated stuff, but the best part is his misdirection. He installed three layers of equipment. Layer one was obvious. It was easy to find if someone looked. If they were looking for a bug, the average person would think they'd found it. Layer two was harder to spot, and it required a military-grade specialist to find the third layer. The guy who did the work is an expert. Not as good as me, but good."

Chapter 34

Kathleen sat with her father in the White House's family quarters, showing him photos on her iPad while telling him about her trip.

She gushed about Oregon's beauty, described Roman's home, and how perfect he was for Julia. She mentioned feeling humiliated by Smoke and how she felt like a spanked girl.

At which President Myers said, "Good for him."

Her father thought, *"Kathleen's traveled worldwide, dined with heads of state, and is more excited about a trip to Oregon to see Julia than any of those."*

After half an hour of listening to her, he smiled, "There's one photo here you didn't talk about."

It was a photo of her, Andy, and Brutus, with her arms around Andy.

"Who's this?"

Quietly, she looked at her father and said, "He doesn't know it, but that's the man I plan to marry."

Her father sat back and looked at her. "Just like that?"

At her nod, he asked, "Is this Andy, the man who sang to you on the video, which went viral?"

"Yes."

She spent another half-hour talking about Andy and Brutus and told him she invited Andy to sing at the Christmas tree decorating party. Her father just raised his eyebrows and asked to see her videos of Andy singing.

She said, "I've got a lot."

He answered, "If no one shoots off any missiles anywhere, I've got whatever time we need."

Kathleen showed him video after video of Andy singing. She gave him long descriptions as she introduced each clip and told her father the background and context of each video. She talked nonstop, pointing out the nuances of everything.

Her father thought, *"Either she's devoured one too many triple lattes, or she's really in love with this guy. I have never seen her like this."*

When Kathleen wound down, Alex asked her, "OK, so what's your plan? I know you well enough to know there is something up your sleeve. What's your plan for this poor unsuspecting fellow?"

Looking sheepish, she said, "Before I answer, let me ask you a question. Did you think Andy's as excellent a performer as I do?"

Alex nodded. "He's good. It's unfair to him, you filmed it on your phone, but he's good."

Giving her father a little girl's smile, she said, "I hoped you could call your buddy at PBS. Just ask him if he'd like to film kids decorating a Christmas tree in the family quarters. You could fill him in on Andy and Ablah's video going viral. PBS could film the event. If it turns out well, your buddy could put it on the air, and if it's a bust, it would be no big deal to anyone."

As Alex nodded approval, Kathleen shivered with excitement.

Chapter 35

Julia enjoyed lunch with her mother after they spent the morning working on wedding plans. Reaching a stopping point, they went downtown for lunch and to look at wedding dresses.

Julia said, "I don't understand how people take months to plan a wedding. We know who we want to invite. People will always be added, but the initial list is with the Secret Service for clearance. We've met with Darci and Gwen about catering the dinner. They will handle everything connected to the meal and drinks. Roman said not to worry about the chairs or the sun awnings, that his mother would have family connections for those. It's way too soon to worry about the flowers."

Julia took a breath and, grinning, said, "Roman and I are shopping for rings this weekend, so what else is there?"

"Lots of things, sweetie, but something's bothering you. What is it?"

Julia sighed, "You know me so well. I'm bored. I don't know what I expected. We're engaged, but I seldom see Roman. He's busy on this project for Dad every day, speaking in a different town every night. We talk late in the evenings as he's driving home or on his way to a motel room. Giving up my job at the preschool was hard, even if it was a volunteer position. But it kept me busy, and I felt useful. I thought wedding planning would require lots of time, and I'd see more of Roman without my job. We talk on the phone late at night, but it's not enough. I feel disconnected."

"I see. Your dad is thrilled with the results Roman is getting. He has many small towns starting disaster preparedness programs and is doing an outstanding job. I understand your frustration, though. After all these years, you meet the man of your dreams. In your mind, you're already married, but you haven't moved in together, and the wedding is almost a year away."

Julia groaned, "Yes."

"I have a few suggestions. First, I think it's essential you start your marriage by telling Roman whatever you are feeling instead of bottling it up. In this case, tell him you're bored, frustrated, and miss him."

"I don't want to sound like a spoiled rich girl who always needs her man around her."

"You won't. Just tell Roman how you are feeling. Be careful to tell him how proud you are of him for doing such a superb job."

"I am proud of him, and he's so excited. You can hear it in his voice."

"Good, tell him that. You don't want him to quit what he's doing to spend time with you. Doing so would hurt your relationship long-term. Massage his ego, tell him whatever you want to say, but make him feel proud of what he's doing. Then come back to talking about how frustrated you are and that you want to spend more time with him."

"Ok, just like the books say, be open about my feelings and pay attention to his feelings. I can do it, but how does that fix things?"

Margo grinned at Julia while reaching across the table to pat her hand. "I'd suggest asking him if he's allowed an assistant after you've talked about that. I'll bet he is. You could be his administrative assistant, and your dad and I could loan you our old campaign motor home. You could drive all over the state with him as he does his meetings, and while he's driving from place to place, you could run a portable office for him from the motor home."

Julia's face lit up with a smile, "Mom, you're a genius. That's a fantastic idea. Do you think I could be Roman's assistant and that Dad will be ok with us using his old campaign motor home?"

Margo said, "Of course, why don't we skip dress shopping? Instead, you call Roman and ask him to play hooky. I'm sure you can convince him to take the afternoon off."

Julia did what her mother suggested. Days later, she and Roman drove Stan and Margo's motor home to Corvallis. Functioning now as his official executive assistant, she helped him cart the boxes of supplies and audiovisual equipment into the meeting room.

Julia got everyone signed in with name badges on their shirts. Those who pre-registered each received a packet of supplies in a cloth grocery bag. Ablah got the bag containing an encrypted satellite phone with instructions on how and when to use it.

Julia alluded to their meeting at the bar, where Andy sang and acted like she hadn't seen Ablah since then.

She said, "Ablah, it's so good to meet you again. I was excited to see your name on the pre-registration list. Roman and I hoped you would register for the CERT training program and participate in the disaster preparedness program. I've never completed the CERT training myself, so we are attending here. If you attend, we can get better acquainted over the next twelve weeks. Perhaps you could become a team leader for coordination of the program."

Julia spoke so anyone nearby could hear, thinking the Middle Eastern man coming in after Ablah was eavesdropping.

Ablah replied, "I don't know what the CERT training is, but I will if you want me to do it. I don't know if I can be a team leader of anything, but I will do anything you ask."

When Roman started the meeting, the room was packed. By now, he'd polished his routine.

"Let me introduce myself and my fiancée and tell you about myself. I want to share some of my experiences, which made me believe in preparing for disasters in advance."

He ran through the presentation he used in Gates. When he got to the end, he asked if there were questions.

A man wearing a construction company's tee shirt asked, "Did you bring Brutus?"

Everyone, including Roman, roared with laughter. "No, No, I didn't. I don't need him tonight, do I?"

Someone shouted a question from the back of the room, "When

are you going to run for office?"

Roman said, "What?"

The crowd immediately got into the give and take, "Yeah, we need someone like you in Washington. Hell, we need someone like you in Salem too."

"No, you don't want me. I'm not a politician."

"That's good. Just take Brutus along to chew the arms off the rest of the politicians."

It took a while, but Roman regained control of the meeting with all but five people signing up for the CERT training.

Roman said, "I will need a local person to help coordinate things with this many signing up. Someone to help make this work. Ablah, you are the only person I've met in the room. Would you be willing to work with my executive assistant to coordinate the meetings, etc.?"

Ablah hesitatingly nodded her agreement, thrilled at the request. Roman said Julia would contact her later to discuss her responsibilities.

Rashid found Khalil, Fathi, and Chawki in the mosque.

He said, "I saw your former girlfriend tonight, Chawki."

Chawki looked up as Rashid continued, "I went to the disaster preparedness meeting like you asked, Iman. It was interesting. They talked a lot about the potential disasters Corvallis faces. A lot of the stuff, like floods and earthquakes we couldn't influence, but fires, road closures because of landslides, and collapsed bridges, we could cause."

Khalil raised his eyebrows, then said, "Good job. Let the infidels tell you how to destroy them."

Rashid continued talking to Chawki, "I saw your old girlfriend sucking up to the program leaders, the ones we saw at the bar. She signed up for a stupid twelve-week program as a team leader. It sounds like a twelve-step program for disaster preparedness. I don't get it and don't see the addiction."

Chawki said, "Perhaps you will find out in the classes."

"Nah, I won't be able to go back to the classes, the group is too small, and I'd stand out. They were all middle-aged white people."

Rashid stayed focused on creating a disaster, "Iman, listening to the program gave me an idea on how we could do serious damage with minimal effort or risk. If we gave everyone on the team a drone, carrying gasoline and a timer, we could fly them into the forests surrounding Corvallis and ignite them all at once. If we did it late in the fall when it's dry, we could set the farm fields on fire the same way. Each of the major roads leaving town goes over a bridge. We could blow them up and surround the town with fires."

Khalil appeared to give it some thought before saying, "Good idea, Rashid, but to what end? How would that help us with our primary goal, which is reigniting the war to free our homeland?"

Chapter 36

Over the following weeks, Roman and Julia traveled around Oregon, conducting meetings. At every session, the question of Brutus and political office came up.

Roman became experienced at deflecting those questions and bringing the conversation back to the disaster preparedness issues. Small town after small town established preparedness committees. So many communities requested the CERT training, a backlog of three months to offer the class developed.

Gates organized active groups which engaged in neighborhood visitations to educate residents on minimizing the fire risk on their properties. In addition, the community worked with the Detroit Dam and Big Cliff Dam officials to establish shrieking whistles, which would echo down the canyon if a catastrophic drop in water level occurred. The sirens were solar and battery-powered and would function if there were a power loss.

They set the sirens up on a relay system. When the first siren sounded at the dam, it would trigger a second siren miles down the canyon. The sequential sirens were like dominos, with the sound echoing in the narrow canyon. As soon as one went off, the next one further down the canyon would trip and alert communities in the water's path.

Gates negotiated with the installers for an upgrade to allow the sirens to be triggered manually in the event of a catastrophic forest fire. There were two different siren tones, but both meant to evacuate.

Julia was much less frustrated. She and Roman were now

spending hours per day in the motor home. While he drove, she would make and return phone calls. With internet capabilities through their phones and iPads, they could even photocopy and print documents while traveling. The motor home was an ideal mobile office.

Julia felt like she contributed to Roman's success with her organizational skills. Proud of Roman's development as a speaker, when she heard the political questions, she became suspicious of her father.

Stan discovered an unknown individual where circumstances thrust him into a series of high-profile roles showcasing him as a 'hero.' Defying standard hiring criteria, Stan took that individual, Roman, and turned him into a State of Oregon Department head.

Stan sent Roman out in Stan's former campaign motor home, crisscrossing the state and building relationships with political and community leaders at the grassroots level. Julia questioned if her father could be so Machiavellian that he plotted a political career for Roman. She decided her father wasn't that devious. He'd just lucked out in appointing Roman, who was doing an outstanding job.

In either case, Roman's natural leadership skills surfaced. He could wear a business suit and impress people in high profile, big city meetings, but he was just as comfortable in the ranching, farming, and logging towns in a pair of jeans and a plaid shirt. He could do 'good ol boy' with complete ease.

Surprised, Roman found he enjoyed his job. After being discharged as a 'wounded warrior,' he'd wondered if he would ever find a career that could capture and hold his attention. He and his family owned three successful businesses, but Roger Harper ran those as CFO to a large degree. Roman and Roger met every Monday and reviewed the books and the goals for the upcoming week. Roman was the visionary, the idea person of *Nelson Timber, Boy Toys & Her Toys Too*, and *Nelson Boat and Tackle*. But Roger, or Roman's mother, ran the businesses on a daily basis.

The three businesses produced extensive profits, but they were not Roman's passion. His excitement waned after the initial activity of getting them started. The day-to-day activity at the boat dealership bored him to tears. He enjoyed playing with the 'toys' at the store but was more interested in the timber division. He was happiest if he could run up and down the forest on his grandfather's D8 Caterpillar.

After much thought, Roman accepted Stan's appointment to his new position. The only reason he agreed was his passion for pre-planning and preparing for life's upsets or disasters. When Stan broached the subject, he hit the right buttons. Stan talked about Roman's responsibility to help Oregonians prepare in advance for natural disasters. Roman knew he was hard-wired to help and serve, and the proposed job was something in which he believed.

Knowing that it was a new position appealed to Roman's nature. He knew he enjoyed the start-up aspect of the job and his ability to shape it and create it as he thought best. He could design the blueprint for tomorrow's leaders and hoped the position would hold his long-term attention.

Accepting the project, he tackled it like he did everything else, in full-speed attack mode. Having Julia in the motor home with him was a dream for Roman. She was exceptional at the detail-oriented organizational part of the job. Her attention to detail and advance preparation made him look polished when he showed up for a meeting. Roman knew they were enjoying a pre-wedding honeymoon traveling the state despite the presentations.

Oregon's vast distances required hours of drive time between towns for his presentations. The scheduling often created free days, which they spent in campgrounds near the town hall meetings.

Roman took the time to arrive early and join each town's residents for coffee or dinner in a favorite local restaurant. They arrived in a new town three or four days a week. He believed his success in the program primarily came because he took the time to meet people and form a relationship before starting his meeting. As a result, when the meeting started, they were already friends.

Each evening after the meeting, Roman found an isolated parking spot for the motor home. He always parked far enough away from people that they couldn't tell if the motor home was 'rocking.'

Chapter 37

Mid-November

As they drove from town to town in Eastern Oregon, Roman said, "There's something we need to talk about."

Julia said, "Uh, oh, is this bad news?"

Roman laughed. Thinking a moment, he said, "No, I want to tell you how much I love you. I fell in love with you on the Santiam while we did the river rescues. I thought you were hot, and no, it wasn't your standing three feet in front of me all day long in a skintight outfit."

Pausing, he added, "Although that didn't hurt."

She swiveled her head to look at him as he continued, "I fell in love with you again the night of the assassination attempt on your dad. When you stabbed Hank Miller, I knew you could understand me and the killing I've done. Knowing you would understand freed me up to release the ghosts haunting my emotions and my heart."

Julia's face softened with compassion as she reached over to hold his hand.

Roman squeezed her hand but put his hands back on the wheel to drive the motor home on the winding mountain roads. "I fell in love with you again when our friends came up for the BBQ. When I saw the ease with which you mingled with our friends, the class you exhibited as you made everyone feel comfortable. I was proud of you and proud to introduce you as my fiancée to my friends. However, that is nothing to how I have fallen in love with you as we've traveled the state. I love our time together. I love how you make me feel when you are on my arm, how you treat me, and how you make love to me."

Julia moaned and felt tears flowing down her cheek.

"I love who you are at your core. You are a kind, loving person who has great instincts and always tries to do what's right. I just love you and needed to tell you that."

Julia thought she would melt on the spot, "That is so sweet. I got warm and tingly just listening to you. How far are we from our camping spot? I want to show you how wonderful you just made me feel."

"Great idea, but you need to hold that thought. I think we're an hour away from setting up camp. What I wanted to talk about is our schedule for the rest of the year."

She rolled her eyes, "How can you talk about schedules? You are so exasperating. You just said the sweetest things you've ever said to me and got me hot and bothered for you. So now you want to talk about our schedules? MEN!"

Shaking her head, she asked, "What about our schedules?"

Roman said, "Well, we've got Thanksgiving in two weeks, with Christmas and New Year's a month later. What shall we do about those? Also, I think we're about done running around the state in the motor home. We're lucky there is no snow on these mountain roads already. I knew from a map that Oregon was a large state, but I'd never driven all over it as we did this month. People in the big cities don't know how many mountain ranges there are or the altitude of the passes. We could wake up and see snow outside our window any morning. I think it's time to return the motor home to your father. It's been an enjoyable honeymoon, though."

"It has been wonderful. I've loved spending all my time with you. But, returning to my condo and seeing you on the weekends will seem strange."

Roman said, "That's one possibility. Another possibility is you move in with me at Hawkeye Ridge."

Julia looked at his profile as he continued to drive, "I would love that, but it's a difficult decision. I know we're living together while traveling, but I still have old-fashioned ideas about living together before marriage. How archaic is that, given what we've gone through?"

Roman shrugged and nodded his head.

Julia continued, "Honey, I would love to move into Hawkeye Ridge with you. I'm ready to marry you today. However, the decision to have a fancy wedding or live together affects our parents. I'm the governor's daughter, and your mother is prominent in her community."

They discussed those issues as he drove and decided they would live in her condo in Salem during the week while he worked out of his office at the capitol. They would both then live at Hawkeye Ridge during the weekends. Both residences would function for parental reputations.

Julia said, "Back to the scheduling, I always go to my parents for Thanksgiving, and my family has a tradition of renting a home at Sun River for two weeks over Christmas and New Year's. We ski every day. I never asked. Do you ski?"

"I would have to say no. I went to Hoodoo a few times in high school, but never took lessons. Let me guess. You're a black diamond skier."

"Of course, you mean there is an area I may outperform you?"

He laughed, "Only until I get lessons."

"What are your holiday traditions?"

Roman replied, "I don't have any. I left home right after graduating and could seldom return for Thanksgiving or Christmas. I was always halfway around the world. Since I've returned, my mother, Alexia, and I have gone to my Uncle Russ and Aunt Alice's. It's getting crowded, though, since my cousin Dennis comes with his family."

Julia asked, "If we're functioning as a couple, even if we're not yet married. Would you like to host Thanksgiving at Hawkeye Ridge? Your kitchen and dining area are large enough. We could invite your family and mine. And we could ask any of our single friends without a local family to join us for the holidays."

"Perfect," Roman said. "Let's see who that is. There would be you and me, my mother, your mom and dad, Alexia and Smoke, and Andy unless he's going home to Pittsburg. I think Dink's family is in Portland, and I'm not sure about Roger. He has a girlfriend, but I don't know if they are at the point of attending family functions together or not. I suspect Bridger will go with Cindy to her family home here in Gates. Is there anyone besides your parents we should invite?"

"I think Alexia's friend Rebecca. She may be broadcasting. But if she isn't working, I bet she would appreciate an invitation for dinner. I think she's alone in Oregon. If we invite her, your buddy Dink may show up."

Roman grinned.

Julia continued, "What do you think about Ablah? I'm getting to know her at the CERT classes we're taking in Corvallis. She's done an outstanding job as a team leader, and I like her. But, the thing with her boyfriend is so awful. He still sends her a broken-hearted emoji every evening. Anyhow, she is at OSU and will be alone for Thanksgiving. Her family is in the Chicago area. I know she is lonely."

Roman said, "She took a significant risk telling us about her boyfriend's family. I don't know what Smoke knows, but he says they're bad people. I know Jimmy well enough to know he has his eyes on them. Sure, invite her. What shall we cook, turkey, ham, prime rib, salmon? What shall we create as our tradition?"

"Turkey, of course. With plenty of mashed potatoes and gravy, sweet potato casserole, and lots of pies to roll us out of the dining room. We can ask everyone to bring their favorite side dish."

Julia continued, "If it's ok with you, one family tradition I would like to continue is our ski vacation at the end of the year. Mom and Dad have skied since before I was born. They always rent an enormous house in Sun River, and we celebrate Christmas there. Various family friends show up for a day of skiing over the holidays. Everyone always knows where my family will be at Christmas. So, I know Mom and Dad will invite not just us, but your family. There would be plenty of room."

Julia sent out invitations for Thanksgiving with the plans made and asked everyone to bring a side dish for the table.

On Thanksgiving Day, uninvited guests popped by throughout the afternoon. Cindy and Bridger, Roger and his girlfriend, and Dink with Rebecca missed the main meal but came for dessert. Not even on the invitation radar screen but dropping by were other retired SEALS in the area. Thomas and Samantha showed up from Portland. People kept dropping in for leftovers or dessert. The fire pit blazed, and football games were on television.

Chapter 38

Thanksgiving Dinner

J ulia was beside herself with happiness. Her holiday party with Roman in her future home was a success. Their friends were mingling and creating new friendships. Everyone welcomed her into their lives. She felt a sense of being part of a large family.

Julia looked around the room and saw Ablah off by herself, looking sad. Julia came up to her and asked her how she was doing. Ablah expressed her gratitude for sharing Thanksgiving Dinner with new friends, but she felt lonely.

Ablah said she missed Chawki every day, "It's so hard to get a broken-hearted emoji from him every day and not be able to send back anything besides a stupid emoji. I want to talk to him and hold him."

Julia said, "That's silly. You should be able to text him."

Julia waved Roman and Jimmy over to the conversation.

"We need your help, guys. Ablah loves Chawki and wants to communicate with him. He told her not to talk to him for her safety, because Rashid cloned her phone. But Chawki gave her a prepaid phone to do what he said not to do. So quit thinking like security freaks and start thinking about a young woman in love. How can she safely communicate with him?"

Jimmy and Roman talked about it, and then Roman said, "I'll get Ablah an encrypted satellite phone to mail to Chawki. You should mail it to Chawki, special delivery at the post office. I'd suggest you send him an emoji signifying, 'shhh, mail coming.'"

Ablah got excited and gave each of them a hug of thanks.

As the evening wound down, the temperature dropped, and people stood closer to the fire. The initial snowflakes of the season came drifting down on a soft breeze.

A week later, Chawki received a notification to go to the post office to sign for a special delivery package. Nervous, he cautiously and discretely opened it after ensuring his privacy.

Inside the package, an encrypted phone shocked him. The instructions said it didn't use standard cellular service but sent its signal via satellite. He read the instructions carefully. One button called emergency services if pushed. Ablah's letter asked him to call and gave him her satellite number. She told him the emergency number did not ring to the 911 center, but to a specialized center that Roman and Jimmy accessed.

Reading that, Chawki grinned and nodded. He thought his uncle and brother underestimated Roman and Jimmy. Neither Roman nor Jimmy were flashy, so they impressed no one in Khalil's inner circle.

Chawki followed Roman's career and Jimmy's business since Ablah first met them. He saw both appeared well connected inside the governor's office and, amazingly, the White House. He saw the newscasts of the medal awards and the paparazzi's eviction from Roman's property. Chawki expected the emergency button on the phone would ring through a military communications network, and someone would monitor the calls.

Chawki went to OSU and found a private bathroom in the library. Entering, he locked the door and called Ablah. After expressing his love for her, he again said the danger was too great for him to phone her.

"Rashid and my uncle don't trust me. I can't call you because they could observe me with video or audio surveillance. Your phone will always be with me in case of an emergency, but I must stop texting you, and I'll no longer send you emojis. Know I love you, but for your safety, we must not talk."

Uncertain of what to do with the phone, he turned it off and placed it in his underwear. He thought, *"This may work for today, but*

I don't want to always walk around with a bulge in my underwear."

Later that evening, he told everyone he registered to take an upcoming concealed carry licensing class. It shocked them that quiet Chawki would carry a gun, and they were curious why he thought it necessary to get a permit.

He told them, "I think we're getting closer to an action date. If so, we'll be carrying weapons. If a police officer stops me, I don't want to give any reason for suspicion if he observes me with weapons."

His uncle said, "I'm surprised and impressed with your forethought. I didn't think you were that committed to our objectives. You are correct. I think everyone should get their concealed carry license."

Chawki went to a local gun shop to purchase a weapon. When the shop owner asked what he wanted, Chawki said he didn't know. He wanted to choose a holster, and if he found a holster he wanted, he would get a gun to fit it. Chawki found a concealed carry holster that would clip on his belt and hang inside his trousers in the front. It was small enough that a loose-fitting shirt worn over his pants covered a Glock 42 subcompact semi-automatic pistol and hid a second compartment behind the gun, which held a cell phone.

Loading the semi-auto, he placed the phone and the gun into the holster inside his pants and went to show it off to the others. Then, walking into the mosque, he interrupted his uncle, talking to Fathi and Rashid. Chawki said, "Check it out."

Spinning around, he modeled his new purchase. With his shirt untucked, the pistol was unseen. He then lifted his shirt and showed them it remained difficult to see, even when uncovered.

Patting his crotch, he said, "All anyone will see is an extra bulge where it counts. Maybe the girls will like me better now."

Pulling the Glock 42, he showed them his purchase. Rashid grabbed it and, shocked, said, "Holy Crap, it's loaded. You didn't tell me you loaded it."

"Of course, it's loaded. It doesn't do any good unloaded."

Chawki thought that even if his relatives got suspicious and searched him, they wouldn't search the bulge in his underwear.

Chapter 39

Khalil made his holiday plans and began growing out his beard. He booked first-class tickets for himself from Portland to London on the internet, knowing he would book a flight to Rome upon his arrival in London. Once in Italy, he would take a series of roundabout connections, ending in North Africa.

Arriving in Libya, he intended to rent a Range Rover and disappear into the interior. He wanted to coordinate the plans in his mind with someone with vast experience and resources.

Gathering his disciples around him, he gave them instructions.

He said, "Rashid, you must re-connect with the newscaster, Alexia Nelson. Earlier, you cloned her phone and hacked her devices. Through her, you tapped into her entire network of friends and family. That was good. But, within days, everyone changed their phones and their passwords. Someone in the group discovered your activities, and our information stopped."

Rashid seemed embarrassed, "I know, Iman."

"You must succeed again at connecting to their communications. This time, you must learn discretion and be more subtle. We need the information you can gather."

"Yes, Iman."

"While I'm gone, I want each of you to develop three sets of plans for your respective targets."

Khalil privately assigned each of them a target and instructed them not to share their objective with anyone else in the group.

He told Rashid to develop plans to knock out cell phone

communication in Western Oregon and shut down Western Oregon's electrical grid.

He instructed Fathi to develop a plan to destroy both dams in the Santiam Canyon. "I want three scenarios for rupturing Big Cliff Dam and Detroit Dam. Then, I want an estimate of the mass casualties. Second, how far will the floodwaters destroy towns? Third, how deeply will the floodwaters cover the state capital, Salem?"

Khalil instructed Chawki to develop their escape plans. If the dams burst, how were they going to escape?

Later, when they were alone, Rashid approached Khalil. "Iman, I am concerned. I don't think Chawki is with us in what we plan. He broke up with the Iranian girl, but he's not the same since then. His heart is not in our cause."

"I know."

Rashid continued, "Yesterday, I followed him, as you instructed. I saw him stop and text someone. I have cloned his phone, so I should see his text. There was none. I think he has another phone. It must always be with him. I searched his apartment and couldn't find it."

Khalil said, "It's so sad. He is my nephew. Keep watch on him. Discuss nothing of importance around him. We must not allow him to compromise our mission. He must not know our core plans. What we do will start the war to retake our homeland."

Scanning the room to make sure no one could overhear, he continued. "If you see any behavior that would compromise our anonymity or our plans, let me know. We cannot allow him to jeopardize our operation even if he is family."

Chapter 40

On the Saturday following the Thanksgiving dinner party, Andy dropped Brutus off with Roman and Julia and headed for the Portland Airport. He was excited. Andy planned on stopping for three days in Pittsburg to see his parents. From there, he would fly to Washington D.C. for the tree decorating ceremony at the White House.

Andy and Kathleen spoke or texted every day. He still couldn't believe he was developing a relationship with the president's daughter. Their kisses on Roman's patio occurred so naturally. He kept waiting for her to realize he was nobody compared to the people in the circles in which she traveled.

She, however, seemed just as attracted to him as he was to her. She told him she had a surprise for him when he arrived. Her one request was for him to bring a black tuxedo and wear it with black cowboy boots, a white shirt with a black string tie, and a black cowboy hat. Andy thought the request strange but agreed.

Talking to Roman and Jimmy, he asked, "Would you guys go shopping with me? She wants me to bring a tux. I've never worn one and don't know where to get one."

They chuckled at his request and then asked Dink where to go.

It thrilled Andy's parents when he showed up without Brutus. Convinced that dogs belonged outside, they couldn't understand Andy wanting Brutus to sleep in the house with him. So, they were ecstatic when he showed up without a dog. Crushed, his mother cried when she learned Andy intended to stay home for just three days. He told them a friend invited him to sing at a family function. His parents were not social media savvy and hadn't seen the video of him singing to Kathleen.

His mother, as he left, asked the perennial question, "When are you going to get rid of that dog, come back home, and find yourself a girl? Your father and I are ready for grandchildren."

With sadness in his voice, Andy said, "I know you don't understand, Mom, but my home is now in Oregon. I will not be coming back to the Pittsburg area to live. I'm sorry. My life is elsewhere."

"But Andy, don't you want a wife and children? You act like that dog is more important than having a family."

"Mom, in the military, we talk about our 'brothers in arms.' I can't tell you the details about Brutus, but he saved my life more than once. His home is with me forever. I will never give him up. He may be a dog, but he's my brother. So, any woman that wants me must take Brutus as well."

"Good luck finding a woman like that," she said with a frosty edge to her voice.

"Maybe I've found her," he thought, walking into the airport.

Arriving in Washington, D.C., a government limo met him at the airport and delivered him to the White House.

Kathleen texted him the entire time he was en route in the limo. Just as excited as Andy, her excitement bordered on fear. Yes, she was eager to see him, but feared the plans she put in place might offend him.

She met him at the elevator to the family quarters. Their meeting was private as she came into his arms for a hug and a kiss. After the kiss, Andy took one look at her and said, "OK, what's up? It's so wonderful to see you, but you look stressed. What's going on?"

Kathleen hemmed and hawed before telling him the truth, "I may have overstepped my boundaries. I did something I thought you would like as a surprise, and now I think I should have talked to you before doing it."

Andy raised his eyebrows in a question, and a nervous Kathleen explained what she had done.

Andy asked, "So, is there a Christmas tree being decorated by kids?"

"Yes."

"What's the problem?"

She said, "PBS is filming it, and depending on how well it turns out, it may be broadcast nationwide just before Christmas Day."

"I see. WOW, that is a surprise and scary." His eyes widening, he took a deep breath.

She continued, "There's more. Besides Dad and me, there will be thirty guests, including politicians and half a dozen executives from the entertainment and music industry. You told me you would like a break in the music industry but didn't want to waste your time trying to meet the person who could propel your career. I want to help you reach your dreams. The people you need to meet will be in the room. Think of it as a mass audition."

Her voice trembled, and she couldn't meet his eyes, "I'm afraid you may be mad at me for setting this up without talking to you. I may be the president's daughter, but I'm just a cowgirl at heart. With your talent, I'm afraid you'll become famous and not be interested in me. You may wind up with your choice of movie starlets."

Andy pulled her into a hug and ended her fears by kissing her. Then he said, "It sounds like you pulled a lot of strings and did a bunch of work to give me my chance. Thank you, that means a lot. But, instead of just relaxing and getting reacquainted, I think I better see the room I'll perform in, check out the sound system, etc."

Kathleen led him to the room with the undecorated tree. The strands of lights were already on it. All the children needed to do was place the ornaments. The kids decorating would be the children of various senators and congressional representatives. The PBS lighting and sound equipment were already in place. Andy knowledgeably flipped switches, and the sound equipment came to life. Grinning at Kathleen, he started doing a casual run-through of a song to settle his nerves.

When he paused, he heard clapping. President Myers walked forward, with Admiral Seastrand by his side. "You're as good as she said. Andy, it's good to see you again. You remember Admiral Seastrand?"

Andy didn't know whether he should salute, stand at attention, or run.

Alex Myers reached for his hand and shook it while pulling Kathleen forward. "You were right. He's every bit as good as the superstar singers out there today. Andy, you have a real stage presence. Your personality shines through your singing. Just be yourself, and you'll be fine."

President Myers continued in charge, "What's your agenda for him, Kathleen?"

Kathleen said, "We haven't talked about any of it, but I thought we could have someone from PBS here tomorrow to run the equipment and do a dress rehearsal. The filming will be this coming Friday night."

Her father asked, "Who's in the audience tomorrow for the dress rehearsal?"

"No one."

"That's a waste, and besides, he needs an audience to bring out the best in him. So, Admiral, why don't you get a group of veterans from Walter Reed to come in for the dress rehearsal? I'll bet there's a bunch who would like to hear Andy sing before he's a star."

♦ ♦ ♦

Andy showed up for the dress rehearsal wearing his black tuxedo, cowboy hat, and boots. It was just a rehearsal, but nervous energy kept him pacing.

Andy walked into the back of the audience and shook hands with the vets. While doing that, he saw the projection screens in the room's front scrolling a montage of his military career. He didn't know who compiled the photos or where they came from, but they included pictures from Afghanistan, North Africa, shots from onboard ships, his graduation from SEAL training, and Brutus. The last photo showed him receiving his Unit Citation medal from the president in the Oval Office.

The veterans mobbed him. They were all injured in some fashion and proud to meet him and shake his hand. Andy was one of them and proof there could be life after the trauma.

Andy strolled onto the stage and started chatting with the vets about the Christmases they'd missed with their families. They discussed the pain of spending Christmas in foreign countries with guns in their hands. Then, acknowledging their sacrifices, he played them the Christmas songs they hoped to hear.

There wasn't a dry eye in the house.

They presented the program Friday night as scheduled. The moguls of music and entertainment were in the room, as were a handful of senators. But the president reserved the front row for another group of veterans. He knew Andy would be comfortable with them in the audience.

When it was over, the PBS producer said he would mix the children decorating the tree into snippets of Andy talking to the vets at the rehearsal program in the editing process. Then, he would intermix the children talking and hanging ornaments with the wounded veterans crying as they listened to Andy talk and sing.

Later, remembering the evening, Andy had images of Frankie Valli and The Four Seasons singing, 'Oh, What a Night.'

The tremendous emotional high following the performance culminated with Kathleen entering his bedroom late at night and crawling under the blankets with him. 'Oh, What a Night?'

Chapter 41

Brutus came barking and running when he recognized the sound of Andy's car coming up the gravel road. Andy got out of the vehicle, and Brutus stood on his back feet and tried to climb into Andy's arms.

Roman invited Andy into the house, and Brutus climbed into his lap as Andy sat down. Andy was still in a daze. He felt his life had turned upside down in less than a week.

He wanted to tell Roman and Julia everything, but knew he couldn't and shouldn't tell them about his evenings with Kathleen. He filled them in on the performance details and its broadcast schedule.

♦ ♦ ♦

"Kathleen invited all these important people to be in the audience. The head of PBS was there with some assistants. I signed pages of forms, allowing them to show the program if it looks alright after editing. There were agents for recording artists and concert promoters in the audience. It was like a big audition. I don't know how she did it, but everyone gave me their cards and told me they would call me."

Julia said, "Andy, that is wonderful. I'm so happy for you. You deserve success, and Kathleen told me she is so proud of you."

Andy said, "You guys are my family out here. Why don't we get everybody together at my place, and we can watch it together? I'd love to share the experience with you and the team."

Roman said, "I hate to disappoint you, bro', but we can't come to your place. President Myers called today. He needs Smoke's crew and our SEAL team for a two-week security detail over Christmas. He hoped you and Brutus were available."

Julia joined in, "Uncle Alex said Kathleen has whined about how little time she spent with you. Although she let me know, the two of you enjoyed some 'quality time.' Uncle Alex's Christmas present to her is he's sending her to join us for two weeks of skiing over the holidays."

Roman jumped in with a laugh. "Would you be interested in being part of her security detail? Maybe the up close and personal security detail?"

Andy thought it was an even better idea when he found out he would share a bedroom with Kathleen for two weeks. The team would escort the vehicles, ski with Kathleen, and provide perimeter security for the house at the Sun River resort outside of Bend.

The team members would combine work with a ski vacation. President Myers told Roman the Secret Service could provide security, but his hunches still wanted 'The Ghost' and Smoke on the job.

Roman added, "He told me to tell you he's sending a form for you to sign. For whatever reason, his hunches want you appointed as a Special Reserve U.S. marshal upon presidential activation. So, you'll have the same appointment as Smoke and me.

Shaking his head, he said, "I don't know what's up with him and his hunches, but I'd humor him. It's almost like he's creating an off-the-books team of SEALS and marshals with no record-keeping or accountability."

Chapter 42

Ski Lessons,
Hoodoo Ski Resort

At the next Challenge Weekend, the team members loaded in an SUV and headed to Hoodoo Ski Resort at the top of the Santiam Pass. The elevation at its peak was 5,733 feet. Drizzling in Gates, the higher elevation, had Hoodoo picking up snow since Thanksgiving. Still early in the snow season, its three-foot snow base added a couple of inches daily. It was adequate for beginner lessons, but the team knew Mt. Bachelor, their Christmas destination, would measure its nightly snowfall in feet, not inches. Hoodoo, however, was close enough to Gates for day skiing trips.

◆ ◆ ◆

Jimmy and Roman discussed the security risks the team would face. They decided the most significant risk was that the young women would out ski their security, leaving them without a nearby guard. Roman called the school earlier in the week and reserved a private instructor for each of them for the entire day. The ski school scrambled to come up with enough instructors. The team all rented skis or snowboards. One of Roman's core beliefs was that many lessons close together in anything sped up your learning curve. Jimmy and Roman figured they needed to speed up their skiing ability to provide security for the black diamond ski bunnies.

Of them all, Andy was the one who could ski. Before his discharge, he took a month's leave and spent it at St. Moritz in the Swiss Alps.

Andy was poetry in motion on a giant slalom run. Even so, he rented an instructor for the day. "I can always get better, and I don't know Kathleen's skill level. I don't want her to out ski me."

You wouldn't know they'd never skied before at the end of the two-day Challenge Weekend. Everyone agreed to sneak away three days a week before Christmas for additional lessons. Of course, no one told the women what they were doing.

◆ ◆ ◆

Khalil was en route to Libya when Rashid entered Fathi's apartment without knocking.

"I got her," he said. Fathi knew he meant he'd cloned Alexia's phone. Rashid always let everyone know he was the best at what he did. He told Fathi how he used the same method as before.

He waited outside of Alexia's news office, texting on his phone. When she approached, he fell in behind her. She texted as she walked, and he appeared to do the same. She entered the elevator, and Rashid rode up with her. Neither spoke, but Rashid was back in the eavesdropping business when she got off the elevator.

Rashid penetrated everyone's accounts except Roman and Jimmy. His inability to access their information frustrated Rashid. It never crossed his mind that they were using encrypted phones.

Rashid muttered, "Why did the Iman leave now? He knew I'd be getting her information again. With whom does the Iman consult? Why is a consultation necessary? We don't need anyone's approval to do whatever we want."

Fathi said, "But we don't yet know what it is the Iman wants to do. He asked us to develop our plans for the targets he assigned us. He's developing the plans for what he claims will be the event which will reignite the war for our homeland."

Rashid argued that Kathleen would visit Roman and Julia over Christmas at a rental house in Sun River.

He said, "I met them when I attended Roman's meeting in Corvallis and the first CERT training class. They didn't impress me. It sounds like Julia invited her friends on a skiing vacation. We could take them. They would surrender at the sight of us with our guns."

Fathi brought the conversation back to reality, "Then what? Suppose we break into the house, hold them up, and get them all in a room. Then what do we do? What have we accomplished? Nothing, we must wait on the Iman to return. His plan will change our world."

Overruling him, Fathi said, "We will use your information to follow everyone involved once again. We will sharpen our surveillance skills and learn about our targets."

Chapter 43

Admiral Seastrand called Jimmy Stockade, "Yes, there is a file on Khalil and each of those attending the Corvallis mosque. Use the communication equipment I shipped to Commander Nelson a while back. I'll send the links and passcodes to your satellite phone. It's encrypted if I remember, right?"

"Yes, sir. It is."

Admiral Seastrand said, "You'll see what we know. It's damning. None of it was in the United States, and we can't disclose what we know about anything he did elsewhere. If we did, we'd compromise our sources, which we can't do."

Admiral Seastrand continued, "The FBI keeps their eyes on him now and again, but he's lying low so far. I wouldn't expect any action from him while Kathleen is in Oregon for Christmas. He's on his way to Libya. He bought tickets on the internet for London, which is his normal stop. His usual pattern is to go from London to Italy or Turkey and then to Libya."

Jimmy asked, "Why, Libya?"

"There is nothing to go on, but we hear rumors that Abu Bakr al-Baghdadi, the elusive head of IFF, the Iraqi Freedom Fighters, is hiding in Libya. We'd take him out if we knew where Abu Bakr al-Baghdadi was for sure. The problem is that we're never able to pin down his location. We hear a rumor he's in Indonesia, and then we hear he's in Afghanistan and then Pakistan. He's always moving. We hear nothing for months, and then he gets credit for an event a thousand miles from his last known location."

"Let me guess. Baghdadi claims credit for everything happening in the world, even if he didn't do it?"

"Exactly. We know that Abu Bakr al-Baghdadi was Khalil's religious trainer as a youth in Iraq, and he followed Khalil to England. You can see the CIA's intelligence files. It's grim. This guy, al-Baghdadi, acts as though Osama Bin Laden trained him. He uses the same method of having no electronic or social media contact. Whoever Khalil's meeting in Libya, he arranged the meeting by courier. So, there was nothing for us to eavesdrop on."

"Well, if you have the time and your courier is trustworthy, it's a secure way to communicate."

"Yeah, I never said they weren't good. It's too bad there's no way to share the information you'll see on the boy's father with them. But we can't. The information is still Top Secret. We'll keep you posted if we hear anything new."

◆ ◆ ◆

Jimmy met Roman in the logging equipment shed. They opened up a padlocked storage pod labeled 'bulldozer spare parts.' Inside was a sophisticated military communication setup. They used the passwords provided to view the files Admiral Seastrand sent.

Jimmy said to Roman, "This guy is a genuine piece of work. He may lie low, but we must remember he's less than an hour away. It's too bad we can't pretend we're SEALS still acting on secret presidential orders and go take him out."

"That would be too easy."

◆ ◆ ◆

Kathleen, Julia, and Alexia were crushed when the men got their skis and started putting on their equipment in the lodge parking lot. The women looked forward to skiing rings around their escorts, but they became suspicious when the retired SEALS seemed confident as they put on their equipment.

Kathleen whispered to Julia, "I thought you said none of these guys could ski? They act like they know what they are doing."

Andy and Dink carried a set of Giant Slalom skies over their shoulders. Roman and Jimmy held shorter, softer skis for skiing moguls, and Bridger stepped onto a snowboard.

As soon as they got off the chairlift, Stan and Margo took the lead, with Kathleen, Rebecca, Julia, and Alexia nearby. No matter where Stan, Margo, Julia, or Kathleen turned, a SEAL shadowed them.

The SEALS kept up with the best the girls could do. At lunchtime, Julia was miffed. "I thought you said you'd never skied."

Roman chuckled, "I hadn't. I told you, that you would beat me until I took lessons. So we took a lot of lessons in a short time frame to keep up with you."

◆ ◆ ◆

Leaving the parking lot, they got into a long line of traffic. Traffic crawled on the snow-packed road. They rounded a bend and saw the police and three tow trucks. An older minivan without chains or traction devices spun out and hit two cars head-on. No one seemed to need an ambulance, but Stan drove past the accident with caution.

Roman, observing, said, "Jimmy, doesn't that look like the Iraqis from Corvallis?"

"Looks like."

Roman raised his eyebrows, "Coincidence?"

Jimmy said, "Doubtful. You always told me never to assume a coincidence."

Roman said, "We need everyone to stay alert. This trip is more than a ski vacation."

That evening, everyone gathered in Stan Anderson's luxurious lodge-style rented home in Sun River. The lodge overlooked the golf course, with miles of snow-covered bike trails doubling as cross-country ski trails in the winter. They were getting ready to eat and then watch Andy sing on PBS when it came on. He was more nervous now than during his performance.

"I told my mom to gather her friends and watch the show." Andy worried, "What if it's horrible? What if it bombs?"

Kathleen snuggled up close to him and said, "It won't bomb. I told you the producer is ecstatic. He told me a star would be born tonight. Just don't forget me when you become famous."

With no warning, phones everywhere rang. The president called Kathleen, Andy's mother called him, and former SEALS from across the country called everyone they knew to get a hold of Andy.

The PBS show finished broadcasting on the East Coast, and the broadcast was tape-delayed three hours for the West Coast. A nervous wreck, Andy waited to see the finished product as the phones rang.

Andy was becoming a star, but his mother gave him hell on the phone for holding out on her. He hadn't told her about Kathleen or performing at the White House. His mother wanted to ask questions about Kathleen but couldn't, since her friends kept shouting congratulations in the background.

Three hours later, the house became silent as the program began with Andy talking to the wounded veterans. Then, the scene switched to Andy alone, strumming his guitar and singing hymns while the children decorated. Intertwining scenes from Andy's military career, his conversations with the veterans, and the children decorating, the producer finished with Andy looking into the love-struck eyes of Kathleen as he finished once again with 'Happy Trails.'

Chapter 44

Fathi, Chawki, and Rashid did not see the PBS broadcast. As they searched each of the parking lots at Mount Bachelor, Rashid drove, looking for the governor's ski rig. Going downhill from one lot to another, Rashid hit his brakes when the minivan slid, making the problem worse. With his car out of control, Rashid skidded into two oncoming SUVs.

The two experienced snow drivers with the SUVs were driving at a slow, safe speed in four-wheel drive. The impact was not life-threatening. Exchanging insurance information and calling tow trucks would have ended the situation.

However, inside the car, everyone yelled at Rashid, and he started yelling back.

Fathi screamed, "I thought you said you knew how to drive on snow. I could have wrecked the car myself."

Chawki shouted at him, "I almost got killed. That SUV hit right where I was sitting."

The two car drivers knocked on his window, asking for Rashid's driver's license number and insurance information. As tempers rose, a woman in a wrecked vehicle called the police. The police were always in the neighborhood during ski season to keep speeding down on the icy roads. They arrived within minutes.

The police officer asked, "Who drove which cars?"

Rashid pointed at Chawki, "He drove."

Chawki and the people in the SUVs denied it. The second police officer separated the individuals and started cross-checking the stories.

It took no time to determine that Rashid was driving and didn't have a driver's license.

Looking at the registration, the police officer asked, "Which of you is Khalil?" and then, "Where is Khalil?"

Fathi couldn't say he was in Libya.

Fathi didn't know what to say when the police officer asked for the proof of insurance card required in all cars. He suspected Khalil didn't have insurance on the minivan.

The police discovered Fathi and Chawki were in the United States on student visas, and Rashid claimed U.S. citizenship but carried no identity papers. The Deschutes County deputies took Fathi and Rashid to jail for the night while they sorted the situation out. They dropped Chawki off at a motel near the police station.

The police gave Rashid a series of citations. He got one for driving without a valid driver's license and another for driving without insurance. The third was for failure to keep his car under control, and the fourth was driving without chains in a zone that required them. Fathi received a citation for lying to a police officer when he claimed he owned the minivan.

The police impounded Khalil's van and told Fathi, "When your Uncle Khalil shows up to claim his car, he will need to provide proof of insurance for the accident."

Released by the police, the three made their way to the bus station for a slow ride to Corvallis.

Chapter 45

O ver the upcoming months, Julia, her mother Margo, and Roman's mother, Rose, spent countless hours planning and revising the wedding plans.

Roman focused his efforts on his job as Director of Natural Disaster Preparedness, and in his spare time, if the weather cleared, he worked on getting the road on his property ready for the wedding.

Jimmy and Alexia became inseparable. About a month after she started counseling, she said she wanted to cook Jimmy a celebratory meal at his home.

He asked, "Celebration of what?"

She answered, grinning, "I think my biofeedback training is working. We can start another lesson in my healing process."

Alexia showed up with the ingredients for a romantic dinner, bringing grocery bags with boneless chicken breasts, wild rice, mushrooms, and her secret chicken and mushroom sauce. In addition, the makings for a light salad and two chilled bottles of Pinot Gris rounded out the meal.

The problem was that she wore a light-yellow shimmering sheath that flowed with her curves and highlighted her tanned form. Braless, her sheath teased her nipples erect with every step as she prepared dinner.

She poured Jimmy a wine and stepped close. Each of them held a glass of wine in one hand. She rested her free hand on his chest, keeping them apart and looking into his eyes. A moment later, she shivered as he raised his free hand and scraped the taunt protruding fabric of the sheath with his fingernail. She leaned up and kissed him, nibbling on his lower lip. Jimmy used his free hand to grip her buttock and pull her closer.

He asked in a husky voice, "Is this part of the homework assignment?"

Alexia stepped back and said, "It is. First, my counselor asked if I wanted to make love to you, and I told her I did. Then she asked if I trusted you and believed you would stop if I asked you to stop. I told her I knew you would. Finally, she asked a question you need to answer. She asked if you would give up control tonight. Would you be willing to stop if I develop an anxiety attack and then restart when I regain control?"

Jimmy nodded, "Sounds like fun."

Alexia continued, "She asked if you would be willing tonight, and perhaps for a while into the future, to allow me to be dominant? Can I be on top? So, I will have a sense of personal control."

Jimmy asked, "When do we start?"

Alexia moved back into Jimmy for another kiss and said, "How about now? We can always eat later. I've thought about making love to you for weeks."

Minutes later, they were in the bedroom with a fire in the fireplace and music playing in the background.

Helping Jimmy unbutton his shirt and nibbling her way around his neck and chest, she said, "In my fantasy, I see you ripping my clothes off me and pouncing on me, but I think tonight we need to go slow. My heart is already racing, which could be anticipation."

◆ ◆ ◆

As the fire in the fireplace burned low, Alexia lay in Jimmy's arms and stroked his body with her fingernails, "That was spectacular. When can we do it again?"

Jimmy said, "I don't know. My experience is no greater than yours. But, if you keep stroking me like you are, it might be right now."

He rolled onto his side. Alexia's eyes widened as Jimmy kissed and touched her. When the hysteria went out of her eyes, he took control.

By eight o'clock, their lovemaking relaxed and became less frantic.

Alexia said, "Maybe we should get up and let me finish fixing the meal I promised you."

◆ ◆ ◆

Jimmy's home became a second rendezvous point. The former SEALS referred to themselves as 'the team' and expanded the concept to include Thomas Jefferson, Mark, and Kelly. As former Rangers, they fit right into the group.

The team still held their Challenge Weekends monthly, alternating between Hawkeye Ridge and Smokes Place. However, events no longer went around the clock, but stopped at a reasonable hour to include a potluck with the wives and girlfriends.

Jimmy started alternating with Roman and Julia hosting the training and monthly potluck. The two home's monthly potlucks became scheduled events, with Alexia assuming the hostess's role at Jimmy's house.

Jimmy's business exploded. Without his ever telling anyone, it became known that whenever Kathleen flew to Oregon to spend time with Andy, Jimmy's company, *SOS Inc., Special Operators Security Inc.,* provided security.

The unspoken presumption was that if *SOS Inc.* could guard the president's daughter, it could handle your issue.

Dink, Mark, and Kelly quit their jobs at The Benson and worked full-time out of the renovated barn at Smoke's Place. Dink and Thomas Jefferson were kindred spirits when they talked about electronics and hacking into secure systems. The more levels of security they found, the greater their excitement. The more complexity they found in a challenge, the more intoxicating the excitement became. The need for court orders and search warrants did not enter their thinking. What they did was illegal, but if their client's threat remained unidentified, Dink and Thomas would poke around the edges of the lives of the involved individuals until they figured out the source of the danger.

Dink, Mark, and Kelly conducted once-a-month training classes on poise and sophistication. They taught the new agents how to blend into high-class environments. For the prices Jimmy charged, the agents needed to be the best.

Roman and Jimmy coached hand-to-hand combat skills and knife fighting on the Challenge weekends.

Jimmy's clients were high-profile individuals. Their security needed to fit into a variety of environments. Dink joked about wrapping the agent's brass knuckles with a feather pillow.

Andy was a rising star in the music industry. His agent wanted him to move to Nashville or Southern California. Andy refused. He agreed to do a series of concerts that would feature the songs on an album he released. He was concerned with not selling out to fame and staying true to himself.

Andy still sang once a month at The Fishing Hole, his friend's bar in Mill City, where he started singing. He said, "They gave me a place to sing when nobody knew me. I'll keep singing for them as long as they want me."

The Fishing Hole now was standing room only on the night's Andy sang, and open tables were scarce the rest of the time. The owners continued to put out a tasty burger and sell the beer by the pitcher.

Chapter 46

Khalil was furious when he returned from Libya at the necessity of going to Bend and posting a bond to release his car. The law requiring proof of insurance gave the option to post a substantial cash bond. Khalil wanted nothing on his record, not even a charge for not having insurance on his car. He posted the cash bond and then purchased insurance, which would cover the minivan in the future. The police released the vehicle to an auto body shop.

The body shop told Khalil, "It'll be ready for you to pick up in two weeks. We need to order in the parts to do the repairs."

Khalil was specifically angry with Rashid. "You acted without thinking. The police database now contains the photos and fingerprints of you and Fathi. You have a blot on your record. What have I tried to teach you?"

"Yes, master, I know I didn't have a driver's license, but why did you not have insurance on the car?"

Khalil fumed for days and then asked to see the plans he requested they draft on their projects.

Rashid and Fathi put minimal effort into their projects. Neither believed it was possible to shut down all electrical and cell phone capacity in the Willamette Valley, and they didn't think their group could blow up two major dams. They each scribbled a plan on one page for Khalil at the last minute.

Chawki, however, approached his project as though it were a college thesis. As he handed the printed and bound report to Khalil, he said, "What gave me the most difficulty was determining where we are when the dams fall. I decided for your project, we must cause the dam failures. If we do, I assumed we're at the dams as they break. If we're downriver from the break, our problems would be the same as everyone else. We would need to outrace the rising waters while experiencing electrical and phone loss and highway gridlock. I think our chances of survival are negligible if we are downstream when the dams go."

Khalil interrupted, "Why do you think there will be a problem with the phones and electrical grid?"

"Ooops, I shouldn't have said anything. I overheard Rashid and Fathi talking about their projects."

Glaring at Fathi and Rashid, he said, "I see. Continue with your escape plans."

"Well, if we're at the dam or upstream from it, we could attempt to escape up logging roads and forest service roads unseen. It would be best if we used high-wheelbase 4x4 vehicles. Then, we could get into the network of gravel roads in the mountains and come down either near Mt. Hood or head east into Central Oregon. The challenges would be not to get lost, and it would be slow."

"Ok, other options?"

"Yes." Chawki handed Khalil his report. "We could continue up the Santiam Highway to the junction with McKenzie Pass and turn south towards Corvallis or Eugene. I would recommend Eugene. Corvallis could become covered with water from the collapse of the dam. Another option would be to get to the airport at the junction of the Santiam and McKenzie Passes. It's a dirt field and not long enough for our King Air. We would need a smaller plane."

Chawki's plan impressed Khalil, "This is good, it's not good enough, but it's a starting point. I expected more from the two of you." He said, pointing at Rashid and Fathi, who stared daggers at Chawki.

He continued looking at them, "I thought you were dependable leaders. I was wrong."

Shaking his head, he ranted, "Our trainees are progressing in their jihadist religious beliefs. Our brothers overseas are providing extraordinary support, and both of you let me down. You could cause the collapse of our entire mission because your plans aren't ready."

Khalil refused to tell them about his trip overseas. He said, "You lost the right to inside knowledge when you did not develop the plans I requested."

He paused and then said, "I will give you another chance. I will give each of you one week to produce the requested plans. I want detailed plans this time. Chawki, your ideas provide a starting point but expand them. Focus on the minutiae of your projects."

"Thank you, Uncle."

"Each of you has six people in your classes at the mosque you identified as people wanting to take action against the Great Satan in Washington. Assign each of them a secret project. Ask them to think of a way to create a massive impact in this area. It could be massive casualties or enormous property damage. Let them provide your inspiration. Then, ask them to prepare a report on their idea, just like I'm asking you to do."

"We'll do better this time, Iman," Rashid said.

"I hope so. Also, I want you to discuss the concept of martyrdom in your classes. We may need half a dozen individuals willing to martyr themselves for the cause."

Khalil acted like a professor reading the reports. He sent each report back with comments on its possibilities but challenged the individuals to expand their details, to cover every aspect of what they would need to put their plan into action.

Most of the ideas dealt with forest fires, explosives at football games, and poisoning the Willamette River in Eugene, which would poison the water supplies for the cities downstream. The estimates in that plan predicted that a million people could be without water.

Khalil called each of the report writers in for a one-on-one discussion. Khalil told those wanting to poison the Willamette River that it would take too long to develop into a disaster. Instead, he challenged them to develop a plan with an immediate impact.

He told them, "We're looking for maximum impact in the shortest time frame. So, what would you do, and how would you do it?"

Some ideas were unexpected, but each young future jihadist was excited about taking action.

Over and over, Khalil challenged them, "Is your plan practical? Tell me where and how you'll get the required supplies. Who will assist you? What time of day would be best? What would it cost? You need to micro-plan your proposed action."

After weeks of preparation, he picked six of his followers. He met each of them for a private conversation. Khalil told each of them, "I see greatness in you. I believe you have what it will take to help me in an activity that will jump-start the war to reclaim our homeland from the American imperialists. We will kick out the Americans and their puppets and set up a caliphate in our homeland. Your name will go down in our nation's history. Young boys will honor your deeds, and old men will be grateful."

He reminded each of the need for total secrecy, even from their mentor at the mosque. Finally, he supplied each with the required materials and challenged them to keep those supplies safe.

His final instruction was to stay ready. "We're within months of a monumental accomplishment. Stay ready. Keep your cell phone charged and with you always. When the time is right, I will send you a text with a date and time. When you receive the text, go into action. Know that your plan is key to our success."

Chapter 47

With classes over for the summer, Rashid again received an offer to work on a maintenance crew for cell phone towers. Khalil instructed him, "Get copies of the maps showing cell phone towers in this part of the state. Visit every tower if you can. Show on your maps which towers you could knockdown. Start thinking about which towers are the keys to the system working. Think about how you would put each tower on the ground, and then tell me how to take them all down at once."

Fathi got reinstated with the Oregon Department of Transportation, working in the Santiam Canyon. Khalil challenged Fathi, "This year, I want you to get copies of the keys in the vehicle garages. Get the keys to every vehicle or piece of equipment. Also, access the keys to the sheds, where they keep the signs and uniforms."

Fathi found a mobile locksmith who wanted to sell his business. He purchased his truck and equipment along with lessons on making various keys. Fathi asked a trainee from the mosque to meet him each morning. Fathi would hand over a set of keys and leave on his job. His protégé would hand the originals back to him two hours later and drive off.

Chawki no longer fought forest fires. Instead, three mornings per week, he left Corvallis in the dark for a 5 a.m. arrival in Newport.

Newport was on Yaquina Bay and home to a working fishing industry. He arrived in the morning three times per week as the sky lightened and purchased crates of fresh fish caught the night before. The crew winched containers out of the trawler's hold and placed them on the dock near Chawki's Mercedes Sprinter. The Sprinter identified the truck as belonging to a Central Oregon fish wholesaler and party supplier.

On those mornings, crew members from the trawler helped load the crates into the Sprinter. No one paid close attention to the fact that a crew member remained in the back of the Sprinter on two separate mornings.

Chawki had trouble speaking to the crew members he smuggled into the country. Neither of them spoke English. Chawki realized his native Arabic language was fading into the background. He thought in and spoke English. He was also losing his British accent. Fathi had spent time in North Africa, which re-familiarized him with his Arabic language. Even he, however, wasn't fluent.

The first stop on returning from picking up the fish was a large storage unit Khalil rented in Corvallis. Capable of holding two trucks, Chawki could pull his delivery van into it and close the door with room left over for storage. Each time he pulled the Sprinter into the storage unit, Chawki unloaded heavy crates before resuming his trip. Rashid, however, was in and out of the storage unit daily. Each time Rashid left, he removed boxes, leaving the storage unit empty.

Chawki next stopped at Detroit Lake, where Khalil purchased a pontoon boat as a party boat built to his specifications. They now held the weekend parties on the party boat on Saturdays and Sundays. During the weekend parties, the opening in the deck stayed closed. During the week, however, a large space with a ladder disappeared into the lake. It was an entry point for scuba divers. The storage racks which hung under the boat and above the water were unseen from the surface.

Three times a week, Chawki unloaded cases of beer and fish crates dripping with melting ice out of his truck and onto the pontoon boat. The covering layer of fish in each container went to the freezer, and the fish boxes made their way under the deck to the storage racks. From the storage racks, they would disappear underwater towards the dam. The containers, even underwater, were heavy. The pontoon boat always smelled of a fish barbeque.

One of the illegal immigrants stayed on the pontoon boat.

Whenever there were guests, he remained in the storage compartment below decks. An expert diver, the crates of explosives were his responsibility. Conveying the containers to the dam, he guided them into a pile where the cliff met the dam. It required consummate skill to conduct a dive going 50 feet deep and steer the heavy crates to drop in a heap at the 400-foot depth. When asked, he explained to Khalil what he did on his dives.

"I use a deep-diving drone to steer each crate as it descends. Before releasing it, I set it on a glide path that should land it near the cliff's edge and the dam's bottom. I will drop hundreds of crates into a pile. Packed with explosives, they also contain a firing or ignition mechanism in a waterproof container. I can't use a timer since the date of the action is unknown."

"How will you trigger the explosion?"

"Do not worry. When it is time, I will take the final truckload of explosives and drive it off the cliff's top onto the pile of crates. Then I will trigger the explosion in the truck and the crates on the bottom. I look forward to being martyred for the cause."

He did not go into the details with Khalil about how he would trigger the explosion, thinking Khalil did not need to know the fine details of how he would set off the explosion.

Chawki delivered an illegal immigrant to the ranch. He was an explosive expert specializing in martyrdom explosions. Soon, six recruits arrived for him to train. He started talking to them about the mystical reasons to martyr themselves for a cause they believed in, the re-establishment of a caliphate in Iraq, the land of their fathers. The idea of creating a country based on their religious beliefs, with one supreme spiritual leader drawing his authority from Mohamad directing the country, and a country ruled by Sharia law inflamed the new converts.

Khalil flew his King Air 350 to the ranch once a week to talk to the young jihadists. He explained that the date for their martyrdom wasn't determined, but expressed how valuable their sacrifice would be. He told them they would know when the master plan was underway. It would be on the news.

He said, "Two hours after the attack starts, I will arrive with 'guests.' The enemy could follow a short time later. You'll be my security force until I can leave with my guests."

They trained with firearms at the rifle range all summer, and their explosive vests were always ready to wear.

Khalil said, "We can hope the enemy does not follow us here. If they don't, leave the ranch as soon as I'm gone. Then, wait two days after I leave with our guests to start your attacks."

They each chose a target to destroy, which would pressure the enemy to capitulate to Khalil's demands. The jihadists would kill one victim per day.

Chapter 48

Roman relaxed. His road neared completion as his logging crew graded the dirt road and placed culverts to control runoff and erosion. A constant series of dump trucks spread gravel as they dropped their loads. Road graders and heavy rollers compacted the rock into the firmness of asphalt. Julia was ecstatic over the road. She still wouldn't drive her Mercedes on it, but she could if she wished. The alternative route shortened the drive time from top to bottom to 15 minutes.

The runway behind the hangar resembled a golf course with freshly mown grass. Rose collected family favors and scheduled Renaissance Fair tent tops to arrive two days before the wedding. The poles and anchoring pegs for the tents were on site.

The rows of portable pink and blue toilets were in place.

Darci and Gwen commandeered the hangar as the interim storage shelter for the pots, pans, and tableware boxes.

The Secret Service set up an airport-type screening system at the gate, packages went through a separate screening set up in the equipment shed, and they reserved every limo shuttle bus in the area to shuttle arriving guests to the top and back down later.

The Secret Service conducted background checks on the guests and staff scheduled to work at the wedding.

President Alex Myers planned to arrive in Oregon a few days before the wedding to spend time with his friends, Stan and Margo.

He would stay at the governor's mansion with them until it was time to helicopter onto Hawkeye Ridge for the wedding.

Andy agreed to sing while the crowd gathered. The long-range weather forecast was even favorable. Everything and everyone was ready for the event.

Roman and Julia decided they did not need or want a drunken 'bachelor's or bachelorette's party.'

Alexia coordinated with the members of the wedding party to plan a girl's spa day. Samantha and Kathleen were Julia's Matron and Maid of Honor. Alexia, Cindy, and Ablah were her bridesmaids. She told Roman, "I have not known Ablah long, but I have gotten to know her well in such a short time. I like her and feel close to her."

Ablah asked if she could invite her parents to attend the wedding. She said they were so proud that Julia asked her to participate in the marriage ceremony.

Roman sent the parent's names in for vetting by the Secret Service. When the report came back, he whistled. Showing it to Julia, he told her, "It's no wonder she has hard feelings for the hardliners in the Middle East. Her family was the Middle East version of royalty under the Shaw of Iran. It was a secular dynasty, with educated women filling roles in both business and government. Her family enjoyed great wealth. When the revolution threw the Shaw out of power, her grandfather got his family out alive, but forfeited his assets. They were destitute. Her family is a typical immigrant story. Her grandfather and grandmother arrived with nothing but ambition and bought a bankrupt combination gas station and convenience store. Living in the store's storage room and sleeping on the floor, they outworked their competition and eventually made enough to buy another store. By the time Ablah's father was born, the grandparents expanded by purchasing an older motel. Thirty years later, when her grandfather died, he passed on to Ablah's father a chain of small motels and gas stations with attached convenience stores. Her father expanded his inheritance and is now worth millions. They hate the religious fanatics who run their old country."

♦ ♦ ♦

When Andy found Kathleen planned to come to Hawkeye Ridge for two weeks, he asked Roman if he could bring his motor home.

Roman grinned and said, "So you think Kathleen might be more comfortable in your motor home than in our spare bedroom?"

Andy couldn't help grinning back, "Well, I'm hoping so. Otherwise, I think it would be awkward knowing you and Julia are just down the hallway."

Chapter 49

The night before the terrorist attacks, Kahlil gave Chawki, who knew nothing of the upcoming events, precise instructions.

"Your team has just completed their training and can now be certified 'flaggers' on road construction jobs. Let us give them a test tomorrow. Tell them this is their final exam. Tell them I want to see if I can trust them to do a job with no mistakes. Take your trucks with your signs. Start putting signs out as you leave Salem warning traffic of the closure of Highway 22 at milepost 54, which is near Idanha. Block the side roads which come into Highway 22. Drop off flaggers at the barricades and close the road. The flaggers can re-route cars and tell people the detour is because of a landslide. Leave your flaggers in place when you've blocked the highways and take a side road to Highway 20. When you get there, head to the ranch in Paisley, which is about a five-hour drive."

Chawki followed instructions. The next day, he took his Sprinter to the storage unit, where he selected a magnetic sign for his truck.

He had not yet picked up his team of flaggers, so there was quiet time to think.

"Empty, the unit is empty. There were four crates here yesterday, but none today. They must contain explosives. I wonder how many tons I've moved this summer. The fishing trawler I meet isn't large enough for everything I've moved. It probably refilled each time I loaded fish. Where does it get its load? I know my uncle hasn't trusted me since he made me break up with Ablah. He always has a project to occupy my time, but everyone is secretive, and no one tells me anything. Something is about to happen. Like it or not, I'm a part of it. I moved those explosives and am

an accessory to whatever he's doing. I think life's about to get even uglier."

Leaning against the empty storage unit wall, he thought while crying.

"I wish I could leave, take Ablah, and go somewhere, but I couldn't leave even if I wanted to. I have no money. He pays for everything and gives me an allowance for spending money like I was a kid. I don't know what to do. I wish I could talk to Ablah."

Chapter 50

Bridal party festivities
The week of the wedding

P ampering facials, manicures, pedicures, and massages occupied several hours at the spa. Julia, Alexia, Kathleen, Samantha, Cindy, and Ablah were relaxed and excited.

Trays of hors d'oeuvres and glasses of champagne flowed throughout the morning. Three large black SUVs with blacked-out windows waited with their doors open. Two Secret Service agents stood by the open doors, watching everyone approaching.

The women exited the salon and entered the middle SUV. All three vehicles entered the street and headed west over the Cascades.

Cresting the top of the pass, Julia said, "I can't believe how little traffic there is. I thought tourists would pack this road with pickups, towing boats, and trailers, heading to their favorite camping spot. This road shouldn't be deserted."

Alexia asked, "Ablah, what do you hear from Chawki?"

"Nothing. Every few days, I get a broken-hearted emoji, sometimes a pair of lips blowing me a kiss. But there's always a pair of lips with a finger across them. I know Chawki's telling me not to contact him. It's so disheartening. I cry every evening."

They continued chatting and paying no attention to anything until a comment from their driver focused them. Looking out the windows, they realized they were approaching Marion Forks. The SUVs slowed as they came up behind a slow-moving gravel truck. Their driver looked in his rearview mirror and attempted to pass the dump truck, which was impossible. The truck stopped, blocking the far end of the bridge over Marion Creek, and reversed, backing up towards them. The SUVs attempted to back up and escape, which was also impossible. Following the three SUVs was another highway department dump truck filled with gravel. It lowered its snowplow blade and pushed the three SUVs together. The dump truck in the front backed into the lead SUV and dumped its load of gravel over the car, burying it over the roofline.

Pushing the vehicles together from the rear, the second truck backed up to the rear SUV and began dumping its load of gravel.

Weapons drawn, the Secret Service agents tried to call for help. "There is no cell phone coverage. Everyone get on the floor."

At the mention of no cell phone coverage, Alexia and Julia pulled out their satellite phones and pressed the emergency button. The phone answered on the first ring. Each left a quick message and turned the phones off so they wouldn't ring. They squeezed the phones into the top of their yoga pants, which was tricky since they were skin-tight.

The Secret Service agents kept telling them, "Stay down, stay on the floor. We will be alright. These doors and windows are armor-plated and designed to repel an armed assault. I don't know how the guys are in the other two rigs. They covered their SUVs with gravel. I don't know if they're safe or if the roofs have collapsed."

And then he said, "Oh my god, what is he doing?"

The women lay on top of each other on the floor. Julia stuck her head up to see what was happening. She told the others, "It's a large bulldozer on treads. It's rolling over everything. It's got a backhoe in the rear and a blade on the front. Oh NO, it just used its backhoe and poked a hole in the front window of the SUV in front of us. All the gravel poured into the car. The agents must be dead. What a horrible way to die."

The bulldozer then did the same thing to the rear SUV before the operator turned and looked at the middle SUV containing the wedding party. He positioned the dozer with the backhoe centered on the front window. Stepping into sight were four Middle Eastern men with rifles. Two were on each side of the SUV, and the one in charge gave the operator, Fathi, a nod. Fathi drove the backhoe into the front window. Gunshots filled the air.

Julia said, "Roman will find us. So whenever we can, we need to leave him clues."

Alexia said, "I wouldn't be those idiots for love nor money when our guys find them. Smoke will tear them apart. We have got to be brave and try to stay together."

"Oh no, what's he doing now?"

The backhoe positioned itself at the passenger window, broke it out, and drug the door off its hinges.

A cultured voice with a British accent said, "Ladies, you are safe now. The excitement is over. Please step out, so we can chat."

As they stepped out of the car, he continued, "Ahhh, there you are, Alexia. I've looked forward to seeing you again. I have fond memories of the time we shared. You must be Julia, and you are Kathleen. I'd know you anywhere. Your photo hangs in my bedroom. You, my dear, are the key I've searched for my entire life. You'll help me unlock my dreams."

He turned to Ablah, "I see why you have Chawki so enchanted. If you and he are both smart, you may yet get to spend your lives together. You will love our homeland."

With a growl in his voice, he said, "Now move. We're in a hurry. Get in the van and do it now."

Stepping into the van, their wrists were fastened with zip ties. Khalil said, "I suggest you not struggle against these. Struggling will make them tighter and increase the pain."

The entire action took less than five minutes. Khalil rehearsed his crew on the ranch repetitively until everyone knew what to do and could do it without thinking.

The van sped up the highway with Khalil talking to someone on the ham radio. They pulled into the dirt airstrip used by the forest service in fighting fires just as a small Cessna landed. The van pulled up to the plane, they tossed the women inside like sacks of potatoes, and the plane took off, heading east.

Chapter 51

Overloaded, the plane struggled to lift off the dirt field and then flew them to the ranch outside Paisley. When the plane landed, the suicide squad met it and removed the women, dumping them in the back of a pickup. Rashid drove the women to the ranch headquarters.

Kathleen asked in a loud voice, "I know this is crazy. But does anyone have a Kleenex? I'm so allergic to the dust and pollen I can't breathe."

She rubbed her eyes until they were bright red. She sniffled and coughed, clearing her throat as she got to her feet. She then spat what came out onto the ground. Samantha reached for a Kleenex in her pocket and handed it to Kathleen, who blew her nose and wiped her eyes. She then rubbed it on her forehead before crumpling the tissue and throwing it on the ground. Finally, she kicked dirt over the tissue, burying it.

♦ ♦ ♦

Khalil searched their handbags and purses. He located their cell phones and searched for concealed weapons. Handing the phones to Rashid, he also found a packet of tissues. He tossed those to Kathleen, saying, "Try not to spit on the floor."

Smiling with anticipation, he said, "Let's see what the news is." The phones and the internet on the east side of the Cascades still worked. Minutes later, he began cursing in Arabic.

"They blacked out our ransom demand. The internet is full of what we did and the damage we caused, although I don't know why Detroit Dam is still standing. They must receive another lesson."

Speaking to the leader of the suicide squad, he said, "Abdullah, you know what to do. Take Mohammed, drive to Salem, and wait until you see a crowd in the Capitol Rotunda. It would be superb if you could take the governor with you into the afterlife."

Julia screamed with tears flowing down her cheeks, "No, no, why are you doing this? He's done nothing to hurt you."

Khalil responded by slapping her across the face, "It is time for you to learn manners. In my culture, you speak when I permit you to speak. All of you, go into the bathroom and do what you must to prepare for a long trip. While you are in there, wash your faces and remove your makeup. You look like a group of whores."

Minutes later, they were crowded into a tiny bathroom. Their hands were still zip-tied. They needed to help each other undo their slacks and use the toilet. It was humiliating and painful.

Ablah said, "We should cluster around each other as a shield. I would bet money the little snoop Rashid has a bathroom video camera."

Julia sat on the toilet with everyone crowded around her. While using the bathroom, she pushed the emergency locator button on the satellite phone. She turned it back off as she stood and buttoned her clothing.

Chapter 52

The women were gone from Hawkeye Ridge for their spa day in Sisters. On this trip, the Secret Service provided the escort duty with screening done well in advance.

The entire team hung out in Roman's logging equipment shed. Roman, Jimmy, Bridger, Roger, Andy, and Dink were from the original group of SEALS. Along with Thomas, Mark, and Kelly, who were now regular members of the team.

It was a gorgeous late summer day as they watched football games, drank beer, and played cards. Darci brought a tray of munchies as a treat. The men were letting their beer buzz wear off. The women would be home in another hour, and no one wanted to be 'under the influence.' Bridger begged everyone not to tell Cindy that he'd drunk a couple of beers.

With no warning, a piercing siren wailed. Next, it was a shrieking whistle, followed by EVACUATE, EVACUATE. Then the siren started again.

Moments later, the lights went out, and the television blinked off. In seconds, the auxiliary generators kicked in, and the lights came back on.

Everyone grabbed their phones to call someone, but no one had cell phone coverage.

The chairlift started running on emergency power. Roman's mother, Rose, exited the chairlift at the midway point, the equipment shed within minutes of the sirens blaring.

Without thinking, Roman fell back into the command role.

"Kelly, take the Argo, get down to the gate, open it wide, and start directing people up the driveway. Tell them not to stop here but to walk or drive clear to the top. We don't know what's happening, so tell them it will be safer to go to the top."

Looking at his team, he saw who he was looking for, "Bridger, we don't know if this is real or not, but we could end up doing a lot of water rescues. Hook up my truck to the trailer, take the forklift, put the pod with our scuba gear on the trailer, and lash it down. We don't know what equipment we'll need. Maybe it's a lucky thing you're storing your Zodiac up here. Get your truck hooked up to its trailer and ready to go. Before you do, somebody take both rigs under the gas storage tanks and top off the tanks and auxiliary tanks."

Jimmy stood by, quiet but alert, poised for action. You could see him processing Roman's commands and running down his own mental checklist.

People began streaming up the driveway. Roman walked out and waved them up the hill. He asked them what they saw. Each said, "The river's rising."

Roman reached for his satellite phone to call Governor Anderson. He thought if anyone knew what was going on, it would be the governor with his access to the state's emergency communication system.

Instead of making a call, he answered one as both his and Jimmy's satellite phones rang. He heard, "Commander? We just received two quick phone calls, one from your sister and one from your fiancée."

Jimmy and Roman listened while focused on each other's eyes.

"What did they say?"

"They both said their vehicles were under attack, they were on the bridge crossing Marion Creek, near the Marion Forks Fish Hatchery, and their driver was dead. Someone dropped a load of gravel on the car's hood to stop it. Julia sent a photo. I'll forward it to you."

Roman asked, "When did you get the call?"

"Just moments after the electrical and cell phone grids in western Oregon went down. We don't know what caused any of this, but we can see a drop in the water level at Big Cliff Dam. The cell phone towers are on the ground, as are the electrical towers. Everything occurred at once."

Within minutes, a caravan of pickups pulling trailers left the equipment shed. Roman drove his GMC with the Argo, Jimmy drove Roman's Super Duty with a pod of SEAL diving gear, and Bridger's rig towed the Zodiac, Lifesaver 2. They jammed each of the pickups and trailers with containers of weapons, ropes, camo gear, and parachutes, everything which they could fit into the trailers in minutes. They were heading on a mission but didn't know what they would need, so they took everything.

As they exited Hawkeye Ridge onto Highway 22, they could see the Santiam River rushing over its banks. The floodwaters flowed over the opposite side of the river into the lower farmland. The elevation rose as they raced East, up the canyon towards the dam and parallel to the river. They saw the river below and heard the siren screaming at people to EVACUATE.

Before leaving, Jimmy asked Thomas to stay behind and run the communication network. "Call in all the *SOS Inc.* team. We don't know what's happening. Tell them to rally at Hawkeye Ridge for deployment if they can get here. Tell them to show up fully armed and ready for action."

Using the equipment in Roman's machine shed, Thomas accessed the internet via satellite phones and tapped into the military communication network, which did not depend on local service.

Jimmy asked Thomas to hack into the phones of the people they watched in Corvallis and the women in the bridal party.

Roman used his satellite phone and called Governor Anderson to tell him they were heading for the bridal party and asked the governor what he knew.

Stan was in a frenzy, "It is like someone declared war on the state of Oregon. They attacked Corvallis about half an hour before whatever happened to the electrical and phone grid. Half a dozen fires are blazing right now in the forests surrounding Corvallis. Highway 20 is the primary route neighboring towns would use to send help. They blew up both the bridges across the Willamette River in downtown Corvallis. Any fire truck going to assist must make a huge detour. We're still uncertain what happened to the electrical grid or phone grid. I'm getting preliminary reports that someone has destroyed the towers across western Oregon. The Guard did a quick flyover, and it looks like everything is on the ground."

As the team approached Big Cliff Dam, the rupture was apparent. As much as Roman needed to go after Julia and the bridal party, he knew this was even more important. Tens of thousands of lives were at risk if the dam completed its collapse. So, pulling in, he stopped where a group of dam workers stood watching the water flow.

The supervisor explained, "This guy pulled up in a highway department dump truck with an attached snow blade. He got out of the truck, and I watched him pull out a shoulder-fired RPG, a Rocket-Propelled Grenade launcher. He tossed two rounds into the metal lift gates used to control the water level behind the dam and blew them off their hinges. Unfortunately, there is nothing we can do to stop the water flow. We were fortunate, though. It appears the dam structure is undamaged."

Pointing up the road to Detroit Dam, which appeared intact, he said, "However, I don't know what happened up there."

Stopping at the top of Detroit Dam, Roman spoke to the person in charge, who explained, "It was a damn noisy morning. First, we started hearing a series of explosions in the distance. The explosions occurred within a minute. Then, looking up the hill, we saw the cell phone towers and the electrical towers hauling electricity from the dam drop to the ground."

He pointed toward the mountains above them, where the towers lay in piles of twisted, wrecked steel.

He said, "When the explosions happened, the phones went out, and the electricity turned off. Backup generators run the station, but even the phone landlines are down. I guess somebody took out those lines too. We can't call anybody."

He continued, "About then, we heard two gigantic explosions down at Big Cliff, and we saw water pouring out of the dam. Then, a few minutes later, this dump truck with a full load came up the hill, pushed over the barricades, and drove into the reservoir. I don't understand why. The guy must have known he was committing suicide."

At those words, the team members shared a worried look.

Roman said, "Bridger, we need to keep going. You're our explosives expert. You keep the trailer with the diving gear. Get in the water and see what you can find. Roger, you stay as his diving buddy. I expect you'll find an attempt to sabotage the dam, which may yet happen. Be as safe as you can, but if this dam goes, it would be catastrophic. See what you can find."

Turning to the bridge superintendent again, Roman identified himself and his position in state government. He then told him, "On my authority and as though it was an order from the governor, start emptying the dam. Pay attention to the Big Cliff Reservoir below you. The truck driver blew out the metal control gate regulating the water level. It's emptying itself as fast as it can. Start emptying Detroit Lake into Big Cliff Reservoir when you see it's about as far down as it can go. If Detroit Dam blows up, there will be less water to deal with."

Waving at Bridger and Roger, who were suiting up, they left.

It was eerie racing up Highway 22 with no traffic. No lights were on in any of the houses they passed. Then, as they approached the Marion Forks bridge, they saw a crowd gathered around a large gravel pile.

It was a strange but ominous sight. Two sizeable yellow highway department dump trucks were each backed up to an SUV on the bridge onto which they dumped a load of gravel. Between the two cars, covered with gravel, another SUV sat with its doors ripped open. The drivers and officers in the Secret Service vehicles were dead.

The women were nowhere in sight.

Chapter 53

Using his satellite phone, Roman called the governor to update him and see what he knew. He knew very little. The governor said State Police were en route to process the crime scenes, and he would update the president about Kathleen.

Roman said, "You call the president. I'll call Admiral Seastrand. You know, every government agency is already processing data. I'll see what the Admiral says. Unless he knows something we don't, we'll return to Hawkeye Ridge and get ready to go where he sends us."

Minutes later, Admiral Seastrand told him there was no communication from the kidnappers. He stressed that ALL the state and federal government resources were in use, attempting to track down any group connected to today's events.

Bridger and Roger came out of the water with smiles as the team pulled back into the Detroit Dam parking area.

Bridger said, "I think we dodged this bullet, Skipper. There's a dump truck down there about a hundred feet. From the shore, this looks like a sheer cliff, but it's not. The cliff slopes out underwater. The driver went over the side, wearing a suicide vest with his cell phone in his hand as the detonator when he drowned. I guess he intended to dial the number for the detonator and drive off the cliff. My hunch is that there are tons of explosives on the bottom, which it would trigger. Of course, I'm guessing here, but I bet he didn't know the cell phone coverage was going down."

With caution, Bridger took the battery out of the cell phone and put it and the phone in a bag for the investigators who were just now arriving.

Roman called Stan again and asked, "Please call the president and ask him to get a Navy crew out here right away with deep water diving gear. Tell him the explosives may be at a depth of 400 feet, and we expect they are armed with live detonators. I'm headed back to Hawkeye Ridge to discover what Thomas has found."

◆ ◆ ◆

As soon as he got to the equipment shed, Dink Lindsay collaborated with Thomas Jefferson. Thomas told him his focus was on the guys from Corvallis. His explanation, "I didn't like them when I heard about them, and I don't like what they did to Chawki and Ablah. The eavesdropping equipment in her apartment was sophisticated technology. It wasn't equipment your average snoopy guy in a college town could access. It was costly, professional-grade equipment. So, where'd they get the stuff?"

Dink and Thomas divided the individuals whose names they knew and started doing background searches. They tried hacking every email, social media, and phone they could find. They found nothing recent. However, they discovered the large transactions of the past, including Khalil's purchase of the apartment complex, the ranch outside Paisley, and the King Air 350. None of the purchases required financing. They found the checks used to rent the storage unit by hacking Khalil's bank account. The owner of the storage unit refused to accept cash. Dink and Thomas showed the information to Roman. Roman called the governor again. Stan agreed that the state police would break down the storage units and apartment complex doors as soon as the judge issued a search warrant. He wanted everything legal on his end. As far as the judge needed to know, a concerned citizen called in a tip.

◆ ◆ ◆

Rebecca called Jimmy on his satellite phone. She was at her station in Portland, which still had working electricity and cell phones. She told him her station had just received a communique from an organization calling itself the Iraqi Freedom Fighters. It claimed responsibility for kidnapping her friends and demanded the release of 200 prisoners from clandestine federal prisons. The Freedom Fighters claimed the

CIA operated the prisons across Eastern Europe and on the steppes of Asia.

She said the communique claimed today's violent actions in Oregon were just the beginning. It claimed an attack would occur every day in the state until President Myers released the brave freedom fighters he held in illegal prisons.

Jimmy asked her to talk to management at her station and coordinate with the competing stations. He said to ask the stations to hold the story for 24 hours since the bridal party's safety may depend on it.

◆ ◆ ◆

Jimmy paced back and forth like a caged lion. Pausing in front of Roman, he spoke quietly, "When the Admiral finds them, we will go anywhere in the world to get them back."

Roman nodded.

Jimmy said, "I want a promise from you, no matter where we go to get them or how much of a hurry we are in, I get five minutes alone with Khalil before we leave."

Looking at the knots in Jimmy's jaw and wondering what he knew, Roman said, "You got it."

◆ ◆ ◆

Admiral Seastrand called Roman, "I ordered a flight of Blackhawks to Hawkeye Ridge an hour ago from Joint Base Lewis–McChord, outside Tacoma. They should be overhead soon. Three are armed gunships to transport troops and supplies, and one is a medevac ship."

"Good."

"President Myers has activated you, Smoke, and Andy into active duty with the U.S. Marshals Service. Anyone who goes with you on the upcoming mission can consider themselves on temporary assignment to the U.S. Marshalls Service by presidential order. The guys from Corvallis are the perpetrators. They left fingerprints in the trucks at Marion Forks and on the SUV's doors. Last winter, the police arrested two of them on minor traffic charges, giving us a quick, positive ID.

"Anything else?"

"Not yet, there is no information on where they are, but we can start the search with the apartment building in Corvallis and the ranch outside Paisley. The Oregon State Police get the apartment. You get the ranch. We've already issued a federal search warrant for the ranch, the apartment, and anywhere else they go. The intel is accessible to your computer. You can review it while in flight. Once you get close, we suggest a low-altitude flight through the mountains to minimize the sound. You can land about a mile away. It's behind a forested ridge that should muffle the sound. The birds will drop you off and then withdraw to a safe zone, about ten miles away. They can be there in minutes if you need them. Good Hunting."

While Roman briefed everyone on the team, they changed into their SEAL or Ranger work clothes. Minutes later, as the Blackhawks arrived, they unloaded from the pickups at the airfield behind Roman's garage/hangar. Armed with 7.62mm mini-guns, Hellfire missiles, and visible rocket pods, the Blackhawks settled to the ground on Roman's airfield. The crowd of hundreds at the wedding site went silent. Everyone in town knew the team members were former combat warriors, and most had seen movies with make-believe SEALS. Civilians, however, never experienced how intimidating a persona they presented when battle-ready with the Blackhawk rotors idling overhead.

The team was in full camouflage gear, painted faces, and communication helmets with Night Scopes mounted to their helmet. Everyone wore body armor and carried weapons.

Andy, Roman, and Jimmy prominently displayed U.S. marshal badges pinned to the front of their vests.

Chapter 54

The Blackhawks lifted off the ground at Hawkeye Ridge. Roman was on the radio, coordinating an expanded search. Thomas and Dink, remaining behind, attempted to hack every person connected with the mosque in Corvallis, which they assumed was a cover for a jihadist cell. Going from one associate to another, they looked at their online calendars, hoping they could find anything suspicious. Blatantly profiling based on national origin and religion, Thomas and Dink didn't worry about the law. They intended to find the bridal party and knew what they found would not be admissible in a court of law. Neither, however, expected the kidnappers to wind up in a courtroom.

Admiral Seastrand spoke in Roman's helmet, "Commander, we just received an emergency bleep from Julia's phone. It was on for seconds, but we got a fix. She is at the ranch outside Paisley. Your touchdown should be in about 45 minutes. It will be near dusk as you land."

The King Air 350 was out of the hangar and fueled.

Khalil brought the women to the airstrip. He kept looking at his watch. Chawki's Sprinter pulled into the ranch driveway and up to the plane.

Pointing at the women and then to Ablah, who cried his name for help, he asked, "What are they doing here, and why is she here?"

Chawki walked over and hugged her, "Why are her hands tied? What is going on? Untie her!"

Khalil's frustration showed, "We're on the verge of restarting the war to liberate our homeland, and you worry about women. You are a weak putz, just like your father."

Fathi stepped into the conversation, "What do you mean he's like our father?"

Kathleen said, "I can answer that. Before I came out here, I saw the classified government report, which shows that your father and grandfather were high-ranking officials in the Iraqi government. So, when Saddam Hussein seized power, they supported him. But in the run-up to the Gulf War, the war of Shock and Awe, your father switched sides and collaborated with American intelligence."

With horror on his face, Fathi said, "No."

Kathleen said, "Yes, your father agreed to be the interim prime minister of the new Iraqi government. He made it across the desert with his wife and daughter when the attacks started. They cleared the final checkpoint. He said he made plans with his younger brother, Khalil, to meet in North Africa so they could go back into Iraq as a family."

Khalil turned and abruptly slapped Kathleen, "Shut up, bitch."

Kathleen continued, "It was your father's misfortune that he met his brother, your Uncle Khalil, who had his mentor Abu Bakr al-Baghdadi with him. They took your family back to his camp where your uncle is the one who beheaded your father, mother, and sister."

With his eyes bulging, Chawki yelled in disbelief, "What? Uncle, is this true?"

Stunned, Fathi said, "No, it can't be true. Uncle, tell me this isn't true."

Khalil turned and, slapping Kathleen again, knocked her to the ground. He pulled a pistol and shot Chawki, who collapsed, holding his stomach and groaning. Fathi rushed to Chawki as Khalil shot him in the head. Fathi fell in a loose, blood-soaked pile covering Chawki.

Cindy grabbed Ablah and held her as Ablah screamed and attempted to rush to Chawki.

Khalil turned to Kathleen, "You, I will take great pleasure in breaking. After Alexia and I finish our fun, you and I will get well acquainted. Even when the president meets our ransom demands, you, Kathleen, will never return. Of course, none of the others will either."

Kicking Kathleen in her stomach, he motioned for two men to pick her up and put her on the plane. The rest of the women struggled and screamed. Kathleen cried and threw Kleenex after Kleenex to the ground as they carried her to the plane.

In moments, the King Air was airborne, leaving Chawki moaning on the ground. Feeling himself fading, he pulled his satellite phone from its secret compartment. He pushed the emergency locator button and sent two emojis before losing consciousness.

Chapter 55

Admiral Seastrand called Roman, "There's a change in plans. We just received an emergency call from Chawki. His transponder is still on and stationary. He pushed the button, sent two emojis, and nothing since. So our planners think you should go in 'hot.' Come through the mountains as planned to keep your sound down, then when you are close, shoot up and over the last ridge, and 'fast rope' to the ground. You could be under fire going in. It might help if you kept one bird in the air with a sniper."

Roman replied, "There are two ex-Rangers stationed at both the doors of the Medevac ship. They can stay up and provide sniper fire until we're on the ground. What were the emojis?"

The Admiral replied, "They made no sense. We know he's not Christian. He sent a picture of a fish and a boat or ship."

Roman asked, "Any other news?"

Admiral Seastrand replied, "Somebody, we're assuming it was Khalil, sent a ransom demand through a Portland TV station. He claimed responsibility in the name of the Iraqi Freedom Fighters. You know about them from your time in the Mideast. You don't know that he included the names of 200 supposed prisoners of ours. Prisoners, he believes, we are holding in 'black prisons' overseas. CIA prisons he claims we have on the steppes of Asia, or in Eastern Europe, Poland, the various 'stan's,' places like that."

Roman asked, "And?"

Admiral Seastrand said, "His intel is out of date. We captured them initially, but we no longer hold any of them. We turned the prisoners over to other countries in the area, and we don't know where they are. They may be in the prisons I mentioned, or they could be dead."

Roman asked, "How is President Myers holding up, and what is our response?"

Admiral Seastrand said, "I've never seen him so angry. His public response is that we don't negotiate with terrorists. His private response was for us to find them and for you to go get the women back. Once the women are back, it will be another story. He is furious. You have full access to whatever resources you need. He told me he believes this is the reason for his hunches about you and Smoke. You are authorized to do whatever is necessary, and he will cover your back with a presidential order."

Admiral Seastrand continued, "He prefers the U.S. Marshals Service handle the rescue and wants to keep the military out of the spotlight. However, he knows you are the best hostage rescue SEAL team we've ever had. You may be marshals, but he expects you to act like SEALS. The military, however, will provide the logistics and support you need. If it weren't for your involvement with the women, this would be just another rescue for you guys. On the president's order, the rules of engagement of your Philippine action will apply. We will find them, and you go get them. You don't leave any witnesses, and everything about this mission stays classified forever."

At 175 mph, the Blackhawks rapidly approached their target. Smoke waved to Roman to wrap up the call.

Roman nodded and asked, "Where did they get the RPGs they used, and how did they get them and the explosives into the country? Where did they find that kind of firepower, and how did they get the explosives here, with no one noticing?"

The Admiral replied, "Unknown right now. We're working on it."

Roman turned to Smoke, who had the team in their 'fast rope' gear. Jimmy helped Roman into his equipment while Roman spoke with the group about the plan.

Roman turned to Andy, with Brutus strapped to his front for the 'fast rope' drop. Brutus wore specialty earmuffs to protect his ears from the copter's noise and a Kevlar flack vest. "Andy, you bring up the rear. We need you to keep Brutus safe. He may be the one who finds them."

The pilots were functioning in combat-level alertness. Knowing of the RPGs at the dam, they kept their electronics peeled for air-to-ground missiles. Crossing the Cascades at maximum speed, they closed on the target, then dropped their speed and altitude. They flew through the last set of ridges and canyons below ridge level to buffer the sound.

The lead pilot came on the intercom, "We're in position. Is everyone ready? Ok, brace yourselves. We'll be shooting up 1,000 feet, going full speed for 1 mile, then dropping to a 'fast-rope' height of about 20 feet. It will happen in seconds, so get your snipers ready."

The Blackhawks flew about 100 feet above the ground behind a ridgeline. They then jumped 1,000 feet at full acceleration, flew over the forested ridge, and dropped like a rock.

The jumpmaster counted the elevation down, "900, 800, 700, 600, 500, 400, 300, 200, 100, and slowing 50, 40, 30, throw the ropes over, 20 GO, GO, GO, GO."

Two bags of coiled rope dropped out of both sides of the helicopter, and before the bags hit the ground, the entire team slid down the lines. They were on the ground, dispersed in firing position in seconds.

Nothing happened.

The Blackhawks dropped their cargo and exited a potential firefight at full speed. Silence surrounded the team.

Roman knelt by Fathi and Chawki. Fathi was dead, and Chawki kept seeping blood from the shot to his abdomen. He was unconscious and limp, with a weak pulse. Roman motioned Bridger and Roger to apply pressure bandages to both sides of the wound while Roman called in the Medevac.

The team gathered around Chawki, with everyone facing outward. Andy struggled to restrain Brutus as he raced to find the multiple Kleenex. Brutus froze and alerted to their rear. Everyone turned to see an individual wearing robes approaching with his hands raised. Brutus growled.

A shot rang out, and the individual fell to the ground, shot through the head. Everyone on the team dropped with weapons poised as a Blackhawk settled to the ground near them, with dust flying. Mark and Kelly jumped out, followed by the medics.

The medics rushed to Chawki while Mark explained. "I saw him come out of the shed as we came down. My sniper scope covered him the minute he stepped outside the shed, and I watched him adjust his robes. I'm betting you'll find a suicide vest under those robes. That's why I took the headshot."

Roman said, "That's a safe bet, given Brutus's reaction. Everyone stay a safe distance from the body. Let a bomb squad worry about defusing him. We need to stay focused on the important task of finding the wedding party."

While Roman talked to the medics starting IV fluids in Chawki, Smoke's team cleared the area. Andy turned Brutus loose, and he raced around, finding Kleenex after Kleenex.

Andy said, "From Brutus's action, Kathleen was here. I'm guessing they've flown out by how he's acting."

Roman agreed, but the team cleared the entire ranch premises, including the tents and ranch house. Dink opened the computers at the ranch house and started looking for anything significant.

Bridger put a detonation cord around a safe and blew it open. It contained account ledgers, but no address books. Bridger put everything in a sack for retrieval. Dink put the computers in a bag for further analysis, and they reloaded onto the helicopters and headed for Hawkeye Ridge.

Chapter 56

Khalil and his hostages lead over the rescue team as they left the ranch was substantial. His King Air 350 top cruising of 350 mph compared to the Blackhawk's airspeed of 175 mph. Moreover, his lead was expanding since the rescue team didn't know where he was going.

The Blackhawk pilot came onto the intercom, "Heading over Detroit Dam in two minutes, Commander, if you want to see what's going on. We'll touchdown at Hawkeye Ridge five minutes later. We'll drop you and your team off and fly to the Air National Guard Base in Salem for fuel.

"As soon as we fuel up and service the 'birds,' we'll return to Hawkeye Ridge. The Medevac chopper is en route to catch up with us. They dropped their patient off at St. Charles Medical Center in Bend. He was still alive when they dropped him off, but I understand it will be touch and go. I gotta say, though, if he had anything to do with these kidnappings and attacks, it might be better for him if he doesn't make it off the operating table. He'll spend the rest of his life in solitary confinement."

Flashing blue lights filled every parking spot within a half-mile of Detroit Lake, which was a beehive of activity, with police boats crowding the dam area. Roman asked the pilot to circle for a better look. He watched the police pull a party boat from the water and onto a trailer to take to the crime lab. Dozens of police with clipboards in their hands were talking to the locals.

There were no private boats allowed on the water. Navy divers and their equipment crowded every foot of the deck space on a barge anchored at the far end of the lake near the dam. A C-5 Galaxy military transport flew the barge and a crane from the Naval Shipyard in Bremerton, Washington, to Salem. A Sikorsky CH-53E Super Stallion, a heavy-lift helicopter, ferried them from the Salem airport to Detroit Dam, where Navy Seabees assembled the crane and barge. When completed, it would lift from the water the dump truck and any explosives the divers located.

The dam at Big Cliff poured water from where the damaged control gates dangled off their hinges. No other damage was visible, and the dam itself looked sturdy. The damaged gates were in the middle of the dam, height-wise. Since it was a smaller reservoir, it should be empty to the halfway point by now, with no further water flowing. Instead, the reservoir behind the dam appeared full and spewed water out through the damaged control gates as fast as the water would flow.

Roman saw that and said, "Good. They're attempting to lower the level of Detroit Lake into Big Cliff as fast as possible. Let's hope it wasn't necessary, but it could lessen the damage downstream if those underwater explosives were to blow."

Minutes later, they landed at Hawkeye Ridge. They found the entire town of Gates evacuated to the mountaintop. The townspeople found and used the tables, chairs, and other supplies intended for the wedding reception.

Brave souls went back down the driveway, went to their homes, and picked up supplies. Roman saw portable BBQs and a lot of picnics going on.

As the choppers landed, the crowd gathered. A groan went through the group when the team exited without the women.

Cindy's mother yelled, "Bridger, did you find Cindy? How is she?"

Bridger shrugged, "Not yet. We'll find them."

The team climbed into pickups to drive to the logging equipment shed, where they kept their supplies.

Roman turned to the pilot and asked him to wait a minute. He waved his mother and Darci over to him.

He said, "Mom, why don't you and Darci fly into Salem with these guys?" Both women hesitated, looking at the Blackhawks bristling with Stinger anti-aircraft missiles and 7.62 machine guns.

He continued, "They're flying into the National Guard unit for gas. The pilot can request that two taxis meet you. Darci, you could go to Walmart's grocery store across the street. Mom, you could go down the road to Costco. Buy both stores out of meat, get lots of toilet paper and cases of water. Get whatever you need for Darci to handle feeding these people for two or three days. Buy anything else you can think of, which is quick. People should not go home until we get an all-clear on the Detroit dam, which could take days. I would give yourselves 15 minutes to load your grocery carts and leave. We need these helicopters back right away."

Hugging his mother, he jumped in the pickup and left her, stepping into the helicopter. The crowd watched as a crewmember strapped in Rose and Darci. The helicopters lifted, hovered briefly, and left in a rush.

Chapter 57

T he team lounged in the garage, waiting for Roman to tell them where to go and what to do. Armed and ready, the team could be out the door in minutes.

Additional operators from *SOS Inc.* straggled in from Portland as soon as they could get through the valley's traffic gridlock. None of them knew what was going on or if Jimmy would need them. They received a message to rendezvous at Hawkeye Ridge, armed and ready for a mission. As soon as they arrived, Dink assigned them to perimeter guard duty. He gave them one order, "Protect the hilltop from outsiders. We don't know who the bad guys are or if they are in the vicinity."

Dink and Thomas attempted to hack all individuals connected to Khalil without regard for privacy laws or search warrants. Jimmy paced back and forth.

Jimmy asked, "Did Admiral Seastrand get back to you on where they got such sophisticated explosives and how they got them into the country?"

Everyone stopped and looked at Jimmy. Roman said, "No, but I can call and ask."

Jimmy said, "I think you should. I bet they got the explosives off a fishing boat, which is where the girls are, back on a fishing boat, and headed out of here. I think that's what Chawki tried to tell us."

Roman put on his military headset and pushed a button. Without a pause, a voice answered, "Yes, Commander?"

"Can you connect me to the Chairman of the Joint Chiefs, Admiral Seastrand?"

"Yes, sir, my orders are to put you through."

As the Admiral was connected, Andy Baker's satellite phone rang to a ring tone of 'Hail to the Chief.' Roman looked at Andy with raised eyebrows as he answered his phone. Everyone in the room now watched both Roman and Andy.

Andy answered, "This is Andy, sir."

"I'm doing ok, sir. I'm worried sick and angry as hell, but I'm ok."

Andy started pacing in a circle, "I know she does, sir. I love her too."

He stopped pacing and looked at his friends watching him, "No, sir, we haven't talked about that yet. But, I promise it's the first thing we'll talk about when she returns."

Clenching his lips to stiffen his emotions, he said, "Thank you, sir. I appreciate that. If you guys can find them anywhere in the world, we can get them. The Ghost is on the phone waiting to talk to Admiral Seastrand. Smoke thinks he knows where they are, but we need Admiral Seastrand to run with it and find them for us."

"Yes, sir, I'll tell him."

Hanging up, Andy shrugged as he looked at Roman. "Kathleen doesn't know it yet, but I think we're now engaged. The president said, hurry up with the rescue. You and Julia are getting married in four days, and he plans on performing the ceremony. I can't believe what a normal guy he is. He called to find out how I was holding up."

Roman motioned to Andy. His own phone was picking up.

Admiral Seastrand said to Roman, "Sorry to keep you waiting, Commander. I was pulling together the latest Intel for you. Oregon State police and the Corvallis police executed search warrants on the apartments, mosques, and storage units. The storage unit is off the charts for explosives residue. There's no question it was a storage point for the explosives. The storage unit is empty except for dozens of magnetic signs which could attach to a truck and various highway traffic control signs."

Roman asked, "What businesses were the signs for?"

Admiral Seastrand started reading from his list, "Let's see, there is a lock and key company, a highway flagger company, and a Central Oregon fish wholesaler and party supplier."

Roman said, "Another link to a fish. That's it. Jimmy thinks Chawki's message was to tell us the hostages are on a fishing boat. Jimmy believes it's how they smuggled the explosives into the country. They came off a fishing boat. If the signs went on their truck, they were picking up what looked like fish somewhere. I'll bet those fish covered the explosives."

Admiral Seastrand continued looking at his reports, "We have a preliminary here from the investigators at the lake. People mentioned they were always barbequing fish. So, Jimmy must be correct; the connection has got to be a fishing boat. Otherwise, it's just too many coincidences.

"Thank, Chief Stockade, for me. We'll start working backwards to see if we can find a source for the fish, and we'll pull the satellite photos of shipping off the Oregon coast for the last four months. It won't take long, but we will need to look at each of Oregon's coastal cities with a fishing industry."

Roman interrupted, "Start with Newport, sir. Dink just handed me copies of checks payable to a fish broker out of Newport. We can email them to you right now."

After hanging up, Jimmy and Roman started discussing the best attack plan for a rescue from a boat.

Jimmy said, "Well, we could parachute and land on the ship. But, given we don't know what we're up against, that could be too slow. We could helicopter in and 'fast-rope down' as we did at the ranch, but it's noisy, possibly getting the hostages killed. We did it at the ranch because of the emergency call from Chawki's phone. I wish the girls would turn on their phones again, but that would be way too easy."

Roman offered, "We could do a standard boarding off a Navy or Coast Guard vessel. I know the Coast Guard Cutter 'James,' a National Security Class Cutter, operates out of Astoria. She's patrolling the Pacific waters for fish poachers. The question is, where is the 'James' right now? She could be off Alaska for all I know. The problem with a standard boarding would be the same as with a helicopter assault. The terrorists would have time to kill the hostages."

Jimmy said, "We're just talking for the sake of talking. We don't know what we're dealing with yet, so we can't decide anything."

Roman said, "I know. Let me see what kinds of resources are available to us."

Chapter 58

Half an hour later, their mission coordinator called, "Commander, we've compared satellite photos of the Oregon coast for the last four months. We've located the ship we think they're on. It's a fishing factory ship that has cruised back and forth off the Oregon coast all summer. It's been off Yaquina Bay and Newport three days a week all summer.

"The factory ship purchases the fish from a trawler and processes them into frozen fillets. That is standard practice with fish poachers. Most poachers are surrounded by an entire fleet of trawlers supplying the mother ship. Here, there is one trawler, and whenever they pass Newport, the trawler goes into the harbor and sells fish off the boat to a fish broker. We think this is where Chawki got the fish for his truck. The assumption is that the fish crates contained explosives. Questions so far?"

"No."

"The assumption is that the trawler picked up passengers instead of dropping off fish at the latest stop. The police checked parked cars within a one-mile radius of the dock and found a Sprinter registered to Khalil. They also discovered his King Air 350 parked at the Newport Municipal Airport."

Roman asked, "Where is the mother ship now?"

"It is due west of Newport and moving as fast as possible to the west. We do not know its destination, but it's about 100 miles off the coast."

Roman asked, "What about the resources we discussed?"

The mission coordinator answered, "Based on your earlier

inquiry, the Coast Guard Cutter 'James' is tasked with your support. She has the coordinates of the mother ship, and her intercept time is three hours. The James is 'loaded for bear' with heavy weapons and can blow a hole in the factory ship. What's important for your mission is she has a Defender Class Response Boat and a Heliport capable of handling your Blackhawks."

The silence built for a moment as Roman heard the coordinator shuffling papers.

"Now that we know what ship it is, we'll be accessing the blueprints of the factory ship from the builder's database and sending them to you."

He continued, "Do you have a plan of operation, Commander?"

Roman replied, "Not yet. In fifteen minutes, we'll be airborne headed for the 'James.' I'll call you once we're airborne with our plan."

Gathering the team, he told them where the hostages were. The discussion focused on what equipment they'd need.

Jimmy said, "We may need to break down doors, cut chains, blow safes, etc. We'll need waterproof bags for any evidence, computers, and papers we find. The hostages may need fluids, and we'll need grappling hooks and lines if we go up the sides."

Andy said, "And our weapons of preference."

Once again, a crowd gathered, watching them load in the Blackhawks with circling rotors and shouting words of encouragement.

"Bring them back alive!"

"Good Hunting!"

"Do us proud!"

"Kill the bastards!"

"Take no prisoners!"

"We love you!"

"Go get them!"

Chapter 59

An hour and a half later, they landed on the USCG Cutter 'James.' The skipper of the cutter met them in the ready room.

Speaking to Roman, he said, "The captain of the factory ship knows we're out here. He changed his course when we first showed up on his radar. We're about twenty miles off his starboard side. We're ten miles ahead of him, holding station on a parallel course based on your plan. Whenever he changes his direction, we adjust to his new course. The Defender Class Response Boat is ready to launch. With the factory ship radar focused on us, they will never see you approach. Your radar image will blur into ours."

He said, "Admiral Seastrand sent you a message, Commander. He said to let you know the individuals you seek aren't American citizens. The president has designated the ship as a harborer of terrorists who have taken action against the United States. He has classified everyone on board as an International Terrorist. The president just signed your hunting license by amending the 'rules of engagement,' which applied to your Philippines action, to include this action. Off the record, Commander, Admiral Seastrand said to let you know they pissed off the president, who wished you a successful hunt."

Minutes later, the team: Roman, Jimmy, Bridger, Roger, Andy, Dink, Thomas, Mark, and Kelly were in the Response Boat racing to the factory ship. Since the Cutter James's intercept point placed them ahead of the fish factory boat, it wasn't necessary to catch up to it. They only needed to traverse the twenty miles separating them.

With a maximum cruising speed of forty-six knots, the Response Boat took less than half an hour to close the distance. With its low profile and stealthy radar signature blurring into the radar image of the cutter behind them, the Response Boat approached unseen.

Jimmy spoke to Roman as they raced to intercept the ship. "It's not just President Myers. We're all pissed. Any of us would put these guys down for what they've done. The president giving us a presidential order authorizing the Philippines' rules of engagement still surprises me. My assumption is he means no prisoners and no bodies?"

Roman said, "That's my interpretation. He is as furious as we are. These guys seriously miscalculated when they took his daughter. The presidential order may be a case of him protecting our backs in advance, giving us cover for whatever happens."

Coast Guard Chief Petty Officer Alvarez positioned the response boat with the team alongside the floating fish factory. Five of the team lined the railing of their Response Boat with a teammate behind them. Each of the five carried a modified AR-15, which fired a canister with a grappling hook and rope.

Roman checked with Chief Petty Officer Alvarez and commanded, "On three: one, two, three."

The grappling hooks flew upward to catch the ship's railing passing above them. As soon as the hooks settled over the railing, up they went, like pirates of olden times. The first five neared the top deck as the second group reached the halfway point of the climb.

Spreading out, they scouted the top deck. Questions of whether they were on the correct ship disappeared as sparks flew. Gunfire from automatic rifle fire ricocheted off the metal deck near them. Thomas fell sideways as two of the ricochets hit him in the chest. The team nearest the gunfire dove for cover from the racketing shots.

Placing Brutus undercover and ordering him to stay, the team medic, Andy, crawled to Thomas. "You okay, Dude?"

Thomas groaned, "Yeah, sore as hell, but grateful for Kevlar vests."

Andy said as he checked Thomas, "You'll be black and blue for a week, but you earned brag rights with Samantha."

"I'd rather earn my brag rights in the bedroom. Help me up. What's happening?"

Both got quiet, listening to the chatter inside their helmets. Smoke ordered Mark and Kelly, who were in the second wave to arrive on the freighter's deck, forward to remove the threat. Moments later, single shots followed single shots.

Kelly's voice came over the CommNet, "The guards are neutralized. All clear forward."

The rest of the team continued scouting the top deck. Roman climbed an outside ladder to the bridge. Opening the door, he stepped in. The captain turned to see who entered and froze in place, raising his hands.

Roman said to Dink, who followed him, "Tie him and put duct tape on his mouth. Do you think you can keep this ship straight on its current course until we clear the rest of the vessel?"

"Yes, sir, I can't take it into a harbor, but I can keep it straight in an open ocean."

Roman headed down the ladder to join the rest of the team. Jimmy took one squad into the hallway containing the crew's quarters and galley. Roman took a team into the working portion of the ship.

Jimmy's squad drifted down the deserted corridor. In stealth mode, they opened doors and cleared the rooms of occupants. Knives were the weapon of choice if anyone were awake. Any crew found sleeping received zip-tied hands and ankles. A third zip lock bent them backward, connecting the ankle and wrist ties. Finally, their mouths were duct taped. The method was brutal, effective, and fast.

Jimmy paused before the next door. He placed a device resembling a stethoscope on the door to listen to anything inside the room. What he heard chilled him to his core.

Alexia said, "You may rape me, you bastard, but you'll never break me again. You talk about keeping me, but know this. If my brother or boyfriend don't get you first, I will kill you someday. I wouldn't be in your shoes for anything. So, start counting your days."

"After the time we shared," Khalil responded, "How can you talk that way to me, Alexia? You must know I have dreamed of you for years. You are a spitfire and will go home with me. Our sons will be warriors for the cause. So now you may as well relax and enjoy our honeymoon. We have weeks before landfall."

Motioning to his squad for silence, Jimmy opened the door. Naked and tied spread-eagled, Alexia lay on the bunk. She saw the door behind Khalil open. She knew it was Jimmy, but she sensed it was the man she'd heard referred to as Smoke, who drifted in the door like a shadow. Smoke placed Khalil in a chokehold, which rendered him unconscious.

Jimmy cut Alexia's ropes and, monitoring Khalil, gave her a quick hug and told her to get dressed. As she asked questions, he placed a finger over his lips. Jimmy opened the door and told the squad to continue. "I'll catch up. But Alexia, please stand right outside this door and don't move. Don't go anywhere and say nothing. I will be out in moments."

He closed the door and approached Khalil. Throwing him onto the bunk, he spread-eagled him on the bed with zip ties. Khalil regained consciousness but could not speak with the duct tape covering his mouth.

Incapacitating Khalil, Smoke cut his clothing off him. Razor-sharp, it took one tug of his knife for the belt to split in half. Smoke cut Khalil's pants off him as Khalil struggled.

In a moment, Khalil lay exposed. Looking down, Jimmy drawled, "So this shriveled up, little, skinless sausage did the damage to my sweetheart. Now, if Roman found you, he would simply kill you. He's much kinder than I am. I think that's too easy for you. Make no mistake. You'll not live to see another day. But before you die, you will pay for what you did."

He reached down with his knife and gave a quick slice. Khalil's testicles dropped onto the bunk as the duct tape over his mouth muffled Khalil's scream.

Smoke picked them up without saying a word, worked with them for a minute, and walked out the door. Alexia stood there, "What did you do to him?"

Jimmy said, "It was important you did not see what happened. All you know is we rescued you. Legally, the question you can speak to is something you saw. You saw nothing happen. It's called plausible deniability."

He took her arm to leave. Before she went, she opened the door. Khalil lay there and looked at her with horror in his eyes. She saw a pool of blood between his legs. Taking another look, she saw his testicles duct-taped over his nose, blood dripping into his mouth. All Khalil could see were his bloody balls.

Alexia spoke to Khalil, "I hope there is a special place in hell for you. If there were more time, I'd take those balls of yours, wrap them in bacon, barbeque, and feed them to you."

She closed the door.

Chapter 60

Roman and his squad continued into the working portion of the ship. His team had seen him in action before but watching him glide forward reminded them of why they called him The Ghost.

Andy, with Brutus, walked behind Roman.

Andy whispered into the communications network, "Brutus knows we're on a mission. He is signaling the girls went this way."

Looking down, Roman saw a silent Brutus straining at his leash. His eyes were alert, and his ears pointed forward. It was apparent; if he could talk, he was saying, "This way."

Listening at every door before entering took time. Brutus led Roman and Andy forward. As they approached a corner in the hallway, Brutus gave a low growl.

It was a blind corner. Roman whispered, "Get ready to let Brutus loose."

He stepped back down the hallway past the squad, then turning, he stepped into the middle of the hall and started walking forward, humming a popular song. The unsuspecting guard standing in the hallway wasn't expecting trouble from anyone walking and humming. As Roman rounded the corner, the guard saw him, but Brutus was on him before he could take any action. Roman followed a split second later.

Brutus was already signaling an alert at the door the sentry guarded. Listening with his stethoscope, Roman heard nothing other than the hostages. Opening the door, he stepped in and motioned for silence.

Julia, Ablah, Cindy, and Samantha struggled to their bound feet. Questions flew as Cindy hugged Bridger and Samantha, a wincing Thomas. Julia threw herself into Roman's arms, and Ablah stood by herself.

"Shhhh, not now. There is not enough time. Kelly, we should be clear behind us. You stay here and guard them. Do any of you know where Alexia or Kathleen is?"

Julia answered, "Khalil took Alexia taken to his quarters. A creepy old guy in robes with a huge white beard was super excited to see Kathleen. He took her to his quarters, wherever those are."

Kelly left the door open and stood guard in the doorway. Everyone wanted to ask questions, but Roman said, "Please, not now. We'll answer your questions later. Now I must listen and be ready."

Roman heard from Jimmy, "I took care of Khalil. Alexia is safe. We're proceeding to clear the crew quarters. We found no one else."

He responded, "All accounted for, except Kathleen. Brutus is leading us into the cargo hold. It seems strange."

Jimmy replied, "According to the plans I saw, we'll be coming into the far side of the cargo area. We'll meet you there."

There was an assembly line for cleaning and flash freezing the fish in the fish processing area. Huge freezers everywhere contained packaged fish on pallets that required forklifts to move.

Brutus led them in a straight line across the cavernous ship's hold to a sizeable Prevost motor home. Parked near it were a dozen metal pods or containers. Brutus stopped, and lifting his head, started sniffing. His hackles rose, and everyone froze.

Andy whispered into the CommNet, "Sir, he's signaling an IED or explosives."

Everyone heard a quiet, "SHIT! Everybody freeze," in the CommNet.

Roman and Jimmy looked at each other for a moment, and then Roman motioned Jimmy toward the motor home while tapping his ears. Jimmy nodded and stepped to the Prevost, placing a listening device on its wall.

Bridger moved forward, checking the pods. The silence screamed as The Team waited until he said, "I don't think they're booby-trapped, sir."

Monitoring Jimmy, who was intent on the sounds in the Prevost, Roman said, "I guess we won't know what's in the pods until we get them open."

Roger reached into the pack on his back and drew out a set of bolt cutters. He positioned them on the padlock and then cut through the lock, which Bridger held to keep from falling. Nothing happened. Roger opened the door to the pod, and Brutus growled.

Roger looked around and then turned to Roman, "Holy Shit, if these pods are all the same, this ship is a floating bomb. This pod contains explosives and weapons."

They opened the remaining containers, which contained explosives for IEDs, surface-to-air missiles, RPGs, and weapons of all kinds. The only remaining place Kathleen could be was the focus of Brutus's attention, the motor home.

Standing outside the door, listening through his headset, Jimmy whispered, "Not a sound other than two sets of rhythmic breathing. It would be too much to hope they're asleep, wouldn't it?"

Roman replied softly into the CommNet, "Maybe not. It's the middle of the night. Except for the guards we found, the others were sleeping in their quarters."

Roman tried the door and found it unlocked. Easing it open, Roman froze. Tied to a chair, Kathleen made eye contact and nodded towards the bed. Snoring in the bed, an aged man with a large gray beard slept.

Andy stepped over to the sleeper and, ripping his covers off, grabbed the semiautomatic pistol from under his pillow. With a gun in his mouth, the graybeard stayed silent. Taking a sock off the floor, Andy stuffed it into the man's mouth and wrapped his entire head with duct tape to contain the sock.

Thomas zip-tied him while Andy turned to Kathleen. Kathleen tried to talk but couldn't. It was a contest between Brutus and Andy to see who gave her the most hugs and kisses.

She said, "I'm so glad you got here in time. He's crazy. That's

Abu Bakr al-Baghdadi, the mullah of the Iraqi Freedom Fighters. It turns out he has been the mullah and mentor for Khalil since he was a teenage boy. They both bragged about how long they've planned to ransom those they call freedom fighters, and we call terrorists. They believe we hold hundreds of their freedom fighters in various prisons and felt they could ransom me to my father for their fighter's release. They thought that once we freed the terrorists, they would jump-start the war to free Iraq from domination by the U.S."

Shaking off the remaining restraints, she stood with Brutus hugging her side. She continued, "The U.S. has hunted Abu Bakr al-Baghdadi for years. Intelligence has identified him several times in mass casualty attacks. We now know we could never find him because he lives aboard this ship. When he wanted, he would unload the motor home and drive somewhere else."

Roman ordered everyone topside except Bridger, Dink, and Thomas. "Bridger, you open whatever needs opening. Dink and Thomas, you bag the computers, hard drives, phones, and electronics. Grab everything you can ASAP and get topside. I'm calling for pickup in ten minutes."

Roman called his mission coordinator for connection to Admiral Seastrand. The link was immediate.

"Commander, I'm here with the president in the White House war room monitoring the situation. You are on speakerphone. What's the news?"

Roman replied, "Tell the president, thanks to Chawki's emojis of a fish and a boat, the hostages are safe. There are no casualties on our team. The enemy incurred several dead or wounded. We have captured Abu Bakr al-Baghdadi, Khalil, and the entire crew. The mother ship is a floating bomb and is packed with explosives, weapons of all kinds, even Surface to Air missiles."

"That explains a lot. How much do you think is on the ship?" Asked the admiral.

"Unknown, we saw at least a dozen pods without a detailed search. I don't know if it's hundreds of tons, but it's a significant weapons cache."

"The ship is secure?"

"Yes. I just called the 'James' for a pickup. They're sending two other Response Boats, one for the hostages and another to hold whatever evidence we picked up. We got every computer, flash drive, external storage device, and cell phone we could find. I need clarity on the orders for the ship and captives because I don't want to misinterpret the Rules of Engagement."

President Myer's voice floated out of the phone, "Roman, I classified the ship as a base for terrorists and the people on board as international terrorists. Kahlil Zaman abducted my daughter, goddaughter, and the women in your wedding party. By their actions, he and his cohorts declared war on the State of Oregon and the United States. Our computer experts have already cracked the ranch and his apartment computers. From those, we've determined the destinations of his suicide bombers. We're still working to intercept all of them before they kill anyone else."

Roman could hear the anger in the president's voice.

He thought, "These idiots made their war personal with the president. It will not end well for them."

"I understand the ship is the roving base of Abu Bakr al-Baghdadi, which explains why we couldn't find him. The United States put a bounty on him years ago. It's ten million dollars, dead or alive. I would have ordered in a cruise missile if we ever obtained actionable Intel regarding his location. He has funded money and provided explosives for terrorist operations worldwide for years. We could send him and his ship to the bottom with artillery fire off the 'James,' but if we did, the sailors on the 'James' would know what happened. I think it would be cleaner and quieter if the ship just went to the bottom. We don't want the publicity of his death to create another martyr. Can you set a timer in those explosives, so their own missiles take them down?"

"Yes, sir," Roman answered.

President Myers replied, "Consider it a presidential order."

The president continued, "One other item, Roman, be careful what you hand over to your superiors in the marshal's office. As I asked Admiral Seastrand to convey to you, the rules of engagement for this mission are the same as your action in the Philippines. Even though you are no longer in the Navy, those orders are still effective. All reports must flow through your mission coordinator, who reports to Admiral Seastrand. Understood?"

Shocked, Roman answered, "Yes, sir."

President Myers continued, "Before I let you go, I know you said the hostages are safe. I have to ask, is Kathleen, okay? And is Andy, okay?"

Roman said, "Yes to both questions, sir."

Turning to Bridger, Roman asked, "Can you set a timer to blow those explosives in about 45 minutes?"

"Easy. I couldn't help but hear part of the president's orders. We got a treasure trove of computers and electronic storage units. I don't know how President Myers knew the contents of the safe. It wasn't as much as the Philippines, but I bagged up millions in cash, which is in a separate bag from the computers."

Roman said, "Keep it safe and separate. We'll need clarification on that."

While Roman and Bridger talked, sailors from the cutter 'James' got the hostages off the ship and to safety.

Chapter 61

Rose did her best to play hostess on her son's property while attempting not to have a meltdown thinking about the danger he and the hostages were in. Darci and Gwen grilled meat and prepared side dishes to give people a meal while waiting.

While at Costco, Rose picked up two huge bundles of toilet paper. The portable blue toilets arrived the previous week, but the paper products were almost as welcome as the food.

It was a surreal experience with the crowd visiting as though it were an ordinary day at a city picnic. Kids ran around, and mothers gossiped while eyeballing the young ones. All the while, everyone knew of the potential catastrophe that would ensue if the dam burst. However, the kidnapping was the primary topic of conversation.

The supervisor from the dam told everyone about Roger and Bridger, "Heroes, that's what they are, Heroes."

Someone asked, "Bridger and Roger? The guy who lived in the trailer park under the bridge and the manager of the boat store?"

The supervisor agreed, "Floored me. Those two heard me tell Roman about this guy driving off the cliff with what they assumed were explosives to blow up the dam. If I'd thought the truck contained explosives, I'd have been outta there. Instead, Roman and the rest of the team jumped back in their rigs and took off after Julia, Cindy, and the others. Bridger and Roger stayed behind."

The supervisor looked around to gather everyone's attention. "Then do you know what those two did? Bridger and Roger got some gear out of the trailer and jumped into the water without a word. That shocked the crap out of me. They acted like it was no big deal. They were down there for a long time. I swear they were in the water for an hour before they pulled themselves out of the water. Bridger recovered a cell phone. He said he thought the driver planned to use it as the detonator. It was a waterproof phone. I guess the guy didn't know there wouldn't be any cell phone coverage when he planned on using the phone. I asked Bridger what would have happened when the cell phone coverage came back on if he hadn't found the phone and taken the battery out."

Pausing for effect, he asked, "Do you know what he said? Do you know what he said?"

He waited until the group said, "No."

"He said the damn phone might have rung and blown up the dam. Heroes, I'm telling you, they're heroes. Cindy better quit pussyfooting around and get that guy to marry her fast. Heroes like him don't grow on bushes."

He told the story to anyone who would listen. Being at the scene made him the center of attention whenever anyone asked about what happened.

Rose visited with her sister Alice when someone said, "Rose," and pointed.

Pulling onto the top of Hawkeye Ridge was a black limousine. Everyone stopped to check out the stranger. The driver stepping out of the car was tall, handsome, and muscular, with the butt of a semi-automatic poking out of a visible shoulder holster. His eyes alertly scanned the crowd before he stepped back to open the passenger door.

Alice's husband Russ said, "I know the driver; he's an operator of Jimmy's."

The driver escorted a Middle Eastern couple over to Rose. The driver said, "Mrs. Nelson, I'm Frank. I work for Chief Stockade at *SOS Inc.* I want to introduce you to Mahmoud and Azar Ahmadi, Ablah's parents."

Mahmoud was 5'8", stocky, with a full head of black hair combed straight back, and wore a well-fitted, expensive, gray suit. Azar was shorter than her husband, about 5'4", and overweight. She wore conservative western clothing with a long skirt and a headscarf.

Mahmoud looked around at the intimidating crowd and said, "We're sorry to intrude. Is there any news about our daughter? Her cell phone doesn't work. The police called us earlier, asking absurd questions about her. The questions were unkind. I need to assure you and them that Ablah is a good girl. Religious crazy people in Iran destroyed our family. She would never involve herself in kidnapping someone to help Iraqi religious crazy people. We do not know what has happened, but we're frightened for our daughter. Ablah is so proud of her friendship with Julia and Alexia. She often mentioned Roman and Jimmy and mentioned Jimmy's company several times, so I hired them to get us to you. We're hoping you can tell us what is going on. Azar is scared to death, and so am I."

Mahmoud put his arm around his wife's shoulder and held her as she cried.

Rose said, "You, poor dear," hugging Azar. Azar continued crying.

Rose said, "Let's get you both into the house and give you a moment to clean up and refresh yourselves after your trip."

Waving Alice and Russ over, Rose introduced them to Mahmoud and Azar. Alice hugged Azar while patting her shoulder.

Rose turned to Russ, "Russ, please let everyone know these are Ablah's parents. They're friends. Please ask people to make them feel welcome."

Frank stayed near the Ahmadi's until Mahmoud said, "I think we're among friends, Frank. You may relax."

Rose took Mahmoud and Azar into Roman's home and, setting them at the kitchen table, explained everything.

When she finished, Azar said, "So your daughter, your future daughter-in-law, and the president's daughter were kidnapped along with Ablah?"

Rose said, "Yes, and the entire wedding party."

Azar said, "No one thinks Ablah is a terrorist?"

Rose said, "No."

Azar asked, "What do you know of this Chawki person? Could he be part of this?"

Rose said, "I don't know. I have never met him."

Chapter 62

Roman and the team made it back on the Cutter 'James' before the factory ship blew up. The girls were not expecting it, but everyone else knew the explosion was moments away. They stood on the top deck with the factory ship visible on the horizon when the blast sounded across the water.

Everyone watched the ship sink as the explosion blew out the vessel's entire bottom. The cutter shifted direction and headed for the explosion to see if there were any survivors. Roman knew there would be none.

All the hostages, except Ablah, had a pair of arms hugging them. Then, holding Julia but looking at Ablah, Roman said to Julia, "You should tell her. The latest information I had, Chawki, is still alive."

The news surprised Julia, "He is?"

Roman said, "He was, and hopefully still is, but, unfortunately, my information is not current."

He continued, "Let's get everyone together for a quick talk before we head home."

Julia helped shepherd everyone into a conference room, and then she huddled with Ablah, who sobbed.

Roman said, "The former military men know what 'classified and top secret' means. Ladies, until now, no one has ever expected you to keep a secret for your entire life. This horrible experience is, by the president's order, designated Top Secret for Presidential Eyes Only. The people you can discuss what happened with are the people in this room. The White House and the governor's office will coordinate a press release. It will present a sanitized version of what happened. Lots of people know pieces of what happened. No one will know what happened out here in the Pacific except us. Ever. Reporters will ask you what happened. Tell the truth and be frank about the kidnapping and your journey to the fishing factory ship."

Questions came up from the former hostages, with everyone talking at once.

Roman said, "You can discuss what you experienced up to a point. But, when someone asks who rescued you or how the rescue occurred, you tell everyone the U.S. Marshals Service came and got you. Do not go into details of the rescue. Do not talk about the ship's sinking, who was on the team that came and got you, the bags of computers, or other things you saw us retrieve. Those computers could contain information that will save thousands of lives. We do not want the knowledge we have the electronic devices to become known. We may even identify other terrorists around the world. If we do, remember, that knowledge is classified."

Julia looked at Alexia and said, "Hey, we get to use the 'I'm classified' line to dodge saying anything." Everyone laughed as they headed for the helipad.

Chapter 63

It was mid-afternoon when the Blackhawks returned everyone to Hawkeye Ridge. The governor's helicopter holding Governor Stan and Margo Anderson landed close to the Blackhawks.

The crowd gathered in silence to watch everyone get out of the helicopters. There wasn't a sound until the women appeared. Then a raucous cry of welcome rang out as the crowd began waving.

Alexia stepped out, and Rose went racing up to her. A welcoming roar met Cindy, then Samantha, who people did not know. Julia climbed out to find herself embraced by her parents and Rose. Ablah exited last, expecting silence. Instead, she received a massive outcry, and it shocked her to see her parents beckoning her.

Kathleen was the final hostage to get out of the copter. Everyone cheered when she turned and took Andy by one hand and Brutus's leash in her other hand.

Before exiting the helicopter, the team secured their weapons and helmets in the Blackhawks. But their faces were streaked with greasepaint, and bloodstains covered their uniforms.

The exhausted team members began wandering through the crowd, scrounging for whatever food was available.

Bridger stood with Cindy's family, who hung all over him.

Alexia held her mother, but so did Jimmy. Rose hugged one and then the other, with tears of relief streaming down her face.

Samantha clutched Thomas's hand, who walked bent over, holding his ribs. They wandered through the crowd, looking relieved.

Roman's arm wrapped around Julia, and Stan and Margo held them in a group hug.

Ablah continued sobbing in her mother's arms.

Mahmoud approached Roman, "I hate to intrude, but is there any way to determine the status of my daughter's boyfriend? Is he still alive?"

Roman looked at Stan, who pulled out his satellite phone and asked his office to connect him to the doctor caring for Chawki at the St. Charles Medical Center.

He told his staff, "Tell them I want to talk to his doctor, and I don't want any of the privacy B.S. I want to know how he is and what his prognosis is."

Stan waved Ablah over to hear the news and put the phone on speaker. The doctor came on the phone a minute later.

The doctor said, "It was touch and go. He almost bled out before he got here. We rushed him into the operating room for abdominal surgery to repair the damage from the bullet wound. I think he will make it if we can keep an infection from getting into his wounds. He will need to stay in the hospital for a while. Beyond that, I don't know."

Stan asked, "Is he stable enough to fly to the Salem Hospital?"

"Yes, do you want me to arrange for a Life Flight helicopter?"

Stan said, "Yes."

Ablah hugged the governor, who got his hand wrung by Mahmoud.

With no warning, thunderous noise exploded overhead. The empty sky filled in a rush with landing Blackhawk warships with the unmistakable thump, thump everyone now knew. Out of the helicopters raced a company of Marines in full battle gear, establishing a perimeter. Landing in the middle of the Marine helicopters was the presidential helicopter, Marine 1.

Out stepped President Myers, who came jogging across the field to his daughter, followed by Admiral Seastrand. A marine squad flanked the President on each side, weapons ready. Kathleen raced into her father's arms for an enormous hug.

Alex Myers then walked down the line of former SEALS and former Rangers who rescued his daughter. Shaking everyone's hand

and expressing his thanks, he stopped at Andy and gave him a bear hug. Kneeling in front of Brutus, the president hugged him with tears streaming down his face.

"How do you thank a damn dog for your daughter's life?"

Andy said, "I think you just did, sir." Brutus stood on his hind legs, attempting to lick the president's face.

Turning to Roman and Jimmy, President Myers looked at the crowd and asked, "I presume I'm safe here. I don't need an entire Marine company surrounding me as I walk around?"

"No, sir, I think we just dealt with the only crazies in the area," Roman answered.

Dismissing his Marine escort, he asked, "How is the Chawki guy doing?"

Roman told him about the most recent status as they approached the president's Goddaughter, Julia. Julia and Kathleen were talking to Ablah and her parents. After introductions, President Myers asked clarifying questions. Then, turning to an aide, he said, "Tell the Marine hospital chopper to fly to St. Charles Medical Center in Bend and pick up Chawki and his doctor. Fly them here to pick up Ablah and then take him to the Salem Hospital. In fact, Ablah, would you and your parents like to go right now? When they pick him up in Bend, you can be there and fly to Salem with him."

Frank still stood guard in Mahmoud's vicinity. He said, "I can take the limo back to the Salem Hospital, Mr. Ahmadi. I will be available there whenever you need me to take you to a hotel."

Governor Anderson said, "No, Frank, take them back to the governor's mansion whenever they leave the hospital. They can stay with Margo and me."

Shocked, Mahmoud said, "I cannot believe how kind you both are. With the power you both wield, we did not know what to expect or how you would receive us. We thought you suspected our daughter of being a terrorist. Never did we expect this kindness."

Chapter 64

The following two days were frantic as the Navy diving crew defused the explosives, which allowed everyone to return home.

All the team members who saw action spent the next day sleeping. However, Roman and Jimmy huddled with Admiral Seastrand and his team doing an extensive debriefing of the rescue.

Roger sat at his desk at *Boy Toys & Her Toys Too*, counting and recounting the recovered money. An armed member of the team functioned as his guard.

After finishing, he sent Roman a message, "We need to talk."

Roman and Smoke took the chairlift down the hill and walked into Roger's office, "What did you find out?"

Roger said, "Based on what I saw in the computers before I turned them over to Admiral Seastrand's guys, it looks like the cash we found was just their version of petty cash. The serious money looked like it flowed, with encrypted connections, to countries with funky banking laws, which is about what you'd expect from a big-time terrorist. I think the petty cash we found was to cover local graft and payoffs. I know you want to know how much we got, and then the question is, what will we do with it?"

Roman said, "Right, I know the president said the same Rules of Engagement applied to this mission as our Philippines action, but I don't know if he meant the money. I think he did, but I guess we'll find out. How much is there?"

Roger answered, "Well, it wasn't as much as the $50 million we recovered in the Philippines, but $8,600,000 is still a lot of money.

So given what we've seen, there's lots of money in being a terrorist. They all seem to possess fortunes in cash."

Roman whistled.

Roger continued, "If President Myers is serious about handing the money over to us, as he did in the Philippines, it comes to $955,555 apiece for the nine of us. You told me not to give you or Smoke a bonus this time. If the girls hadn't gone through what they had, I'd call it a profitable few days."

Roman looked at Jimmy, "What do you think, Smoke? Would we have found the girls if it weren't for Chawki's clue?"

Jimmy answered, "Maybe yes and maybe no. And if yes, maybe not in time."

Roman asked, "How do you think the team would feel about cutting Chawki in for an equal share?"

Roger interrupted Jimmy, "I can answer that, sir. They'd say hell yes. None of us did this expecting to get paid, but we sure won't turn down the money. The team was frantic thinking about the girls. Hell yes, cut him in for a share. He may need the money for a lawyer."

Chapter 65

Roman rejoined President Myers, Admiral Seastrand, and Governor Anderson. They relaxed while playing cards and sipping beer at the fire pit. They preferred playing poker on Roman's deck to hunkering down in the governor's mansion.

The Marine 1 helicopter ferried them back and forth from the governor's mansion each day.

Roman approached the poker game and, waiting for a break in the conversation, said, "Could I interrupt the game and speak to the Admiral?"

Admiral Seastrand excused himself from the poker game.

Admiral Seastrand said, "You better stay out of the poker game, Roman. The president keeps trying to get the governor to raise his bet by agreeing to run for president when his term is up. You better make yourself scarce, or they'll have you running for governor."

"Not me." Roman laughed, "That's how I wound up as a reserve U.S. marshall. I learned my lesson."

"What did you find?" the Admiral asked.

Roman explained what Roger told him and asked, "Was the president serious about us taking the money?"

Admiral Seastrand said, "Yes, he is serious about it. He's already drafted an executive order, changing the letter he gave you after the Philippine action and before your discharge. The letter will legitimize depositing the cash. I gave him the names of everyone who went on the mission so he can update their letters."

Admiral Seastrand continued, smiling, "Besides the money you recovered, there was a $10 million bounty on Abu Bakr al-Baghdadi, dead or alive. You delivered proof of his death. So, you can add that to the kitty."

Chapter 66

Three days later, Hawkeye Ridge volunteers completed the cleaning and redecorating.

The crowd returned to their homes, the grounds picked up, the portable toilets emptied, and the refuse carted away. Darci and Gwen restocked the supplies for the reception and were racing around, checking on last-minute wedding details.

The renaissance tents fluttered in the gentle breeze, making the 80 degrees feel comfortable. Security measures were once again in place at the bottom of the hill.

Stretch limos carried people up the hill. The bride's party occupied the house. The groom's party got dressed in the apartment above the boat store, *Boy Toys & Her Toys Too.*

Chawki sat in a wheelchair with a nurse in attendance. With pride, Ablah's parents sat with him. Chawki held a file folder on his lap.

Mahmoud said, "The president is a great man. Your family kidnaps his daughter. You helped them, even though you didn't know what they intended to do. Yet, because you love my daughter, you send a message you know will get to the right people telling them how to find the president's daughter. Your love for my daughter saved not only my daughter, but also the president's daughter and the women in the bridal party."

Mahmoud and his wife were weeping, "He not only has forgiven you your actions, but he has given you a full pardon along with proof of what happened to your father and the information you need to regain your inheritance. Chawki, you'll be a wealthy man."

Chawki, his voice thick with emotion, replied, "What makes me wealthy is Ablah sticking with me through everything."

Chapter 67

The assembled crowd got quiet as the groom's entourage entered from the side of the altar. Naturally, everyone expected nervousness from Roman, and they were not disappointed. However, as Best Man, Jimmy kept tapping his pocket to feel the rings.

The president of the United States stepped in front of the altar.

Music began playing, and the audience stood with heads turned to watch the bridal processional.

The Ushers were Roman's cousin Dennis who escorted Ablah, Andy, who accompanied Kathleen, Bridger provided an arm for Cindy, and Dink escorted the Maid of Honor, Alexia. The Matron of Honor, Samantha, walked by herself.

Julia stepped down the aisle on her father's arm with her eyes on Roman.

Thank You

Thank you for reading 'ON PRESIDENTIAL ORDERS.' I hope you enjoyed reading it as much as I enjoyed writing it.

If you are curious about the beginnings of the Hawkeye Ridge series, I hope you will go to Amazon and discover how Roman met Julia. That title is simply Hawkeye Ridge by G.D. Covert.

The third book in the series, Xavier's Tears, will publish soon. If you want me to keep you posted on its publishing date, please email me at my website, **http://www.gdcovert.com**.

Acknowledgments

My wife, Lisa, heads my Gratitude list. This series would never have started without her love and encouragement, which continues every step of the way. From the first, "What are you doing, writing a book?" To the daily proofreading and critique, Thank you, Honey.

Peggy Lowe of Authorgraphics.com deserves a thank you for her eye-catching artwork.

John Lake Jr. and Robert A. Joyce, two High School and College friends deserve an enormous thank you for their critiques. I greatly appreciate your willingness to critique an old friend.

About the Author

As a child, I escaped into the magical world of fiction. The small-town library in Columbiana, Ohio became my refuge.

A Vietnam-era medic in the USAFR, I've always been self-employed. I worked my way through college as a barber, graduating from Arizona State University.

Moving to Oregon, I was a Real Estate Broker and owner of a Real Estate School before spending 38 years in the financial services industry. A book was always nearby.

On vacation, I became disgusted with the books I had with me. Muttering, "I can do better than that," I opened my laptop. Hawkeye Ridge escaped onto the pages.

You can learn more about me or send me an email on my website:
https://www.gdcovert.com

45153056R00162